SILK AND LEATHER

LESBIAN EROTICA WITH AN EDGE

Visit us at www.boldstrokesbooks.com

SILK AND LEATHER

LESBIAN EROTICA WITH AN EDGE

edited by

Victoria Villaseñor

2020

ISBN 13: 978-1-63555-587-5

This Trade Paperback Original Is Published By
Bold Strokes Books, Inc.
P.O. Box 249
Valley Falls, NY 12185

First Edition: April 2020

CREDITS
EDITORS: VICTORIA VILLASEÑOR AND STACIA SEAMAN
PRODUCTION DESIGN: STACIA SEAMAN
COVER DESIGN BY TAMMY SEIDICK

CONTENTS

ALL ABOARD

L.L. Shelton

L.L. Shelton is the indie author of the Our Glass Series, the Nights of Lily Ann Series, and the short story "Cuffed to Her." Her genres have included lesbian romance and lesbian erotica. She lives in the United States on the Eastern Shore with her partner of twenty years.

All aboard!

The words bounced from the speakers above Silk's head. She stopped to listen to any further messages, but when the speaker drew quiet, she continued her journey through the train cars. Dressed in a white silk blouse, she teetered between the crowd in the tightly enclosed space. Bodies pressed against each other with hands straying to forbidden body parts as she tried to find balance. A quick apologetic smile followed each arousing touch. The white silk clung to her body from the heat, with a sensation developing within. Her nipples were ripe from all the contact and ready for plucking.

As she reached the last door, a man and woman stood facing each other in a small corridor. They leaned against opposite walls, restricting the space between them. The woman raised her body as Silk stepped closer. She wore a tight-fitting, green lace blouse. Her long auburn hair flowed down, with little twists at the end of each strand lifting from her bare shoulders. The corners of her mouth turned up slightly, revealing a shy smile. Submissively, her eyes fell as she clearly admired Silk's curves.

Silk took a step toward the man, causing his smile to widen. She smiled back, but with a small shift of her heel she was pressed against the lady in green. Their silk and lace tops were drawn together by static electricity. A different electricity ricocheted through her veins, the type that fires desires. Silk shuffled sideways, followed by a pause. She grabbed the woman at the waist before she pushed her hips into her. She was rewarded with a barely suppressed moan. Eyes met and seduction was firmly in place. Another shuffle and lips lingered inches apart. Breaths held silent. Another shuffle and her fingers ran across the woman's stomach. Breath hitched. Silk stepped free and pulled the door open to the next car on the train. She stepped inside, but not before turning to give the woman in lace a soft, wanting gaze.

Silk found her seat quickly, a back row one in first class where she had a little privacy and a bit more room to move. The train would depart shortly. She second-guessed her decision to decline a sleeping car. The twelve-hour ride to New York City already seemed unbearable. The time would click by slowly unless she could find something or someone to meet her entertainment needs. Maybe an auburn-haired woman in a lace blouse could fulfill that desire. She turned back in search of Lace. She was gone. A large round man stood against the same wall reading a newspaper where she once stood. So much for the hope of auburn hair cascading over her skin with lace fabric gently caressing her inner thighs while Silk held the woman's head tightly between her legs. Silk was becoming intoxicated with the thoughts of pumping until she released in the woman's mouth. A tinge of wetness emerged, and Silk forced herself to draw her attention somewhere else.

Her fingers softly stroked the white silk material wrapped around her neck. With a twist, the back of her hand slipped between her breasts. She watched out the window as bodies rushed to load the train at the last minute. She sat in row sixty-nine admiring her reflection. Her makeup was flawless, with a light coat of red lipstick over full lips. Her long blond hair was half pinned up. A slight dip and deep cleavage reflected in the glass. Yes, she was on form today.

The first drops of rain spiraled down. The outside world soon disappeared under a frost that swallowed the window. Silk swiped toward the left, the wetness from the window smearing over her fingers. The outdoor picture was visible again, the platform clear. Silk was startled by dark brown eyes looking fixedly upward into the window at her. The woman's back was straight, her shoulders squared; her ground held solid. Waves of long black hair flowed down her back. She wore her black leather pants like a painted canvas. Toned muscles were displayed flawlessly from a leather vest she wore eloquently. Tiny raindrops slipped down her bare arms.

If only my tongue could lick the wetness from her skin, Silk thought.

Silk's eyes didn't falter; she kept herself focused on those lusting brown eyes when her fingertip moved over her nipple. She slowly twirled around the outer area of the bud, causing the bump to stiffen. She adjusted her seating as a gathering of juices started to pool. The feeling of Leather's eyes on her caused heat to rise from her warm core. Her thumb and index fingers pinched her now prominent nipple and twisted. Unable to hold the eye contact, her head fell back, and she released a low, soft moan. She forced her gaze back to the window. She lusted to be watched as she touched herself.

But Leather was gone. The platform that was once occupied by the olive-skinned beautiful woman dressed in black leather was stripped of any pleasurable scenery. Silk sighed heavily before falling back into the cushions. Two shortcomings on the same day did not bode well.

Silk kicked off her heels and stretched her legs out, with her feet resting on the chair across from her. Her head tilted back on the hard headrest with a hint of discomfort at the odd position. The engines of the train came to life with a thunderous vibration. The train jerked ahead, and the feel of movement swept over her body. *Oh, this will be a long trip. A very long trip.*

Fingertips brushed over her knee in a downward motion, causing Silk to stir from sleep. A hand grasped her calf, and the sensation of her leg lifting caused her eyes to widen. By the time she focused, her leg was in Leather's lap. Silk blinked a few times to erase the vision, but no. She was real. Leather held her leg and slowly kneaded the muscles. Silk ran her tongue over her bottom lip, which was suddenly dry as a desert. There was a knot in the back of her throat. She swallowed a few times to relieve the strange feeling. Leather's touch was currently unraveling Silk's calm, collected manner.

Leather's touch caused a pulsating throb to radiate through Silk's body, straight to her clit. She watched as Leather lifted her foot and softly licked the pad of her toe. Butterfly kisses trailed down her arch before rounding the heel. Her foot found a resting spot on Leather's shoulder. Butterfly kisses continued, mixed with nibbles over her calf until Leather was leaning forward, licking softly at her inner thigh. Silk shifted and pulled her skirt up, desiring those lips to travel higher. She parted her legs as Leather fell to her knees between the seats, her feet in the aisle. Leather's mouth teased the crook of her leg, a breath away from her center. Only a few more inches and her sweet sex would be tasted. She moaned at the thought of her come filling Leather's mouth. As if she sensed her need, Leather hooked her fingers into the silk panties, pulling them to the side to reveal her sex.

Silk's eyes grew heavy with pleasure but soon widened when Lace appeared beside her. She stood her ground between the seats and watched the show. The warmth of Leather's mouth engulfing her soaking folds, her long tongue licking the nectar flowing freely, caused Silk to arch. She released a soft whimper of pleasure. Heat rocketed through her body. Silk's hand fell to Leather's head and pushed her deeper while her gaze focused on Lace. Silk couldn't help but notice her voyeur's protruding nipples through the blouse that clung tightly to her. They were huge and in need of sucking. Silk's mouth made an "O" shape with a silent moan when visions of sucking them to a peak flashed before her eyes.

Lace watched.

Silk's shoulders raised off the chair when Leather's tongue swirled around her clit. She felt her hood pushed back, and a long lapping lick brought her to the edge. She gritted her teeth to hold back the orgasm. She grasped the armrest with her free hand that wasn't holding Leather in place. She looked between the two women as she started to pump. A finger slipped past her entrance with ease and dove deep into her, up to the knuckle. A second finger joined the first. Silk whimpered at the fulfillment. Leather clamped down on her swollen clit and moans breathed over Silk's hot spot. Her chest rose and fell with each breath sucked into her lungs.

Lace watched.

Silk held Leather's head steady between her soaking thighs. Leather was going to swallow her. All of her. She was on edge. She pumped faster. One hand pushed Leather's mouth closer, and the other grasped the headrest, which was no longer causing discomfort. She pumped. Her eyes were heavy, watching the lust in Lace's gray eyes.

Watch her swallow me. Watch me come in her mouth. The words rang out in her head just as she arched outward. She thrust harder. *Good, so good. Keep watching me*—a quiet scream released as she exploded into Leather's mouth. Her thighs tightened against the sides of Leather's head. Juices released. All of her juices. Just as she was descending from her explosion, Lace licked at her bottom lip; Silk closed her eyes and skyrocketed into an uncontrollable second climax. Leather sucked in the double dose of liquid with fervor. Silk descended for the second time. She opened her eyes with exertion. Lace was gone. Silk's leg fell to the side, releasing Leather from her duties.

Leather kissed her way back over the glistening thighs. She stood and pulled Silk up with her. She slipped the heels onto the feet of the long legs that had held her head like vise grips mere minutes before. Grabbing her hand, she guided her through the corridors at a rapid pace, with Silk double stepping to keep up with her. They soon reached a sleeping car, and with a swift motion, Leather pulled Silk into the small room before closing and locking them inside.

Silk's body thumped against the wall. Leather pressed into the kiss with her tongue invading Silk's mouth with desire. Tasting Silk had ignited an inferno inside her. She needed to come. She needed nipples between her lips as she relentlessly sucked them to their limits. Holding their kiss, Leather clawed at the buttons on the silk blouse. With the fall of the last button and the parting of material, she tore the bra apart, releasing the full breasts, and the sound of the ripping cloth added fuel to her fire.

Breaking the kiss, she pulled Silk's hands above her head and held them against the wall. Her free hand ripped the torn material away, revealing dark pink areolas. Swollen nipples taunted her. She held Silk's arms tight above her head, and the other hand pushed gently on her stomach, keeping her in place, restricting her. A dip of her head and she sucked in her hard, pink nipple, only to release it long enough to flick and roll her tongue around in circles before the nipple was absorbed deeper and harder. Leather's moans rippled over the soft flesh. Releasing the swollen kernel with a deep sigh, she attached to the other breast with urgency. Need and want pulsated through her clit. She undocked from the nipple with a growl. Releasing her hold, Leather pointed to the bed.

Leather watched Silk follow directions like a good girl. Her eyes looked down in hunger at the beautiful woman beneath her. She had one mission, and that was to get some release. She slowly unzipped her leather vest, pulling it apart to reveal her small breasts. She twisted her nipples, making them extend to their limits. Her eyes were heavy from the pleasure. She unzipped her pants, revealing the top of her mound. She pulled Silk's lips to the curly hair; small licks caused a low tug in her center. A tug of the hair and Silk's mouth withdrew from the sweet smell. Leather flipped Silk around, so her legs were up against the wall and her head hung off the side of the bed. Leather pulled her pants down and stopped when the leather reached her thighs. A small patch of curly hair emerged, and Leather spread her legs. Her fingers separated her folds for Silk to admire. Leather slipped her finger in and out of the folds, moaning softly at how desperately she wanted this. She slid her finger into Silk's mouth and watched as Silk sucked the juices with hunger. The leather pants peeled from her body to a final resting place on the floor.

Only wearing her leather vest, Leather moved so she was flanking Silk's head. Silk's heels remained on, and her skirt had fallen to her waist, revealing silk panties. Leather splayed her legs further apart as she prepared to lower herself onto Silk's waiting mouth. She grabbed Silk's ankles and secured them to the wall. Her heels dug into the plaster as anchors. She lowered herself to Silk's mouth.

Her tongue swirled in circles, up and around, grazing her clit before continuing its journey. The wet twisting tongue slipped closer and closer to where she needed it most. A thrust and it dipped in, teasing the spot just inside. Silk was rewarded with a deep moan. Leather spread her legs and the rhythmic pumping started. Her hips were rotating from front to back and gaining speed. Leather spread Silk's legs; the silk panties were wet, the wet spot growing as Silk devoured Leather with her mouth. Watching Silk's pussy getting wet was enough to make Leather want to explode, but she held steady. Releasing this soon would be like eating dessert before savoring the meal. *She likes fucking me with her tongue. That's it. Take it.* The words ran on repeat in Leather's mind. She was climbing. Her breaths increased. Silk's tongue fucked her with every thrust while her hands grasped at her ass. Leather reached down and stroked her own clit. Gripping the swollen bump between her thumb and index finger, she began to jerk. Faster and faster. Her eyes closed, teeth gritted, back arched, she came in Silk's mouth. A scream of ecstasy echoed off the walls. Silk licked her, missing some, the sweet fluid running down her chin. With a heavy sigh, Leather fell on the bed.

Silk twisted to an upright position, steadied herself, and pulled her skirt down. She rebuttoned her blouse and motioned in a "one minute" gesture to Leather before she slipped out of the room.

Lace stared out the window at the passing scenery. Suddenly a hand rested on her shoulder, causing her to look up. Silk stood beside her and motioned at the seat next to her. Understanding the silent question, Lace motioned with her eyes to the lounge where a poker game was currently in the works. Silk took her hand and Lace was guided toward the sleeping car area.

Once inside, the door was locked, and Lace stood in front of Leather with Silk behind her. Two hands wrapped around her waist and undid her skirt, letting it fall to the floor.

Leather watched.

Slowly the lace blouse was pulled over her head and tossed to the side. Then her bra was released, and her nipples tightened in the cool air. She noticed the want in Leather's dark brown eyes. She felt Silk's fingers roll around her swelling nipples before pinching them gently. She rewarded the action with a moan.

Leather shifted and softly stroked herself.

Lace's body was guided to the bed as an offering. She was lowered next to Leather, with her knees spread. Leather twisted her nipple before leaning over and sucking it in deeply. Lace's back arched hard, and a deep moan emerged. When her other nipple was pinched, Lace cried out in pleasure. She was soaked and throbbed with need. She searched for Silk to plead for release.

Silk parted her folds and she took her first finger with ease; then another slipped inside her, followed by a third. Lace was full and ready. Silk started to fuck her at a steady pace, her thumb pushing against her clit with every thrust. Her hips began to rock onto Silk's fingers. She couldn't last at this pace. Her walls were tightening in small spasms. Just at the edge, Silk hooked her arm under Lace's thigh and pulled, flipping her over.

She landed on all fours on top of Leather, with her breasts dangling above her swollen lips. Lips that couldn't get enough of her nipples. She felt them sucked until they ached in pleasurable pain. Leather bit and sucked at them with no mercy. Red, swollen, and throbbing, her nipples were on fire in the best of ways.

She reared back when Silk's three fingers slid back inside her. The same rhythm rocked her again from behind. Small slaps on her ass make her quake with need. With every rock, her nipples were pulled to their limits as Leather held firm. She was dangling over the edge of orgasm. One more push, one more dip, one more nibble, and she would plunge.

She could barely keep her eyes open as she neared climax. With a quick glance she saw the two women who were taking her were also masturbating. Their fingers were rolling and pushing into themselves. They were waiting for her to come so that they could follow.

They need me to come. Harder. Fuck me harder. Lace slipped over the cliff. Cries of ecstasy filled the room. Her walls tightened and her back arched as she released herself. Pain seared through her nipples as teeth clamped down hard. A second wave started to form. She released again. Her orgasm flowed from her like a river.

Leather lifted and brought herself to a thundering climax. Silk's entire body bent over Lace's ass, her wetness rolling down Lace's butt cheek as she released. They descended from their climaxes, gasping for air, limbs tangled and hearts beating hard.

The perfect mixture of Silk, Leather, and Lace.

Silk sat looking out the window. The weather had cleared, and she looked up when the announcement came over the speakers.

"Arriving in New York City."

Her gaze fell back to the window before she felt her lips engulfed in a kiss. The smell of Leather filled her nostrils with a slight hint of Lace. Tongues clashing. Teeth pulled at her lower lip, and Silk couldn't repress her moan. She allowed the sensual noise to fill Leather's mouth.

Silk watched as Leather pulled away with a grin. She slipped quietly out of the room with only a quick nod.

Making her way down the aisle, Silk stopped by a chair occupied by Lace. The man rested beside her with his eyes closed. Silk gently brushed her cheek. Lace lowered her eyes submissively, causing a tingling between Silk's legs. She leaned over, kissing her lips softly and stroking her nipple through the soft lace material. She felt Lace suck air in a short gasp. Silk pulled away slowly and gave Lace a soft smile before continuing her departure.

The conductor's voice rang out of the speakers.

"Welcome to New York City. Hope you enjoyed your train ride."

Silk stopped at the steps that led to the platform. She listened to the message before placing her sunglasses on with a smile.

ENGAGEMENTS

M. Ullrich

M. Ullrich lives at the Jersey Shore with her wife and three feline children. She works a day job out of necessity, laughs to keep her sanity, and writes because there's always a story to tell. Connect with M. Ullrich on Twitter, Facebook, and Instagram.

Family parties always made me nervous, especially when I was about to meet my girlfriend's family for the first time. Allie told me again and again that I had nothing to worry about. We were going to have dinner to celebrate her brother's recent engagement. Her tone matched her easy expression, but we had been together long enough for me to know when she was nervous. She picked idly at the callus on her palm. A dead giveaway. I stopped fixing my long hair and looked at her in the mirror. She looked incredible despite her worry.

"What's bothering you?"

Allie met my eyes in the reflection. She smirked and dropped her hands to her sides. "How is it that we've only been together for a couple months and you already know me so well?"

I turned around and leaned against the marble vanity. "You always tell me my brain was what you found attractive in the first place."

Allie stepped up to me and scanned my body. I pushed my chest out slightly. My black dress was modest, but my cleavage still enticed.

"I guess now would be a good time to confess..." she said,

reaching out touch her fingertips to my throat. "I didn't really notice how smart you were until about our third date."

I dropped my head back a bit, greedy for Allie's delicate touch. For all the ways she could be delightfully rough with me, she was the softest woman I had ever been with. The perfect butch package I never thought to search for. I lost myself to the moment.

"You've been lying to me this whole time?" My skin prickled in the wake of her touch ascending my bare chest. "Are you ashamed of what you noticed first?"

"Your eyes," she said immediately. The quickness of her response made my heart speed up. "Then it was these." She palmed my breasts. My nipples tightened at the sudden stimulation, and my moan echoed in the bathroom.

I wanted to kiss her. I wanted to take her confidence and turn it on its head in a way that would leave her on her knees begging, but we didn't have time for that. I ran my hand over the short hair on the back of her head. "You're trying to distract me."

Allie smiled. "Is it working?"

I leaned in, bringing my lips within millimeters of hers. I could taste the mint on her breath. "No."

Allie stepped away and rolled her shoulders. I felt cold and regretted letting her go. But watching her black oxford shirt stretch across her broad back was enough of a reward for the moment.

"I'm just a little nervous. That's all."

"It's more than a small case of nerves."

"How can you tell?"

"We live less than two hours from your parents' house, and you insisted we get a hotel room."

"It'll probably be a long night, and I don't want either of us to drive if we're tired. Or drunk."

"And staying with your family wasn't an option?" I knew my question struck a nerve when Allie didn't answer. She only shook her head. I watched again as she started to scratch her palm. "Your callus gives you away every time."

Her hands stilled. "My family is dysfunctional, like most, but my mom isn't very accepting."

Panic started to creep in. "Will she have a problem with me being there? I don't want to cause any problems."

"Oh no," Allie said, taking my hands. The warmth of her fingers laced with mine calmed me. "She'll love you, I have no doubt about that. She just doesn't like how I look. I'm not a *woman*."

I would've found Allie's use of air quotes while holding my hands funny if she didn't look so worried. "But you're all woman, baby." I pulled my hands free to wrap my arms around her waist. I grabbed her full, muscular ass and dug my nails in. I licked my lips at the urge I felt to sink my teeth into it next. "And I happen to really love the way you look."

Allie kissed me softly. Her expression grew a fraction lighter. "My mom sees the world differently and has no problem vocalizing her opinions."

I knew this was the perfect time to share my latest bright idea with Allie. "Lucky for you, you're dating a woman who thinks ahead to solve problems before they arise." I walked out of the bathroom with Allie in tow. I searched my overnight bag and smiled triumphantly when I found the little plastic rectangle in the side pocket. I held it up and laughed at Allie's confusion. "This is for when you, or we, need a distraction." I tapped the remote to her strong chin, ran it down the center of her chest, and then grabbed her hand to place it in her palm. Just the way the small remote was dwarfed in her big hands turned me on. "Press the button once for low, two for medium, and three times for high."

Allie looked between me and the remote. "What is this to?"

"My panties."

Her eyes flew wide open. "They turn on?" I nodded. "Like, vibrate? You're wearing vibrating panties to your first dinner with my family?"

I started to second-guess myself when Allie's face gave me no hint at what she was really feeling, other than complete shock. "I kinda figured the night may be tough since you've been worrying so much, and I thought this would help—" I stopped talking as soon as Allie held my face in her hands. I smiled back at her brilliant grin.

She kissed me hard and said, "I think you may be the perfect woman."

I laughed loudly as I gathered my purse. "Just promise me you won't set it too high for too long. That'll make me come really fast."

"You've already tested it out?"

"Of course. Last night after you dropped me off."

"*Fuck...*"

"Let's go. We can't be late." I started to leave the room, feeling incredibly sexy, wanted, and powerful even after literally handing over control to Allie. That was the beauty of our relationship—she had all the power, and I had all the control.

"Miranda, wait." Allie's voice jolted my clit. Just hearing her say my name combined with my anticipation made me wet. "There's something else I need to tell you."

I grinned wickedly. "Another confession so soon?" When I looked back at her, I knew whatever she was about to say was going to be the opposite of sexy. "What is it?"

She looked down. "Remember the girl I told you about? From college? The first girl who broke my heart?"

I knew my brain was moving slowly from arousal and nerves, but I also knew these dots were impossible to connect. "Yeah, you were madly in love for four years and then she dumped you before graduation. She was straight, supposedly, and you were devastated. What about her?"

Allie took a deep breath before looking me in the eye. "Her name is Eve, and she's my brother's fiancée. And no, no one knows about our past."

My stomach dropped along with my jaw. I didn't know what to say. But the most surprising detail in that moment was the flare of jealousy in my chest that traveled lower and lower and ebbed as a throb in my pussy. Apparently, I had a thing for meeting exes.

"Well," I said much more calmly than I felt, "let's go show Eve what she's missing out on, shall we?"

We arrived fifteen minutes later than we wanted to, but we still beat the guests of honor. A small win. I wanted to meet Allie's parents before the distraction of Eve entered the picture. Allie's father, Simon, was everything I imagined he'd be: a big, broad, burly man with eyes that matched his daughter's in kindness but not in color. Allie has the most hypnotic cerulean eyes, but Simon's were a vibrant emerald. I was much more nervous meeting Jeanine Boyle. From the very little Allie had told me, she'd be the hardest to win over. But when she opened the door and greeted us, she enveloped me in a shockingly strong hug and hesitated to let go.

"It's so nice to meet you, Miranda." Jeanine looked like she wanted to applaud me. "You're so beautiful and girly."

I kept my smile pleasant and face as neutral as possible. "Thank you, Mrs. Boyle. I'm so happy to meet you both." Allie placed her hand on my lower back, and she led me farther inside. Her touch grounded me.

"Where are Alan and Eve?"

I bit back a laugh. I had so many forbidden fruit jokes to make but knew better. I considered making a note of them all in my phone to tell Allie later.

"You know how your brother is," Simon said.

"Only aware of the importance of his time and no one else's?" Allie's tone held a chill I had never heard before.

The door swung open then and a man who looked exactly like a younger version of Simon walked in. I knew this was Alan, which meant the gorgeous blonde behind him was Eve. I leaned into Allie and whispered, "Blonde, huh?"

She looked at me with a pinched smile. "My type has changed over the years."

"Good answer."

Alan extended his hand to me in a jabbing motion. "You must be Miranda, whom I've heard nothing about."

I took his hand in a firm hold. "And you must be Alan, whom I've heard very little about." I turned to the woman next to him and waited for her to take my hand. She was hesitant. "And you're Eve, someone I've heard a lot about." Eve held my hand tightly. Her narrowed eyes and pleasant smile contradicted one another.

"Let's eat!" Jeanine's announcement broke the tension.

I was seated next to Allie at a modest-sized dining table. Unfortunately, we were across from Alan and Eve, with Allie's parents taking their rightful spots at the heads of the table. The conversation was boring as Alan recounted his clichéd proposal at a baseball game. Kiss cam, seventh inning stretch, blah blah blah. Eve finally spoke up when she declared the evening was like a fairy tale. My panties started buzzing the next second. I whimpered into my water glass.

"I thought you hated baseball, or all sports, for that matter." Allie sipped her red wine slowly and I felt dizzy while I watched her throat flex as she swallowed.

Eve stared at Allie. "I've changed a lot in ten years. You'd know that if you kept in touch."

Allie casually reached into her pocket again, and the pulsing between my thighs increased. I wasn't sure I'd make it to dessert.

"Who cares about the past when we have a wedding in the future? We should start planning. Allie, dear, I hope you plan on dressing appropriately for the occasion." Jeanine managed to look sugary-sweet even as she offended her daughter.

I reached over and grabbed Allie's free hand on the tabletop. "I can't wait to see you in a tuxedo." I subtly pressed into my seat to cause more friction between my wetness and the vibration. "You'll be the most gorgeous woman there." Allie winked at me, and my pleasure intensified.

"You will not wear a tuxedo to your brother's wedding."

Simon pointed his glass in Allie's direction. "My tailor would be happy to help you out."

"Allie will be in my wedding party," Eve said. She grabbed Alan's hand and mirrored our pose. "We'll pick something out. Together. She'll look stunning."

The speed of the vibrator reached high and I was a minute away from having an orgasm for dessert. With an audience. "Excuse me," I said as I stood. I placed my hand on Allie's shoulder. "Will you show me to the bathroom?"

"It's right up the stairs. You can't miss it," Alan offered.

I tightened my grip on Allie's shoulder as my inner muscles fluttered. Thankfully, Allie got the hint and stood. She kept her distance from me as we walked and allowed me to ascend the stairs first. It felt like the longest walk of my life. When we got to the top she chuckled.

"You really can't miss it." Allie pointed to the large bathroom. Her eyes were mischievous, and she wore a wicked smirk. She put her hands in her pockets and held my gaze as she turned off the vibrator.

I let out a steady breath and looked down the hallway. Every door was closed. "Are any of those your old bedroom?"

Allie opened the door closest to me. "It's just a plain guest room now, but—"

I practically leapt at Allie. I was done talking. I wanted to feel her everywhere and taste her mouth. I backed her into the room with the force of my kiss and shut the door. I leaned back against the wooden surface and caught my breath. Allie watched me with keen eyes and flexed her strong hands at her side. I knew what she wanted and how she was waiting for me to let her take it. I bunched my dress around my waist and tugged at the hem of my panties. I felt the material tighten and rub against my thumbs as I did a little dance for Allie. I could easily watch her watch me for hours; her eyes moved rapidly with a hunger to devour my every inch and commit the vision to memory. She made me feel sexier than anyone ever had, and in that moment, I felt myself fall further into her. I pulled my panties down, over my hips, and then let them drop the rest of the way. I ran my fingertip through my copious wetness before sucking the digit between my lips.

"I told you not to leave them on high for too long. Now I need to come and you're going to make me." I held my dress up and spread myself wide for Allie, displaying my protruding clit and glistening flesh.

Allie rushed over to a nearby dresser and pushed the ornaments off to the side. She motioned for me stand in front of her, then lifted me easily and set me down. After adjusting my dress, she encouraged my legs apart and stepped between them to claim my mouth. She kissed me deeply and thoroughly, the kind of kiss that lingers and bruises. She made quick work of my dress top to expose my breasts. Allie loved my breasts, and I was lucky for it. She always knew what I wanted before I asked. She knew when to bite and when to soothe, and she always knew when I was about to beg for more.

"Please…"

Allie licked the peak of my right nipple and smiled up at me. "We have to be quick." She held eye contact and licked me over and over. She bit down on my sensitive skin and I had to fight back a scream.

I bit my hand to try and control myself. I caressed Allie's cheek with my other hand before pushing her head down farther.

Allie knelt before me, my favorite place for her to be, and didn't hesitate to dive in. She went right for my clit, understanding that foreplay was far from necessary. I was open, hot, and ready for her. She entered me swiftly with two of her long fingers. The definition of her knuckles stretching me as she pumped in and out drove me to the brink. Her pillowy lips cradled my clit and she'd swipe her tongue across the sensitive nub from time to time. She knew I needed constant stimulation to come. Allie was toying with me and she was lovely while doing it.

"I'm so, so close," I said against the back of my hand, trying desperately to keep my volume down. I wanted to scream my pleasure, her name, and my praise. But I stayed quiet. So quiet, in fact, that the soft knock at the door sounded loud in the room. I froze, but Allie kept working me from the inside out. My head hit the wall.

The door opened and Eve's voice hit my ears before I saw her. "Allie? Are you in here?"

I turned my head just in time to see Eve the moment she caught us. Her mouth was agape and her knuckles white where she held on to the door. She looked away and mumbled an apology.

Allie stood and covered me the best she could, but I was too out of sorts to move. I was breathing heavily and counting each breath like it was a second. It wasn't until the tenth breath that Eve looked back at us. She bit her lower lip and I licked mine.

"We started to worry so I came to check on you. I didn't expect... I'm sorry." She started to leave and something inside me erupted.

"Stay," I said demandingly. "You can watch if you'd like." The idea of Eve witnessing what she'd never have again caused me to pulse. I needed Allie inside me again, filling me, and I needed Eve to understand her biggest mistake was now the best part of my life.

Allie looked at me curiously. "What?"

I grabbed the front of Allie's shirt and pulled her toward me. I lowered my voice and said, "Let's show her what she's missed, what she is missing, and what she'll never have again." I grabbed the back of Allie's neck and pressed my lips to her ear. "I want her to know you're mine." I looked at Eve, who still stood frozen in the doorway, and bit at the side of Allie's neck. Allie's hips bucked into the dresser.

Eve stepped into the room and shut the door. She sat on a small chair in the corner and placed her hands on her lap. She looked utterly innocent. Not at all like a woman who once upon a time fucked her fiancé's sister.

Allie's movements were hesitant at first, but after a few encouraging words she was back on her knees and had me spread wide open in front of her.

I dug my heel into her back while she swiped her tongue over my entrance, my clit, and back down to the start of my ass. The velvety texture against my skin nearly short-circuited my brain with arousal. I was sure I couldn't possibly be more turned on, but then I noticed movement out of the corner of my eye and saw Eve with her hand between her legs. The motion of Allie's mouth matched the rhythm Eve's hand worked inside her panties, and I wondered if she was reliving one of her favorite times with Allie. The idea and the visual took my breath away and I let out a strangled whimper.

"Three and deep, baby, please." I slammed my back into the wall when Allie gave me the three fingers I so desperately needed. No one stretched me like she did, and I bet Eve spent every night missing this feeling. I touched Allie's jaw to relish our connection. She worked and worked, and I was so close. My orgasm was building, my nipples constructed and tingled, and my stomach tightened in anticipation. I knew I was going to come hard.

Eve's panties were pushed aside, and she fingered herself frantically. I watched with rapt attention as her dripping digits disappeared and reappeared. The erotic visual kicked my senses into hyperdrive. I smelled our combined arousal, I heard the slapping of wet skin, I felt my climax igniting every inch of my body, I still tasted Allie's lips, and my eyes feasted on a beautiful woman searching for the pleasure she'd never have again.

I came with a muffled cry. Allie held my hips as I shook and bucked against her. My eyes were clamped shut but I felt tears try to escape. The pleasure was liberating and overwhelming, twisting my stomach with unrelenting waves. I sat limply as the final tremors passed through me. Allie kissed my thighs delicately. I heard Eve come a second later, but I didn't open my eyes until I heard the door open.

Eve paused before leaving. "I'm happy for you," she said sullenly and left.

Allie stood to her full height and pushed a few unruly strands of hair from my face. She leaned in for a kiss, and I swiped my tongue across her lips first. Tasting myself on her was the perfect nightcap to an earth-shattering orgasm. "That was something," Allie said with a chuckle.

"I don't know what came over me. I'm sorry if you were uncomfortable."

"I wasn't. I was barely aware Eve was in the room. All I cared about was you."

I pressed my cheek into Allie's warm palm when she touched my face. "I hope that helped you get over any lingering feelings you may have had..."

Allie kissed me slowly and pulled back with smile. "Since the day I met you there haven't been feelings for anyone else."

My heart warmed and I knew I loved her. "Good."

Allie helped me down from the dresser and straightened out my dress. She picked up my panties and put them in her pocket. "Unless this is what happens when you're jealous. Then I'll have to tell you about the cashier who flirts with me at the grocery store."

I didn't bother to hold back my laughter. We checked around the corner before we left the room. At the bottom of the stairs, I turned back to Allie and pressed my hand to her chest. "Don't think we're done yet. I packed plenty for our night away."

Allie smiled at me, a warm, genuine grin, and I knew she loved me, too. "I can't wait."

INFLORESCENCE

Elna Host

Often quirky, always queer, Elna Holst is an unapologetic genre-bender who writes anything from stories of sapphic lust and love to the odd existentialist horror piece, reads Tolstoy, and plays contract bridge. Find her on Instagram or Goodreads.

I dream of a cavalcade of all the cunts I've ever known. Vaginas, twats, quims, lady parts, honeypots, velvet curtains—call them what you will. They swarm around me, eager as pets, some shy and sheathed, others brazen and dripping, throbbing and ready. I am hot in my sheets, trapped by my own tossing and turning, a prison of fabric I've worked myself into. My temples are pounding; damp ringlets of my hair snake down my forehead, tickling my cheek. My nostrils flare, filled to the brim with the scent of snatch, in all its manifold variations, from the mellow, sweet, drupaceous smell of on-the-verge-of-period to the tart, salty swell of ovulatory heat.

I fucking love cunt. I can't help it—I should wax poetic, no doubt, over the curve of a breast, the swaying of hips, the way her neck turns like a swan's and la-di-da. I would fool no one. At the end of the day, what I want is a generous helping of hot and swollen vulva. I want to fall asleep with my face taut and crusty from its drying outpourings. I want to wake up…not like this.

My fingers play over my pubic mound, but I know it's no use. I can't get myself off. Never could. It's my Achilles' heel.

Frustrated, on the cusp of a dream-induced orgasm cruelly torn away by my own growing wakefulness, I throw off my tangled bedding and stomp toward the bathroom. A cold shower is what I need. Or a crash course in masturbation. But it doesn't work, and don't think I haven't tried. I've scoured the murky corners of the web for tips and tricks on autoerotic techniques. I've spent an embarrassing sum on aids and gear, lotions, and potions, oh my. To no avail. What I need is another woman's wetness, another woman's rapture to spark my own.

I turn the knob, and as usual at this hour the water coming out of the overhead shower is freezing, soul-numbingly so. So much the better. I brace myself and step inside.

❖

After a shower, after coffee and a slice of buttered toast and the whole ritual of tooth-brushing and selecting my outfit du jour, my mind carefully trained on the statistics relating to my latest text-in-the-making, I feel better, slightly. Bordering on human, at any rate.

I try not to think of my thumping clit but instead of rosebushes, hawthorn hedges, the dos and don'ts of autumnal weeding. These are no euphemisms. My day job is as a freelance journalist for several lifestyle gardening magazines.

Learn to cultivate your own garden, wrote Voltaire, and though I have failed in the metaphorical sense, I'll be damned if I'll fail in the literal one. My begonias need watering. My latest article needs pruning. I need to start thinking about soil maturation. There's plenty to do.

Except there's a stubborn shade of arousal seeping into everything I put my hands to. My writing seems riddled with double entendres. I google *fancy* rather than *pansy*. My nipples chafe against my shirt.

Impossible.

Biting my tongue, my nail, my lips, I surrender, at last, to the impulse of picking up my phone and placing an express delivery order with the multinational German logistics company. I have a standing order for tulip bulbs.

It's cheating, I know, but I'm nigh on desperate. I can't think.

The first time I was ever prompted to touch myself *down there*, as we termed it then, I was somewhere around thirteen years of age and had been told by my best friend in the world that it was "nicer than ice cream," a saying we used to refer to *really bloody good.*

I was doubtful, and the doubt leaked into my clumsy fingers endeavouring to manipulate smooth, dry folds. After a quarter of an hour's pointless exercise, I decided, vexed and blushing, that she was messing with me. You can't tickle yourself, they say. The correlation didn't seem far off.

Years later, the topic resurfaced as I was helping her pack up her girlhood room to leave for university.

"You're kidding me?" she said, incredulous—and gorgeous, as ever—where she stood on her bed plucking the fluorescent stars off her ceiling. "You don't masturbate?"

"I just never got into it," I returned evasively, fiddling with the staples still piled on her desk: her coloured pencils, her plethora of scented erasers and decorative tapes. "I don't...I've never found the right way."

"Oh, Millie." She plonked down on the bed and lifted her pleated skirt. "Come here."

As it turned out, I didn't walk out of that drowsy-suburban room with any newfound key to the pleasures of Onan. But I had discovered I was a lesbian—three times over, in the biblical sense.

❖

Rapping my fingertips against the tabletop, I stare in front of me at my plus-sized computer screen, where there's a close-up of a dahlia of the Jowey Winnie variety, flamingo pink.

I have a penchant for ball dahlias. I adore the size and blatancy of them, their rounded petals forming little flutes or tunnels, just big enough to slip your pinkie into. In my middling-sized garden, I have a big chunk of a section dedicated to them, ranging in color from sweet, light powder pink to a deep and rich burgundy. If it were up to me, they would feature prominently in my catalogue of articles. But they're out of fashion, I'm told.

"Too dowdy," one editor informed me. "People want racier stuff in their gardens nowadays."

People must be blind.

I look at my watch. Thirty minutes since my order went out. Another thirty until the appointed lunch hour. I grit my teeth and get up to fetch the watering can.

At my university—another university, in another city, another time—I did a joint honours degree in History and Horticulture. Though some evil tongues would tell you I specialised in Cuntology.

They wouldn't be far off.

My years as a student were spent in a haze of alcohol and pussy juice-induced highs. In between, I read about flowers. Flowers and dead kings.

It's all part of the circle. You bud, you flower, you fuck, you die.

Sure, I craved a steady relationship. But they never seemed to work out. After a while, they all boiled down to: "For fuck's sake, Millicent, you can't come here at all hours just because you've got an itch. I'm behind on my reading as it is. Why don't you give yourself a hand?"

Or worse, teary-eyed complaints. "It's like you're just using me for sex. I feel like a great big blow-up doll. Are you even genuinely interested in me?"

Who would have thought self-stimulation was a prerequisite for long-term coupling? No one questions the foxglove's need for the bumblebee. The daisy's demand for the cabbage white. The bog-standard rose's want of the garden-variety bug.

I needed cunt to keep me going. I needed cunt to take my mind off cunt, if only for a few hours, because there were essays and papers due, there were exams coming up, and what I could use, more than anything, was that blissful peace of mind that only a sound and proper double crescendo can bring about.

Watering begonias takes time. Or perhaps that should be watering *my* begonias takes time. Although, like the dahlia, they are the sort of plant that everyone and their grandmother has had and has thrown away. I stand by the exuberant proclamation put forth in my first published article: "They really are the uncrowned nobility of potted plants!"

I favour, of course, the tuberous kind.

Upstairs, in the master and spare bedrooms, I keep a score of them. A blend of yellows and oranges for the spare; bright stop-signal red for the mistress of the house. There's an office as well, but I rarely go into it. It's overflowing with misguided well-wishers' contributions of Orchidaceae.

Orchids leave me cold. Too elegant, too self-sufficient by far. When I first moved in, I tried working in that room for a couple of weeks, before their oppressive presence drove me to haul my workstation down to the kitchen table, where it has remained since.

I can't bring myself to throw them out. In their own right, after all, they are living, breathing things. I regift them, from time to time; but regifting, too, is a tricky business. For one successfully transferred cymbidium, you might end up with two miniature miltassias to take its place.

This never occurs when I give someone one of my fiercely beloved begonias. A faint smile, a shrug of the shoulders, a breezy "you shouldn't have." No, I end up thinking, I clearly shouldn't have. I'm surrounded by orchid-loving twits.

Downstairs, there's another four dozen Begonia semperflorens, Begonia foliosa, Begonia cucullata, spanning from bridal white to salmon pink. I have a couple of spider plants as well, but those are mainly for the air. Still, they're good little drinkers. They love to please.

Refilling my watering can, I eye the cuckoo clock on the kitchen wall. This too is a present, a tongue-in-cheek prank, but one I treasure, unabashedly, because when that funny little bird makes its appearance with its inimitable clatter and hoot, I know that soon, any second now...

It's five minutes to the hour.

I'm too hot for this. I rub my water-splashed hand over my neck, undoing the top buttons of my shirt to watch the trickle of droplets down my cleavage.

The creases of my cunny lips scrape against the sturdy material of my underwear. A tip I picked up: wear abrasive panties for moments of self-gratification throughout your busy day. If I sit down and rub myself vehemently against, say, the padded arm of an armchair, it almost works.

The key word being *almost*. Excruciatingly, infuriatingly, mind-maddeningly almost.

For my last birthday, which was in May, Violet Krauss, editor-in-chief of *The Reluctant Gardener* (one of these newfangled web journals for city-dwellers dreaming of green-fingered chic), gave me a lily-shaped vibrator.

"You're pushing forty, Miles," she drawled and clinked my glass. "It's time for toys!"

I donated a cattleya to her collection, the next time we met. I don't think she got the message. If anything, she looked positively thrilled.

The cuckoo barges out of its box, shrieking its wood-ball head off, and I'm as close to peaking as I am to wetting myself, or having a heart attack. I drop the watering can into the sink and grab a kitchen towel to dry myself off. I don't know if I'm hearing an engine or myself humming.

I'm hoping both.

There are two seconds of silence. Two seconds in which my morning dream of feminine favours comes crashing back into me full force, until my skin is overrun with rosy excitement, my breath coming in short little gasps. If I close my eyes, I can almost feel them, like something out of a surrealist painting come true: cunts brushing against my arm, my cheek, leaving a snail trail of arousal in their wake. I moan, low in my throat. My finger pads tap against my sweet spot, right behind my left ear.

If I could just…If only…Oh, Jesus.

The doorbell shatters the stillness like an angry alarm. I open my eyes, a slow smile flickering across my lips. It's time. Just in time. At last.

❖

"Ms M. White?"

The woman on my doorstep, official looking and strictly business in her company-issued uniform, studies me archly as she pronounces the three syllables of my foreshortened name, the name printed on the order slip stuck to my package, which she cradles in her arms like a baby animal.

"Yes," I say, angling the door open for her, stepping, pertly, aside. "Do come in."

She hesitates for an instant before taking my cue.

"Where would you like me to put your delivery, madam?" she asks, looking askance at me, craning her neck from side to side. "I'll need you to sign for it."

"Just put it on the table." I bustle her through to the open-plan kitchen, allowing, in the process, the sensitised skin of my wrist to touch her tan, muscular forearm. It makes me tremble. Already, I am losing control.

"Madam," she says, and her chin juts out, working to keep her expression blank, nonreciprocal.

She has the face of an angel. Strong, angular, unforgiving. Like a woodcarving in a medieval church.

But she is alive, radiating her workday warmth, and I want her with every fibre of my being, every drop of my quickly melting core.

I can't remember my lines. I can barely, to tell the truth, remember my name.

"Right there," I stutter, motioning toward the table, before I turn to the kitchen counter, grabbing hold of the kettle to steady myself.

Behind me, I hear the cardboard box swishing across the oilcloth of my tabletop. I peek over my shoulder and catch her square fingers tracing the outline of the stylised floral pattern; a soft, rubbery, squeaky sound reveals that she is pushing at it with a certain amount of force.

I turn on the tap. Lift the lid off the kettle. Wilt against the cool stainless steel of the countertop.

"What are you doing?"

She's right behind me now, not quite touching, yet managing, somehow, to invade every pore of me at once. Porous, that's how I feel. Ready to suck her up through osmosis if that's what it takes.

I turn off the tap and replace the lid on the kettle.

"Water," I say, in a brittle voice. "For tea."

She takes a step closer, the piqué material of her polo shirt just shy of my back.

It's not fair. I know the rules, but it's not fair, not at all.

I am approaching suffocation, my throat and chest too tight to draw breath.

She wields a pen, of the disposable, rollerball variety, and dangles it in front of me.

"I need you to sign the form, madam. Then I'll be on my way."

I snatch the pen from her grip, her teasing the-cat-plays-with-the-rat hold, and turn around, the edge of the counter pressing into the small of my back.

"And what if I don't want you to be on your way?"

❖

I had ordered a special type of potting mulch, tailored for orchids, the first time Rosa Gonzales came to my house.

It was winter, a sleety, bleak kind of day, and I required her assistance with getting the cumbersome bags up the stairs. For real, that time.

"No problem," she said, in her hoarse yet mellifluous voice—that voice which of itself can have me hot and bothered, primed and ready for action, simply by uttering my name in the dead of night. "Just tell me where you want it. No sweat."

In that moment, I knew exactly where I wanted it, and it entailed quite a bit of sweat.

"I…I can't say," I said, confused, violently reddening, ashamed of myself. I counted back the days to my last ignoble fix: a quickie in a bathroom stall at a local dykes-on-bikes bar, with a woman whom, I was uncomfortably aware, I wouldn't have given a second thought in the light of day. Had it been a month already? I wasn't sure.

"Sure, you can," Rosa insisted, and her eyes glimmered in a way that made me weak at the knees.

After she'd left, I put in an order for a shovel, gardening shears, a multipack of black-eyed Susan seeds. And another for green rope netting and mesh support clips. I didn't need any of it.

I half ruined myself, over the next couple of months, hitting the button for Express Delivery, time and time again.

❖

"Well, aren't you a naughty customer today," she says, her tongue clicking for emphasis, her glittering eyes raking down the length of me.

I reach out to touch her. She slaps it away.

"That's against regulations, madam."

I groan. I'm too desperate for games.

Rosa puts her hands on her hips and tilts her head to the side. "You need to come real bad, don't you?"

I nod. I think there might be tears in my eyes. Rosa's eyelids flutter. It's such a slight movement, one might have missed it, might have bought into her whole unaffected façade, her nonchalant pose, her holier-than-thou facial expression.

I suppress a smile.

"Unbutton your shirt for me."

Her command is low but resolute, her eyes narrowing with pleasure as my hands spring to action to do her bidding.

I shrug and let my shirt fall to the floor. Her approving gaze sweeps over the pale, white expanse of me, stopping to consider the soft swell of my love handles, the deep cleft between my tits.

"I want to…" She shakes her head, rephrasing. "Touch your breasts for me. Please."

Pushing the cups of my bra up and out of the way, my hands fill with ample, supple flesh. I grab them, caressing, running my thumbs over the pink pucker of my nipples. Rosa's right hand falls from her hip, clenched tight. I am rocking against the kitchen counter, in time with my own rhythm, my fingers itching to explore further, even as I watch my growing excitement mirrored in my would-be lover's eyes.

"Take off your pants," she rasps out. "Now."

My hands are shaking as they embark upon their newly assigned task—too much, or nearly so, to manage the zip. Rosa's left hand balls into a fist.

Finally, blessedly, I get my slacks open and wriggle out of them. As I put my hand to my underwear, Rosa shakes her head, with a hint of reluctance.

"Not yet," she says, close to a sigh. "Touch yourself through the fabric first. Get yourself warmed up."

"I don't need—" I interject, but she silences me with the merest glance. She falls to her knees on the hardwood floor. She doesn't seem to mind.

"That's quite a picture you've got there," she observes, edging closer, referring to the verging-on-indecent print of a cream and pink peony that covers my genitals. "Why don't you use it as a guide?"

A shock of warmth blooms through my belly at the simple, frankly spoken suggestion. I keel against the counter for support.

"I…I can't," I say, echoing our first verbal exchange.

"Sure, you can." Rosa grins up at me. "Go ahead, babe. I'm right here."

She raises her hand, beckoning me to do the same. Her palm is a hair's breadth away from the back of my hand. Slowly, she moves us into position, not quite touching, never quite touching, yet making every hair on my body stand erect.

"Such a pretty flower." Her fingers' ghost touch coaxes mine into stroking the outlines of each petal. "Let's fondle it. Let's make it sing."

The feel of my own dampness oozing through the cotton makes me hiss. Of my own accord, I run a finger up the puffed-out length of my sex, slicking the fabric against it as I go along. Rosa shudders and drops her hand to her lap, knotting it into her shorts.

"That's right, love. Give us a proper show."

I can't say where the pleasure comes from, whether it's from my own groping fingers, or watching her watching me, her face avid, every pretence at indifference gone, but it doesn't matter. I draw back my shoulders, my nipples tipping up like adventitious buds, and have at it: my fingertips tracing and kneading, patting, and pushing, fervently rubbing the poor flushing flower into me until it's soaking and twisted beyond recognition. I'm glowing and panting with the effort.

So close.

So. Fucking. Close.

I whimper and look down. Rosa has slipped her hand inside her shorts. Her breathing is quick and catching. Her lips are drawn thin as a line. She catches my gaze and looks back at me, helplessly.

"Off," she manages, through gritted teeth. "Fuck's sake, Mill. Take them off."

It practically topples me over the edge. With the last tatters of my patience, I tear at my sticky panties until they're at my feet. I kick them across the room, I don't know where. All my attention, from head to toe, has been pulled into my pulsating centre.

Timidly, I place my hand back over my exposed cunt.

"Move your legs apart a little."

I comply, the air feeling strangely naked against my naked lips. I let out a surprised, involuntary yip as Rosa lies down, her head lodging between my feet.

"Please, babe," she cajoles, though she doesn't need to. "Do it for me. You're gonna make me come so hard."

Through the opening in her shorts I can see her hand working furiously, and I circle my own nub, mimicking her movements, adding a few nuances of my own invention.

It feels *good*.

It feels so good I get floaters of light in my peripheral vision and flames of enjoyment lick along my thighs. The steel counter is kissing the skin of my ass as I slap against it, thrusting into my own hand, my left one coming up to squeeze every last bit of sensation out of my tits. From underneath me, Rosa is bucking, grunting, calling for *madre de Dios*.

I throw my head back and join in the chorus. Even as I feel it, that first tantalising contraction from within, I let my coated fingers slip from my clit and burrow into me, marvelling at my slippery softness, the way I hug myself so wondrously, hungrily tight.

"For the love of fuck!" I cry out, or something to that effect; I can't really say because I'm shaking, my teeth rattling with my first ever honest-to-God and full-blown climax elicited by nothing but my own fair hands.

My knees buckle and I think I'm going to sag to the floor, but I'm swept up by two solid arms pressing me to a piqué shirt-clad chest, my cheek branded, I will discover later, by the machine-embroidered letters that spell out the acronym of the express logistics and delivery firm.

"Fuck," I murmur, as I listen to the rapid heartbeat sounding from inside that chest. Her arms stroke soothingly, tremulously down my back.

"Fuck yeah," Rosa agrees, and I sigh, happily, contentedly, so satisfied it just about hurts.

❖

"Wait! Your sandwiches."

Rosa Gonzales's mouth twitches as she accepts my offering,

wrapped in greaseproof paper, tied around with a bow. She kisses my forehead lightly.

"I'm so flipping proud of you, babes."

I beam beatifically. "Me too, actually."

She starts to turn away again, and I tug at her sleeve, not yet ready to let her go.

"I don't know what I'll do when you start your new job at the office, though," I blabber, feeling fragile, yet pleased, in that peculiar afterglow way. "I mean, I'm happy about your promotion and all, but..."

"Hey." She lifts my chin and rubs her thumb across it. "Don't worry about it, okay? There's always Skype."

Heat spreads across my face, like she's intended, and she chuckles and leans in for a quick peck.

"See you tonight, Milflores. You be good now. Don't do anything I wouldn't do."

I stick my tongue out and shove her, grinning, out the door.

As I turn to tidy the empty cardboard box off the kitchen table—tulip bulbs aren't in season, but you knew that, right?—my mind is flooded with a myriad of images of precisely what Rosa would, in fact, do over a videocall. I have a fertile imagination, the bane and blessing of my comparatively sedentary existence.

I'll get some work done first, however.

At the moment, I'm only moderately moist.

Be Good to Mama

Ali Vali

Ali Vali is the author of the Devil series, including the new book *Heart of the Devil*, and the Forces series, including the new *Force of Fire: Toujours a Vous*. She's written numerous standalones, the newest being *The Inheritance*. Ali currently lives outside New Orleans, where she enjoys cheering LSU and trying new restaurants.

Roselyn Weber sat at the bar of the Saint Hotel on Canal Street and tried to maintain eye contact with Madam Bliss Laroux while also trying not to laugh at what she was trying to talk Bliss into. Bliss had recently moved from Nashville and brought most of her girls with her to set up her burlesque revue, and Roselyn was asking for a unique favor.

"You know my reputation, so that's a lot to ask," Bliss said as she flipped through Roselyn's portfolio again. "You learned from Hazel. Why not try this in Chicago?"

"Hazel thought I'd be more comfortable here since there wouldn't be any familiar faces in the crowd. The classes were a gift from my sister, who thinks I'm boring and who was trying to make me more interesting, and I ended up really enjoying myself."

"Hog-tying your inhibitions and locking them in the basement is usually a freeing experience."

"True, and Hazel said I had a natural talent for it but I wouldn't really graduate until I actually did it in public." The longer she sat in this haven of red velvet and crystal chandeliers, the more ludicrous this sounded. Once Bliss turned her down, she could tell Hazel she'd tried her best and enjoy the rest of her long weekend away from home.

"Ten o'clock show tonight. You can close out the first set." Bliss placed one of her pictures on the table. "Did you bring this one?" Bliss tapped on it with her dark red painted fingernail and Roselyn nodded. "Good, wear it, but Roselyn Weber isn't exactly a catchy stage name."

"How about Rose Devine? That's Hazel's suggestion, anyway."

"See you at ten, Rose, and make sure you leave all your inhibitions in that basement. This is art, and I don't want you freezing up on me. My regulars, as well as the newcomers, expect a certain caliber of performance, and shy hesitancy isn't it. Don't let me down."

"Yes, ma'am."

"It's Madam Bliss. Let's make Hazel proud."

"Is this a high-class brothel?" Dr. Winton Samuel asked the receptionist after glancing around the lobby draped in sheer coverings with suggestive signage on the walls like, "play naughty—sleep saintly."

The receptionist smiled and shook her head. "No, ma'am, it's a Marriott with a bit less corporate stiffness."

"My assistant has quite the sense of humor."

The woman laughed and handed over her keys. She held up a slip of paper and then read from it. "Her message was: Live a little, Mother Teresa. You're not that far from the Hilton, so you can attend your conference and still have a good time." She smiled. "Enjoy your time in New Orleans, Dr. Samuel."

"Thanks," Winton said, planning on dropping her stuff off and heading over to her conference. "I have to get out of here before I lose my sight from all this dim lighting."

The conference at the Hilton was packed, but she figured it was the location more than the subject matter that had driven up the attendance. She walked back four hours later planning to have a drink at the bar and order room service, wanting to avoid the French Quarter for now.

"Dr. Samuel?" the bar hostess at Tempt Bar asked, stopping her in the lobby.

"Have we met?" she asked, changing her mind about the drink because of the size of the crowd in the bar area.

"Not yet, but it's still early. If you'll follow me, your table's ready."

"My table? Who made a reservation? Never mind," she said, seeing her assistant's fingerprints all over this. "How'd you know it was me?"

The woman shook her head and smiled when she stopped at a small table directly in front of the stage. "Your assistant said you were tall, dark, stunning, and too uptight for your own good."

"You figured it was me with that description?"

"Face it, sugar, you ain't exactly painful on the eyes, but you seem like you're tighter than a fifty-year-old virgin. Enjoy the show," she said, accepting a whiskey neat from the passing waitress and handing it to Winton. "You have to promise to stay until the end of the show, or I might have to resort to my handcuffs."

"I promise, but what kind of show?"

"Life ain't no fun without the occasional surprise, Doc, so relax."

She sipped her drink and choked a little when Madam Bliss Laroux came out, introduced herself, then dropped her bra on Winton's head. Leave it to her assistant to pick burlesque as the first outing of her trip. Madam Laroux, though, had quite the swivel in her hips, and as an orthopedic surgeon, Winton could appreciate that. That range of motion was hard to achieve no matter how healthy you were.

A line of dancers all came out after Bliss introduced them and they all had some piece of clothing they wanted to share with her. Apparently, this was the seat that made her the center of attention.

Winton glanced at her watch and the waitress slapped her hand down as she delivered another drink. "All these gorgeous women in here and all you can think to do is look at your watch? What's wrong with you?"

"Sorry, I've got an early morning." She took a sip of the new drink and realized she was way past her limit.

"Or a late night, if you play your cards right." She winked and swished away.

"I've got a real treat for you all, so remember to be kind. Put your hands together for the debut of Rose Devine," Madam Bliss said, winking at Winton. This evening was feeling ever more surreal.

And then nothing else mattered as she watched the petite woman saunter toward the stage and hold her arms out so the two muscular security guys could lift her onto it. She'd never used the word "saunter" in her life, but she couldn't think of any other way to describe the way the woman moved into the room.

"Good God." The sway of her hips could've been the only part of her show and Winton would've been satisfied. Anything more and she knew she'd have the experience seared into her brain—already, all the other performers were a mere shadow of memory.

Roselyn took a few deep breaths to calm herself as Bliss introduced her, but her lungs would only expand so far because of the tight corset under her dress. She was trying to focus on the advice her instructor Hazel had given her and to pretend she was performing in front of her fellow students. A room full of buzzed patrons, though, was certainly a different vibe than her class.

"You'll be fine, and there's plenty of inspiration sitting in the first row," one of Bliss's girls said. "Keep your eyes on the fine specimen at that table," she pointed, "and it'll put some extra swivel in your hips."

"Thanks, I'll try and remember that," Roselyn said and let out a deep breath.

She set off when Bliss finished her introduction and thought about throwing up as she was lifted to the stage, but turning around to face the crowd brought her to life. The music she'd chosen was upbeat and she started by walking from one end of the small stage to the other, leaning down at each end and lightly shaking her breasts at the crowd.

The gloves that came to her elbows peeled off slowly as the lyrics to "When You're Good to Mama" began. She worked the fingers as she moved around the stage mouthing the words.

The gorgeous butch sitting alone at the closest table took a little coaxing, but she finally came up and pulled her glove completely off. Roselyn held her in place to take the other one off, but this time she placed the fingertip of her index finger against the butch's mouth as a challenge. They locked eyes and for once she didn't back down, and she arched an eyebrow when the woman hesitated before taking the edge of the glove between her teeth and gently pulling the glove down.

The softness of the silk sliding down her arm raised goose bumps on her skin, and she knew it was from the sight of her willing participant with the glove hanging from her teeth. She pushed the woman using her fingertip to her forehead and started to feel the rhythm of the routine her friends had helped her put together. It was way more suggestive than she was comfortable with, but the crowd cheered when she unzipped her dress at the side and held it up with her hand to her chest. She smiled coyly.

At the refrain she dropped it so it pooled at her feet. She held her hand out to the woman still holding her gloves, and she stood with no problem this time. Hazel had jokingly told her a corset was the secret to conquering any problem she'd ever face, and maybe she was right. Even a nun would feel sexy wearing this.

She stepped out of her dress and could really move now that her legs were free. She locked eyes with her muse still standing by the stage, but she wasn't sending her back to her seat this time. The chair she'd asked for was front and center, so she sat and shimmied her shoulders as she started unclipping her garter belt from her stockings. Her helper swallowed hard when Rose placed her foot on her chest and worked the fishnets down while wiggling her toes, indicating the woman should finish the job.

The audience started to really cheer when she moved to the ties of the corset, but the intense, hungry look on the woman's face was all that mattered. Achieving the audience's response wasn't why she'd taken the classes, but she'd be lying if she said she wasn't enjoying the attention.

She turned around and opened the corset, waiting for the last few seconds of the song before turning around to show off the red pasties over her nipples. It was the only color she'd added to the all-black outfit. The heat suffusing her face meant she was blushing, but she'd done it, and from the smile on Bliss's face, it had gone okay.

One of the security guys held up her robe as she left the stage for the end of her very short-lived career. She glanced over her shoulder at the butch at the front table, who was still looking at her with starstruck eyes. "With any luck, I have a lifetime fan."

❖

Winton waited for someone to come for the pieces of clothing she had draped over her shoulders, but instead her waitress handed over what she thought was her bill. It wasn't.

The note was short, but it certainly captured her attention.

Room 891—don't forget the gloves.

She read it five times before lifting her head to glance at the entrance, but all she saw were patrons. The performer was gone, and obviously waiting for her in room 891.

"Is there some reason you're still standing here?" the opinionated hostess asked. "You don't strike me as the scared type."

She paid her tab and headed upstairs to see what the performer had in mind. This wasn't her style, not even on vacation in a city that could be the definition of decadence, but maybe she *was* too uptight. The door was held open with the security latch and another note.

Welcome, Dr. Samuel. Have a seat.

There was another glass of whiskey next to the wingback chair, and the music started when the door clicked closed. Rose Devine had to be in the bathroom, so after a moment of hesitation, Winton sat down and gulped the drink for a bit of courage. Maybe this would be better than a massage in the spa.

She unconsciously spread her legs when Rose came out in the corset and a satin thong, and she gulped again at the sight. Rose was stunning, sexy as hell, and utterly mesmerizing as she started a very private dance. The music was slower, and Winton gripped the arms of the chair when Rose turned around to show off the most perfect ass she'd ever seen on a woman.

"It's okay to touch," Rose said, leaning over a little bit as if to encourage her.

She raised her hand and slid it from the small of Rose's back down the slope of her right ass cheek. The urge to put her fingers between her legs was overwhelming, but Rose glanced over her shoulder and winked as if guessing where her mind had wandered.

"Patience, Doc, patience," Rose said and moved a few feet away to continue her dance.

"I'm only human, darlin'."

Rose gave her a good look at her backside before turning around and holding up the lace to the corset. This time if Winton wanted it off, she'd have to do it herself, so she pulled and smiled when Rose shimmied enough to expose her breasts. The pasties were thankfully gone, exposing gorgeous pink nipples.

"Do you like what you see?" Rose asked, moving closer and placing her chest inches from Winton's face. She nodded, having lost the ability to form words. "Then prove it."

Winton chewed through some of her control and sucked her nipple into her mouth, moaning uncharacteristically when it got rock hard against her tongue.

"There's two of them," Rose said, and Winton released her with a pop to treat the other one to the same thing.

With Rose's hands in her hair, Winton cupped that great ass, pulling her closer.

"Not so fast, lover."

The smile on Rose's lips made her relax, and she sat back and waited. She couldn't take her eyes off Rose's breasts when Rose knelt in front of her and unbuckled her belt, unbuttoned her pants, and lowered the zipper as well.

"Dance with me," Rose said, rising to her feet with her hand out.

When Winton stood her pants fell and she kicked them away, leaving her in very plain white Jockeys.

They took a few steps together as Rose slowly unbuttoned Winton's shirt and took it off, along with her bra. She stopped breathing when Rose ran her hands from her shoulders down her chest to the top of her underwear.

"Can I have these?" Rose asked, tugging at the waistband.

"You can have anything you want," Winton said, and Rose tugged her Jockeys down, following them to the floor before pushing her back in the chair.

"This is your last chance to stop," Rose said, dragging her hands from Winton's knees to the tops of her thighs. Winton shook her head and closed her eyes when Rose leaned in and kissed her. "You know what I want, baby?"

"No, but I'll do whatever necessary to give it to you." Winton cleared her throat when her voice cracked embarrassingly.

"I want to make you come with my mouth first," Rose said as she ran her tongue along her top lip. "I'm going to suck right here." She spread Winton's sex open and pinched her clit hard enough that Winton was sure she'd beg if she stopped. "I'm going to get you hard, and then I'm going to suck you until you come for me."

"Okay," she said, knowing she sounded like a complete dork. Thankfully, Rose knew what she was doing and saying, because a witty and suave comeback to make someone wet wasn't Winton's forte. She guessed it was all part of her uptightness, something Rose was cutting through like a hot knife through ice cream.

Rose lowered her head and started; a fantasy come to life. It felt so fucking good, and Winton dug her toes into the carpeting to not come as fast as an inexperienced teenager. Rose was relentless, though, as she switched from a feather touch to sucking like she wanted Winton to feel it in every cell of her body. Just when she thought she'd explode, Rose went back to the feather touch, and Winton wanted to cry from the need to come.

"Please, baby," she said and had to relax the muscles in her legs before she got a cramp.

"Please what?" Rose lifted her head and took the time to gently bite her nipples.

"I need to come," she said, sounding like she'd run around the city carrying her car.

"Then come for me." Rose sucked her in and didn't let up. She trapped Winton's clit between her tongue and the roof of her mouth, and Winton shut her eyes and gave thanks to whatever entity had made this night possible. The tightening in her belly built as the orgasm did, and short of being knocked out cold, she couldn't stop it.

"Fuck," she said louder than she meant, and had to tug Rose's head away when she became hypersensitive.

Rose's wet lips and smug smile were too much, so Winton picked Rose up and gently tossed her on the bed. Asking permission was probably the way to go here, but she ripped the panties off so she could flatten her tongue over Rose's clit and bury her fingers in her pussy, words something she couldn't be bothered with in the moment. Never in her life had she wanted to totally possess a woman, but tonight Rose was going to be hers in every sense of the word.

Her fingers came out slowly and went in as quickly, and she

smiled when Rose's hips came off the bed and she grabbed a fistful of Winton's hair to keep her head in place. "Oh fuck, baby, just like that." Rose writhed, her hands alternating from Winton's hair to grasping at the bedsheets.

"Tell me what you want," she said, and Rose moved her head from side to side when she moved her fingers in and out again, slowly.

"I want you to fuck me," Rose said. She gave her what she wanted and kept pace with Rose's hips, loving how wet she was and how much she seemed to want this.

"Right there, baby...don't fucking stop."

She slammed her fingers in faster and concentrated when Rose closed her legs, trapping her head between them. The moan Rose released before she relaxed and let her legs fall open made her think she'd erased at least a bit of her dorky, egghead image.

"You know," Winton said, as she moved up so Rose could lie on top of her, "when I said you needed rehab after your ankle surgery, I thought you would've used the office's PT guy. Not a burlesque class." Her face hurt from smiling when Roselyn rested her head right under her chin and sighed contentedly.

"What's the fun in that, Dr. Samuel? Those lessons got me back in heels in no time flat." Roselyn slid off her, circled her navel with her index finger, and laughed. "And if you remember, I asked you out when I came in to have my stitches removed, and you turned me down. You should've said yes, considering I was trying to get a good look at your ass when I tripped over the box by my desk. I had to resort to drastic measures to get you to notice me."

"I noticed you every time you came to the office to do our books, so don't think you're invisible. Heels are something I don't recommend, but hell if you don't look sexy as hell in them."

"Then why not say yes? It would've saved me getting practically naked in front of a crowd," Roselyn said, pinching her nipple hard enough to make her hiss.

"Because I'm an idiot, clearly." She lifted Roselyn on top of her again and smiled. "But only private dances from now on, okay? Or I might need a cardiologist."

"I promise, and I want to start another performance right now—only it requires a partner."

"I'm not a very good dancer."

Roselyn leaned over, opened the nightstand, and held up a strap on. "I think you can manage. How else can I demonstrate my bump and grind abilities?" Roselyn slapped her thigh to get her to lift her hips and got the thing in place in no time.

She glanced down and smiled at the new addition to her anatomy and at the way Roselyn gracefully straddled her.

"Fuck me," Roselyn said as she slowly lowered herself until she'd taken it all in.

"With pleasure."

❖

"So, what exciting things did you do on your vacation?" Winton's assistant asked when she got back.

"She learned how to dance, and it went pretty well," Roselyn said as she sat down to start on their financials.

"Dance lessons?" Sean asked Winton. "You have absolutely no rhythm."

"It depends on the partner, buddy," she said, moving closer to Roselyn and getting her ass slapped hard. "The right one can be rather motivating, and with the right incentive you don't mind doing it over and over until you get it right."

"And your dance card is filled, so don't think some other clumsy accountant will come along and teach you any new moves."

"You have a deal, on one condition." She lowered her head and whispered in Roselyn's ear. "Tell me you didn't toss out the pasties."

Taking a Leap

Kitty McIntosh

Kitty is a Scottish writer and poet. She is an avid reader and posts her reviews on her blog, *Kitty Kat's Book Review Blog*. She writes lesbian romance, mysteries, erotica, and poetry. She has been published in the anthology *Our Happy Hours* and in *A Heart Well Traveled*.

I had an itch that needed to be scratched and I knew exactly what it would take. I'd been preparing, getting my special collection together. It was hidden at the very back of my walk-in closet, on a top shelf, in a hat box, underneath piles of violet tissue paper. My flat-mate Josie was too nosy for me to take any chance of it being found. I suspected she'd be shocked and horrified at the thought of her seemingly straitlaced friend being involved in such fantasies. But I had to do something about it, and soon.

I heard the front door click shut. At last, I had the place to myself. I got up on my tiptoes and reached way back until I could grab the box. It was getting heavier. Each month on payday I had bought another item to add to my collection. The latest had arrived in the mail in a plain brown package. I could feel my excitement build. But before I opened it up, I would go through the contents of the box. I had already committed each item to memory, and I had imagined the ways they would be used. Maybe it was a bit OCD, my little routine, but it got me hot and bothered, and I was always ready for some alone time by the time I got to the bottom of the box.

It was my guilty little secret, and I must admit to getting quite a thrill from that fact. Maybe that's why I kept it up. I lifted the things out, one by one, stroking my fingers lightly over the purple silk scarves, thinking of the day I'd finally get to use them. Next came the black leather corset, studded with shiny metal. I hadn't dared try it on. I wanted to keep it special. The heaviest items in the box were the various tubes of flavored and colored lubes. I had read that one could never have enough. Well, I certainly didn't know from experience. All my fantasies were based on erotica and my vivid imagination. This month's addition to the collection was the one I had been most looking forward to. I had chosen carefully, and after much consideration, from the catalogue. Although I had never used one, I knew that I wanted a strap-on, a leather one. And I had booked a special weekend away where I planned to use it.

❖

As I drove through the Scottish Highlands toward the address of the country house on my invitation, the sheer beauty of the area astounded me. On either side of the narrow, winding road, craggy cliffs showed layers of rocks built up over millions of years. Waterfalls poured down mountainsides topped with hard-packed snow, and sheep grazed in the uneven green fields that stretched for miles. Although it was cold outside, I wound my window down, desperate to breathe in the cool, clean air. The sharp cry of an eagle sounded above the whir of my engine and I watched as it swooped down to pick up an unfortunate rabbit for its meal. A large metal sign in the distance alerted me to slow down as I reached Farrington Manor. Turning onto the long, bumpy driveway I could see the house looming above, clearly visible on top of a hill. It was in the style of a Georgian mansion, with a large courtyard in the front. The area was being used to park several expensive-looking cars, and my Mini looked decidedly out of place.

It was at this point that the butterflies firmly took root in my stomach. I tried to look super confident as I walked from my teeny-tiny car up the huge stone steps leading into the hallway of the house. I certainly didn't feel it. I don't know what I expected, but the calm, matter-of-fact reception I received took me aback. Were they so used to organizing sexual fantasy fulfilment parties that no one batted an eye?

Walking through the house on the way to my room was like walking back in time a hundred and fifty years. The wall hangings and carpets were of an earlier era but in beautiful condition. The smell was of beeswax mixed with a floral scent I couldn't quite pinpoint. In a building this old there was no elevator, so I followed a uniformed housekeeper up the wide, sweeping staircase to the first floor. My room was at the end of the corridor. I had tried to sneak a peek at the other rooms with doors slightly ajar, but they seemed to be unoccupied. I was curious about my fellow participants. I'd be getting to know one of them very intimately later. At that thought I shivered—although I was unsure if it was due to anticipation or fear. My bravado was beginning to slip.

If I had been impressed by the public areas of the house, the bedroom took my breath away. A huge four poster bed dominated the space. Luxurious silk sheets and plump pillows made me wonder what might be taking place there in a few hours' time. *If* I could hold my nerve. A log fire burned in the fireplace, warming the room. I was drawn to an envelope on one of the pillows. My name was written in beautiful italic lettering, and on the back a wax seal added to the mystique. It seemed a shame to rip it open. But I was intrigued and carefully peeled it back, removing a card with instructions and a black silk mask.

Dinner will be served at seven p.m. in the dining room.
Wear the enclosed mask.
Bring a small overnight bag with ALL items required as
you may be spending the night in another client's room.

This was real. I was actually going to do this. And despite the somersaults currently taking place in my stomach, I couldn't wait.

❖

The gong in the hall reverberated around the mansion. My room was at the back, miles from the dining room, but I could hear it clearly and almost jumped out of my skin at the sound. Time to face the others. Instead of being paired with our chosen partners privately, it seemed we were to face each other over dinner first. I wasn't sure I could face a roomful of strangers, knowing that we were all there to carry out our personal fantasies. I hoped the lighting was low, as I was sure my face would be beetroot-red the whole time. Well, the part of it they could see.

At the table, we were all wearing our black silk masks covering a portion of our faces. I can't remember what we had for dinner, and I doubt I ate a bite. The resident butterflies in my stomach saw to that. As dessert was being cleared, a tall, slim woman wearing white gloves placed cards in front of each of us. On each card was written the number of the room we were to go to. Furtive glances toward the cards indicated that I wasn't the only nervous participant at the table. That made me feel a little better.

A gong sounded again, and our host made an announcement.

"Please make your way to the room number on the card. Each one of you has been paired with participants open to your fantasies. Those without a pairing, please go to your own rooms and wait. Enjoy!"

It was then that I noticed that only half of us had cards. But that didn't matter to me. I had mine, and I was ready. One by one we filed out. The number fifteen was now imprinted on my brain as I walked through the portrait-filled corridors toward what I hoped would be a life-changing night of sexual bliss.

❖

Standing outside of room fifteen, I slowly lifted my hand and knocked hesitantly on the heavy oak door. It wasn't locked, or even closed. I pushed it open and stepped inside the room. She was standing in front of the lit fireplace. It cast a subtle glow over her face, and I could see she was still wearing her mask. My breath hitched at the sight of her. Her eyes shone and she was looking straight at me. There was a challenge there. We both knew what we were there for, and there was no point in being coy. Her eyes flicked down to the black bag I was carrying, and I could feel the anticipation in the air. A stab of panic hit me. I'd tried to appear so brave, but it just occurred to me that she might be expecting more than I was willing to give—or take. My heart felt as if it would burst from my chest and I thought there was a good chance she could hear it thumping. One more second and I would have turned and fled. But she stopped me. A smile gradually appeared on her face, breaking the unbearable tension. She started to move toward me, never once taking her eyes off mine.

My requirements for this fantasy had been carefully thought out, and the top priority for me was silence. I knew exactly what I wanted to do and didn't want to spoil it by putting my foot in it and saying something stupid. Only now that I was here, that didn't seem important. The way she looked at me pushed all other thoughts from my mind. I wanted to touch her, and as she arrived at the spot I had welded myself to, I reached for her, running my fingers gently down her arm. Her breath hitched. Taking her hand, I led her to the bed and pulled back the sheet. Purple silk, exactly as I had requested. I had a thing about purple. I laid my black bag on the bed and clicked it open. Then I gently removed her little black dress, letting it fall to her ankles. I knelt and lifted her feet, one at a time, removing her shiny black stilettos. A slight change to my carefully choreographed plan occurred to me, and once I had thrown the dress onto a nearby upholstered chair, I put the shoes back on her feet. They were so hot, and I could imagine them wrapped around my neck as my tongue ravished her pussy. I reached into my bag and pulled out four purple silk scarves. I tied one to each wrist, then indicated she should lie on the bed. Once her wrists were tied to the wooden posts, I tied the remaining two to her ankles and then to the posts at the bottom of the bed. I had planned on a blindfold for this fantasy, but her eyes entranced me, and I couldn't countenance removing the mask she had on. I wanted to look into those eyes as I slowly fucked her.

My carefully thought-out plan involved music, soft, sensual music. I connected my phone to the speaker discreetly hidden behind the heavy velvet curtains. Her eyes never once left me as I carried out each small step. I removed my shirt and my black silk trousers and stood naked in front of her. Did she like what saw? I hoped so, because I certainly liked the vision before me on the bed. I put on my tight leather bodice and stepped into the harness I had agonized over for months. I fitted a long, thick, shiny silicone dildo into it, loving the feel of it pushing against my already hard clit. I was so ready for this I could feel the wetness begin to drip down my legs. I wanted to take this slow, that had been my plan, but it was going to be a struggle. I wanted to be inside her, to thrust hard until she screamed. Instead, I made myself stop and take in the view.

Her long blond hair was splayed out on the pillows and the small strip of hair between her legs glistened as she became progressively wetter. I leaned down and placed a kiss on each breast, then took her nipple into my mouth, rolling my tongue around and around until it was rock-hard. She began to moan, softly at first, then more insistently. I could feel her hips begin to move, to buck. If she hadn't been tied down, I was sure she'd have pushed my head to exactly where she wanted it. I wanted it too and wasn't about to make her wait. I made my way to her wetness and I couldn't get enough. I drank every ounce, and still more replaced it. Licking every inch, I found the taste intoxicating, addictive. Her clit beckoned me, and I sucked it hard, encouraged by her increasingly loud moans. My face sank deeper into her folds, licking, sucking, desperate for everything she was willing to give. Her screams filled the room as her body convulsed, over and over again, and a final gush soaked me, covering my face with her delicious juices.

Gradually she stopped twitching and I looked up and saw a satisfied woman staring back at me. But I wasn't finished. I indicated the dildo jutting out from the leather strap-on. She nodded. I untied the silk scarves from her wrists and ankles and flipped her over on to her stomach. My fantasy was to take her from behind, but first I had to have a bite. Her ass beckoned me. I massaged her beautiful cheeks, my thumbs dipping into the crevice, teasing ever closer. I bent down and kissed the soft skin before nipping at her repeatedly until she was squirming so much, I could barely hold her. I could see her pussy was dripping and ready for me. Sliding the dildo through the juices, I made sure it was coated before pushing inside, inch by slow inch. Her cries of pleasure sent a jolt to my clit and I increased my pace, faster and faster until she screamed so loudly, I was sure the whole house would hear. Her ass thrust back into me as she came, pushing the dildo against my clit and pushing me over the edge. Never had I felt such a powerful orgasm. I could barely focus for the stars in front of my eyes as my insides contracted deliciously. I collapsed on the bed beside her, falling into a deep, contented sleep.

❖

As I checked out next morning, I saw the beautiful blonde leave just ahead of me. And I knew that this wouldn't be a one-off. I would be back on the website as soon as I got home, booking the same again for the next month. And I hoped she would too.

Although, I'd found myself, and I was going to keep delving into every fantasy I had, no matter who my masked playmate might be. I'd taken the leap, and I'd landed exactly where I needed to be.

THE BET

Sandy Lowe

Sandy Lowe is the author of *Party of Three*, *Irresistible*, and *Party Games* and is the Senior Editor at Bold Strokes Books.

I could be a cheater. I could be a liar. I could just skip all the drama and run away. No one would find me. Of course, I'd know I was a wussy little coward, but the shame would wear off eventually. That'd be a small price to pay to keep what's left of my dignity.

I steer the Lexus to the curb of the Ritz-Carlton and hand my keys to the hipster-skinny valet huddled heroically against the March wind. The fancy-pants cobbled entranceway was designed by someone who's never worn heels, and mine are killer. Flirting that delicate line between sexy and porn star, the four-inch, midnight blue death traps make my calves thinner and my ass oh-so-perky. Beauty is pain. Right now, I need all the help I can get.

If I didn't love tequila almost as much as air, I wouldn't be in this mess. Like a lousy lover, it sweet-talked me with promises, convincing me that I'm beautiful, and funny, and spontaneous. Then it kicked my ass into next Tuesday.

I'm never drinking again. Tequila and me? We've officially broken up.

I head straight for the bank of elevators when I hit the lobby. I might want to ride off into the sunset Thelma and Louise style, but I'd only hope for such a poignant end if my friends ever found out I reneged on *the bet*. Some people have the kind of friends that send you cupcakes on your birthday. Mine get you shit-face drunk and post the evidence on Instagram. Mercy's got no currency when a good laugh's at stake.

The elevator doors open on the fourteenth floor, and I breathe slowly out through my teeth. Even though I'm already walking down the corridor, scanning for 1425, part of me doesn't quite believe it. That's the sane part of me. The rest of me keeps going.

The churning in my gut isn't all anxiety. Confession time. My deepest, most intimate fantasies have always involved fucking women. More specifically, women fucking me. This is my chance, and I'm still debating whether to seize it or run like hell.

1425. I knock before I lose my nerve.

She's entirely unexpected and my knees wobble. Five-foot-eight with broad shoulders and narrow hips, she couldn't possibly be the… Could she?

"Hi, you must be Meg." Her eyes are so blue I blink. She's not quite smiling, not quite smirking. A lazy half tilt of lips. She's expecting an answer, but I'm two steps behind her, still taking in the fact that she's…well, she's…butch. No one says that anymore, but there's just no better word to describe that way of embodying masculinity in a form so lusciously female.

Her blond hair's short and lighter on top, as if she spends a lot of time outdoors. She looks capable, like I could hand her a power tool and she'd know how to use it. Like she isn't afraid to get her hands dirty. Like she wouldn't break a sweat fucking me.

"Um, hi," I say, smooth as sandpaper. I should leave. Right after I scrape my tongue back into my mouth.

She swings the door wider and motions for me to come in. I do. Tequila didn't give me a lot of choice in the matter.

"I've never done this before. Had sex with a hooker, I mean. I've never had sex with a woman, either. Actually, I've never had sex with anyone. I'm, like, a total virgin," I blurt the instant I'm over the threshold, then immediately clap my hand over my mouth.

Oh my God.

Her sultry ocean eyes laugh. "Sex worker."

That's right. I tell a professional I'm a virgin and she corrects my vocabulary.

"Sorry. I've never had sex with…someone who's paid." Heat

rises up my neck, reminding me why the phrase *out of your depth* was coined.

"That's okay. We can take it as slow as you need. I'm Lane. It's nice to meet you." She takes my hand as if we're on a date and leads me to a couch in a corner of the room. "Why don't you tell me why you're here."

I don't really want to talk, but I can't help myself. I blab when I'm nervous. The three brain cells in my head still functioning are preoccupied, admiring the way her shirt pulls against the swell of her breasts. It looks starched. Do people still starch stuff? It's endearing and I imagine opening it, one button at a time. The heat migrates to my cheeks.

"I'm not really supposed to be here," I tell her, half statement, half apology.

She nods as if this makes perfect sense when it obviously doesn't. She hasn't let go of my hand, and her fingers wrapped around mine set a fire alarm shrieking in my head. Too hot to handle.

"Two nights ago, I was at this club with my friends, Cassie and Jordan. It was my birthday, and I got pretty wasted. Like, can't stand up on my own wasted. Anyway, Jordan bet me I wouldn't be able to down three tequila shots in succession without choking. I'm an idiot and took the bet. When I lost, I knew I'd have to sleep with a girl."

It's that word *girl* that finally shuts me up. There are so many words I could use to describe her: stunning, gorgeous, sexy, but *girl* wouldn't make the list.

"Why?" she asks.

She's rubbing circles over the inside of my wrist. I'm not sure why touching my wrist should make it hard for me to breathe, but if she doesn't stop soon, I'll need a paper bag. My nipples harden and the breath I can't catch expands in my throat. Can she see my hard nipples through my dress? Should I care if she can?

"Because that's the payment for any bet Jordan makes. She thinks it's weird I've never...you know."

She does know. Far better than me. That's exactly the point. How many other fidgety women has she had on this couch? Loads, probably.

"Jordan doesn't understand why I've never had sex. So she's always making bets to try and get someone to pop my cherry," I tell her, like everyone says *pop my cherry* and I'm not completely losing it.

Lane leans toward me and our thighs press together. Even through the fabric, I can tell she's solid muscle.

"Why are you still a virgin?" Her voice is low, intimate. She brushes a strand of hair behind my ear and I forget the question. Her lips are so close. I want her to kiss me. Imagine it. Try to will it into existence.

Please. Kiss me.

"Meg?"

"I didn't really know I was gay until college and I never wanted a girlfriend. But, well, no girlfriend, no sex. I've never met a lesbian who can fuck without getting attached. All my friends' hookups were so much drama." I flush. It's true, but it still makes me sound like an asshole. "Not that there's anything wrong with that."

Why am I explaining my desire for romance-free, drama-free sex to a sex worker? She gets it.

"Is that why you're here? So I'll fuck you without getting attached?" she asks.

I nod. I'm distracted processing the way the word *fuck* sounds coming out of her mouth. I want her to say it again with her fingers moving inside me.

"I figured, well, I figured this arrangement would be perfect. Plus, I have to tell my friends about it later, and if sex is anything like kissing, girls you're dating get really annoyed when you talk about it. I learned that freshman year when Bianca Turner and I made out in the library." I bite the inside of my lip. Next thing you know I'll be telling her about my first crush and my daddy issues.

"Sounds reasonable." She touches a finger to the tip of my chin. "We should make your first time special."

I nod. Words desert me. Too little, too late now.

"What do you fantasize about when you touch yourself?" Lane asks.

I groan. I don't exactly mean to groan, but it comes out of my mouth before I can stop it. This would be a lot easier if she didn't say things like *touch yourself.*

"I don't know. A lot of different things." I'm the poster child for dorks everywhere.

Somehow, I thought I'd be cooler. I'm generally unflappable. I've given a thesis presentation to twenty frowning professors. I don't flinch at needles, I even bungee jumped in New Zealand. But this woman, with her tropical breeze eyes and blunt questions, has me alternating between winning the grand slam for most embarrassing thing ever said and being totally tongue-tied.

"How about kissing? Do you fantasize about that?" Her voice is soft and coaxing.

I dig deep to find my game. "I've been fantasizing about kissing you since the second you opened the door."

Her smile warms. It's genuine, the kind that ends with a twinkle in her eyes. "I like the sound of that."

I smile back and that's as far as my game gets before her lips are on mine. She doesn't waste time, and that's fine with me. I was never any good at talking dirty. The kiss is confident. As advertised, she knows exactly what she's doing. That part's better than fine.

Her tongue slides between my lips, and I get a rush that starts at my mouth and ends between my legs. I'm already wet. Already getting that squirmy, urgent, hollow feeling in my pussy. The one that makes it hard to think about anything but being fucked.

I press my face into her neck before I can find my voice to beg. "God, sorry. I need a second."

"Doing okay?" She slides her hand into my hair and cups the nape of my neck.

I nod even though I know she can't see. "I never expected it to be like this."

"What do you mean?" Her fingers sift through my hair and down my spine to the curve of my ass in one teasing caress. They hover there, not quite touching, before trailing slowly back up again. I squirm. I want her hands on my ass. Would she touch me there if I asked her?

My ability to form a coherent sentence was shot the second she put her hands on me, so I keep it short. "You're hot."

There's a laugh in her voice when she says, "That's a problem?"

The laugh only embarrasses me more. "I never knew how much I wanted to be kissed like that, by someone like you, until right now."

I pull my face from her neck and watch as her eyes widen, and the line of her mouth softens. I've surprised her. I'm oddly proud to have surprised a woman who, I'm sure, has heard just about everything.

"I'm glad it was me who opened the door." Lane brushes her lips over mine. "I'd like to touch you."

I nod. God, yes.

She stands and pulls me against her. "You're very beautiful."

I know she's paid to say that kind of thing, but Lane's sin wrapped in sex, sprinkled with lusty goodness. It makes me giddy. Beautiful women are bold. I press my body to hers and wrap my arms around her waist. "Want to know what else I fantasize about?"

"Oh, absolutely."

"I have this one fantasy that gets me off…"

Her mouth slides over the column of my neck. "Tell me."

"I'm in a bar. It's crowded, and noisy, and I'm not drunk enough yet to find the country music star wannabes amusing. It's the kind of place that has Bud Light on permanent special. Where cowboy hats and belt buckles tussle for dominance in an overcrowded market. Not my kind of place. I'm there for her, for my mystery date. I'm the cautionary tale, the blond chick in a horror movie that's too stupid to live. I'm meeting a stranger I found on the internet for sex."

Lane's breath is warm against my neck as she pushes my hair to the side and finds the zipper of my dress. "Keep going."

Tomorrow I'll be shocked at how brazen I'm being, but right now I don't care about anything except what's going to happen next. The reason we're both here. The part that's less about fantasy and more about pushing, sliding, pumping, fucking. I press my pussy to her thigh.

"I'm circling the room, trying to find her. I start to wonder if I've been stood up. That pisses me off. I went to a lot of trouble to look good. And suddenly, there she is, watching me, a sweaty bottle of IPA dangling from her fingers. The back of my neck prickles. I thought I was the hunter, but really, I'm the prey."

Lane's palms coast down the bare skin of my back, parting my dress and sliding the thin straps down my arms until our bodies pressed together is the only thing holding it up. She kisses me, just a little rough, using her tongue like I pray she'll use her hands. "Not a hearts and flowers type, are you?"

I shake my head. "Do you think I'd be here if I was?"

"What does she do to you, this stranger you shouldn't be meeting?" Lane asks.

"I try to act cool, like I'd known she was watching me, but she's not buying it. She doesn't care about pretenses. About politeness, or small talk. She's after one thing, and the way her eyes rake over me like she's ripping off my clothes leaves no room for misunderstanding. She holds out her hand. The only invitation I'm going to get. My choice. My consequences. I take it."

Lane backs me toward the bed, letting my dress slip to the floor in a puddle. "Leave the heels on," she murmurs, dropping to her knees. My insides do a wobbly somersault and belly flop back into place. I might throw up, or spontaneously combust—both seem plausible. I clutch her shoulders for balance as I step out of the dress. I'm the one who looks like a sex worker, in my black lace push-up bra, whisper-thin panties, and come-fuck-me heels. Lane's breath shudders out and caresses my thighs. She must touch dozens of women in her line of work. It's ridiculous to expect her to be turned on, to hope that my desire somehow singles me out. But I want her to want *me*, and not the cash sitting in the bottom of my purse.

"Are you wet?" she asks.

Niagara Falls is nothing but a trickle of water compared to the rush between my legs. I bite my lip, shy now that I'm as good as naked and Lane's staring at me. I can't quite find the courage to answer her directly. "Why don't you find out?"

She presses her mouth against my panties and her tongue against my clit.

Oh, fuck.

"I can taste you through these. You're soaking." Lane has no problem at all being direct.

My clit throbs under her tongue, and I thrust my pussy into her mouth. I need more. I've never needed anything so much in my life. "Please."

"Do you beg your fantasy woman so nicely?" she asks.

I continue with my tale. "We don't even leave the club, just go around the side of the building to an alley that reeks of day-old buffalo wings and other unmentionables I don't want to think about touching my shoes. She pushes me against the wall. She's between my legs, her hands on my breasts. She slides my skirt up and rubs her thigh against my pussy."

Lane makes a strange sound in the back of her throat. Under other circumstances I would've said it was pain. But I don't need experience to know that it's pleasure. The line between pain and pleasure, between torment and temptation, between waiting and wanting, is so fine it's imperceptible.

"Don't come until I'm fucking you." My soft and coaxing lover disappears, taking my inhibitions with her. Lane's tone reminds me of a drill sergeant, more bite than seduction. It shouldn't have made me even wetter, but it does.

"Okay." I don't have a chance in hell of keeping my promise. I'm already close, and we've barely even started.

Lane drags my panties down my legs and turns me so I can sit on the side of the bed. She teases me, licking my folds and pushing her tongue inside my pussy. My heart rate doubles in an instant, pounding its beat in my ears. Oral is the thing I've wondered about the most. The thing, really the *only* thing, that a sex toy or your own hands can't give you the gist of. That feeling of warmth, and lips, and tongue on your most sensitive place. I open my legs wider. *More.*

When she starts flicking, and dipping, and swirling her tongue from one place to the next, I fall backward onto the bed, unable to watch, unable to do anything but ride her mouth and feel…everything. She lingers just long enough to make it feel good, to make me want more. Just long enough that my hips rise and my stomach quivers. But not quite long enough, not quite hard enough, to make me come. If she doesn't touch my clit soon, I'm going to beg. I know I'll beg with the same certainty that I know she'll want me to.

"What happens next?" Lane asks.

My body answers her question with a thousand helpful suggestions. Next, suck my clit. Next, fuck me. Next, do anything you want, as long as I get to come.

It's only when she pauses expectantly that I remember the fantasy.

"She shoves my shirt up and slides her hands along my rib cage and under my bra. Her fingers are cold and my skin's hot. We're fire and ice. She's all that stands between me and burning alive. She palms my breasts, but we both know that's not why she's here, not what she really wants. She abandons them quickly, sliding under my skirt instead, under my panties, touching me there," I say.

I'm so close my whole body trembles, tense and expectant.

"Don't come yet," Lane murmurs.

"God, please just do it." I'm as moronic as a teenage boy getting his first blow job. It's her fault. Her doing. The woman on her knees in front of me and the woman playing a role in my head merge as lips wrap around my clit.

I cry out. I'm going to come. I start to shake. She presses the tips of her fingers to my opening and I hold my breath, desperate to hold on. "Please."

I have to keep going. "I'm better than this. Better than the dirty alley, better than three minutes of foreplay, but underneath it all, we're the same, her and I. Both ruled by our desire. Both of us looking for the rulers of our limits."

Slowly, so slowly, Lane presses deeper into me. She sucks my clit as she waits for my body to adjust to her fingers. My brain declares a national holiday and shuts up shop. Why bother with fantasy when reality is so much more intense? My hips pump into Lane's hand. She slides all the way in, and it feels better than I'd hoped. So good I come around her fingers, fast and sharp, like the snap of a rubber band, crying, and shivering, and begging in nonsense words I can't seem to stop. Begging her to never stop. "Please."

She starts to fuck me, and before the first orgasm subsides, I can feel a second building. She slides slow and deep, pushing my knees up to my chest and sucking my clit, rolling it over her tongue. I grab her head and thread my fingers in her hair. My entire world is the glide of her fingers inside me. She reaches right through me, surrounding me, encompassing me.

"Come again," Lane says against my clit.

She fucks me harder. When she sucks my clit again, pulling it tight between her lips, I shatter, my orgasm breaking like shards of glass over us, piercing and splintering.

I gasp for breath like a sprinter finishing a race, spent and wobbly. When I've recovered enough to prop myself up on my elbows, she's sitting back on her heels licking her fingers, sticky with my come. It's just about the sexiest thing I've ever seen.

I can't take my eyes off her and Lane smiles. "Tell me, what else do you fantasize about?"

IN A PLACE LIKE THIS

Rebecca Stieglitz

Rebecca Stieglitz is a femme lesbian from Southern California. She loves women, writing, and writing about women. "In a Place Like This" is her erotica debut.

I'm not expecting much when I walk into the party that night. Just a few drinks, some small talk, maybe a little dancing. But as soon as I step into the bar, I see her. And she sees me.

She's only a little taller than me, but her dark leather jacket and casual swagger make her seem larger than life. She's got a buzzcut and an industrial piercing in one ear. When our eyes lock, I feel a chill down my spine and a spark between my legs.

"Who's that?" I whisper to Sasha, a femme friend of mine who makes it her business to know about every butch in town.

"Oh, KT?" Sasha laughs and slaps me on the back. "Good luck, Diana. She's a mechanic down on Sixth Street. Very mysterious, very private. I haven't even been able to find out if she's got a girlfriend."

"Maybe I'll find out." I tug the neckline of my top a little lower. From the way KT looked at me, my money is on no girlfriend. Sasha raises her eyebrows but doesn't stop me as I start to weave through the crowd toward KT.

There's not much room to maneuver, and I keep running into people I know. It is a party, after all. Someone offers me a shot, another friend asks me where I got my skirt, and soon enough I've lost track of my mission. I can't even see KT anymore. I give in to my friends' distractions and try to have a good time, but I keep scanning the room for her. She's stuck at the back of my mind and I can't let her go.

"Diana, come dance," my friend Rachel says. It's not really a question. She hauls me out onto what passes for a dance floor and starts swaying with me, playfully spinning me around and around.

On one of the spins, I see her. She's in a far corner of the room, slouching against a counter and idly sipping a beer. She sees me see her, like before, but this time she sets down her drink and starts walking toward me.

I start to wish I had taken more than one shot. Rachel is still dancing with me, sweet and gentle, but I can feel the heat rising in my cheeks as KT approaches. I don't even know this woman. I don't know if she will dance with me. But I sure hope she will.

"Excuse me." KT is close enough to touch. "Rachel, do you mind if I cut in?"

"Go for it." Rachel actually passes my hands over to KT before wandering off to coerce a new dance partner. I don't see where she went. I'm too busy staring at my slim hands in KT's sturdy, callused grasp. I could think a lot of things about those hands, but I'd better not. After all, I don't know her. Yet.

"So, how do you know Rachel?" I ask, tearing my eyes away from those hands of hers. We start to sway in time to the music. Up close, I can see that she's not as hard-edged as I thought. Her eyes look soft, as does the fine layer of buzzed hair on her scalp.

"I fixed her bike once," KT says. "We sort of hit it off. Her girl and I are pretty good friends too."

I watch her lick her lips, feel her hands tighten slightly on mine.

"You got a girl?"

"No girl." I feel myself grin before I can help it. "I'm Diana, by the way."

"I'm KT." She's smiling too. Actually, it looks more like a smirk. The music changes to a faster beat and she shifts her hands to my waist, pulling me close. I drape my arms over her shoulders and lean in. She smells like sweat and motor oil, but it's not unpleasant.

"So, if you're a mechanic, does that mean you're good with your hands?"

It's about as blatant as a girl can get, and I'm rewarded with a throaty chuckle. The music pulses through my body as her hands start to move lower. She toys with the hem of my skirt.

"I have pretty good reviews," she says, grinning. The music swells, and she pushes her thigh between my legs, and I have to grab the collar of her jacket to steady myself. This is all happening so fast, but that's not a complaint. Sometimes good things come to you when you least expect them. But here, on the dance floor, surrounded by all our friends? I start to wonder just how far KT will go.

My concern must have shown on my face, because KT pulls back. "Sorry," she says. "I guess I—I just thought—"

"No, you thought right." I tug her forward by her collar, wanting her strong thigh back between mine. She breaks into a smile, all hesitation gone, and slides her hand under my skirt. My skin tingles and I sigh at her touch. My hips buck against her leg ever so slightly. I can feel something hard against my thigh: she's packing, even though this isn't that kind of party.

Well.

I suppose it is now.

The crowd ebbs and flows around us. I can see Rachel over KT's shoulder, dancing with a woman I don't recognize. I hope she doesn't see me, because I know my cheeks must be flushed and my eyes half-lidded with the lust flooding through me. I can barely hear the music over the sound of my heart pounding.

"So, what do you do?" KT asks.

I try to answer, but as I open my mouth, she jerks her knee up and grinds her thigh between my legs. My words turn into a gasp and I cling to her as she laughs.

"That was rude," I say as soon as I regain my composure.

"Seems like you liked it, though."

"Keep your voice down." She's a little too loud and a little too cocky, and I don't want Rachel or Sasha to see me like this. KT won't stop smiling, though, so I reach down and squeeze her strap through her jeans. That gets her attention.

"Diana," she starts, but I grind the strap back up against her and she bites back a moan. She doesn't move my hand away, though.

"Not so fun when it happens to you, huh?"

"Still pretty fun." KT is so close. Her breath is hot on my cheek and her gaze is on my lips. I bring my hand back up to her collar as she closes the gap and pulls me into a fierce kiss.

I may not be able to hear the music, but I can hear the cheers and whistles from the party crowd. I just don't care. A handsome stranger is kissing me and I'm not going to let anything ruin this moment.

KT is on me like a force of nature, biting my lip and pulling me closer than close. I do my best to return her energy. When we finally pull apart, both of us are panting and KT's cheeks are a brilliant red. A few people clap, and I shoot a dirty look at our unwanted audience.

"I'm going to the bathroom." I plant a quick kiss on KT's cheek and dart away before she can pull me back in. I just need a breath, a break, a second to get my wits about me.

The crowd parts to let me through. I refuse to meet anyone's gaze, but I can feel their eyes on me as I make my way off the dance floor and through the bar area. I can also feel just how wet my silk underwear has gotten and the way my lips still sting with a pleasant soreness. If this is some sort of contest between KT and my better judgment, I think I know who's winning.

When I close the bathroom door behind me, the noise of the party fades and my head clears. I take stock of the situation while I fix my hair. KT is hot, she's clearly into me, and it's been too long since I've been kissed that well. On the other hand, all my friends are here, and… And what? They'll make fun of me? They do that anyway.

I resolve to ask KT to join me in the bathroom. I splash some water on my face, dry my hands, open the door, and come face-to-face with KT.

She places one hand on my chest and pushes me back into the bathroom.

"What are you doing?" I hope I already know the answer. KT locks the door behind us.

"I want you," she says, simple as that. "Thought this might be a little safer than the middle of the dance floor. Unless you're into that."

"Here is good," I breathe, backing against the sink. KT smiles, but her eyes are hungry.

"Yeah? You want me to take you right here in the bathroom?" She steps up to me and flips up my skirt, revealing the damp patch on my pink silk. "Oh, *Diana*."

"That's your fault." I point out the obvious, slipping her jacket off her shoulders. "You started it."

"I seem to remember you starting it." KT shrugs off the sleeves and drapes her jacket over a handrail. She's wearing a tank top beneath it, and I can't help but run a hand over her bicep as she leans over me. She hesitates again. "Are you sure about this?"

"I'm sure." I pull her into a kiss, tender this time. I don't know much about KT, but I do know that I want her to feel comfortable with me. This is a two-way street, and we're speeding down it.

"Okay then." She yanks my thong down to my knees. Our kiss turns hard and desperate as KT slides two fingers into me with a single thrust, making me moan into her mouth. She falls into a steady rhythm, pumping in and out of me and filling the bathroom with slick noises. All I can do is cling to the cold porcelain of the sink and lean into the pleasure.

I don't know how long it's been when KT finally pulls her hand away. She presses her fingers to my lips, and I take them into my mouth, rolling my tongue over them as I suck them clean. She bites her lip as she watches me.

"You like that?" I ask when she withdraws her fingers. She nods, still biting her lip, not taking her eyes off my mouth. "I can think of something else I could suck on."

KT scrambles to unzip her fly. I'm already falling to my knees, ignoring the way the tiles dig lines into my shins. I want to see that look in her eyes again.

Her strap-on is thick and blue. I hold it reverently and slide my thumb over the head, watching her face all the while. She shudders and, encouraged, I gently take it into my mouth. Now it's her turn to lean back and cling to the sink as I bob my head back and forth. I peer up at KT through half-lidded eyes to see her mouth open as she watches me with a mix of lust and awe.

I take her deep into my mouth, deeper than I would have thought possible. KT twines her hands in my hair and begins to softly thrust her hips, pushing further and further and *further* until I gag and pull back. She lets me catch my breath, and when I'm ready, she starts up again. Her movements get faster and more erratic until she's pounding into my mouth, grunting under her breath.

Then, abruptly, she stops. I sit back on my heels and quirk an eyebrow at her.

"Not like this," KT mutters. She offers me her hand. I take it reluctantly. I was having a good time, and it's not that I mind her change of heart, I'm just a little disappointed. My lips are red and raw, and I feel a pleasant ache between my thighs as I stand.

In an instant, KT flips me around and bends me over the sink. She kicks my legs apart and grabs my hips before rubbing her strap against me, making me whine.

"Like this," she says, pressing into me. I'm wet enough for her to slide in with ease, but I still feel every inch of her. She fills me up and stretches me out and the worst, or best, part is that I can see our faces in the mirror. I can see myself moan and see my eyes close with every thrust. With her free hand, KT grabs a fistful of my hair and yanks my head up, making sure that I can see everything.

"Oh, God," is all I can say. Over and over again. I realize how loud my moans are, but there's nothing I can do about it. If there's someone waiting for the bathroom, they're getting quite a show. I just hope that no one I know is close enough to hear.

"Does that feel good, baby?" KT asks, tugging on my hair as she thrusts harder. I try to nod. "You like this, huh. I bet you even like how dirty this all is, a pretty little thing like you in a place like this. Everyone out there was watching, but now I get you all to myself."

"I'm all yours," I say, or try to. It's a little hard to talk with silicone slamming in and out of me and driving me wild.

"All mine," KT repeats, her eyes fluttering. She lets my hair go and grabs my hips with both hands now, steadying herself as she shudders against me. "God, Diana, you're gorgeous. I'm...I..."

"It's okay," I gasp out. "Don't talk."

The bathroom is loud enough without us trying to speak. I'm moaning, she's panting, and above all else there is the unmistakable sound of sex. KT's fingers are digging into my hips and I can tell she's close to coming. I relinquish my hold on one corner of the sink and reach down to rub my swollen clit, desperate to get off before she's spent.

KT slams into me with a cry and a final sweet thud, thrusting deeper than I thought possible. In the mirror, I see her face as she comes.

It's enough to push me over the edge too. I cling to the sink and fail to stifle a series of loud moans. KT holds me through it, stroking my hair, and whispering sweet things in my ear. The aftershocks course through my body and leave my legs weak and shaking. I couldn't have asked for anything better.

"Thank you," I say when I've recovered the capacity of speech. She pulls out and tucks her strap back into her boxers. I begin to pull my thong back up, but it's still wet and sticky, so instead I take it off and hand it to her. "A souvenir."

"After all that, I think I'll be wanting your number too."

"Of course." I smile and sag against the sink, totally worn out. "Just give me a second. And I need to fix my hair. I'm a mess."

"I like it," KT says with a grin. She retrieves her jacket and slips my panties into a side pocket. I can see that her legs are a little wobbly too. "It was very nice to meet you."

"Likewise." I give her a peck on the cheek, then start the futile process of trying to make myself look like I hadn't just had sex in a bathroom at a party full of people. I hope this is the start of something, but even if it isn't, it will always be the best time anyone's ever had in a place like this.

THE LAYOVER

T.L. Hayes

T.L. Hayes has three books published with Bold Strokes Books, as well as a fourth with KDP. Follow her on Facebook for event updates or visit TLHayesweb.com for all the news that's occasionally not fit to print, and while you're there make sure to subscribe to her blog.

The text had come in as soon as her plane had landed.

You have one hour to get here, or I won't play with you.

As soon as the cab driver handed back her credit card and receipt, Tanya quickly thanked him, grabbed her backpack on wheels, and exited the cab.

She had hurried into the first taxi she found at O'Hare and had given him the downtown address, which she knew could take upward of forty-five minutes to get to in heavy traffic. Now, on the sidewalk, she briefly looked up at the façade of the John Hancock Building, at its crossed steel beams. It was a building she had always admired and always tried to stop by whenever she was in the city, even if it was only to have lunch. Now that she knew someone in the building, she counted herself lucky that she got to sleep here occasionally, instead of in some bland hotel out by the airport.

When she walked up to the Delaware Street entrance, she was greeted by a doorman, who opened the door for her as he tipped his hat. She didn't come often enough for him to call her by name, but maybe someday, if she played her cards right, that would change. Via a series of elevators, she finally reached her destination on the sixty-third floor. She stepped out of the elevator into a private hallway and pushed the button next to the door to the condo.

It was only a moment later when the door was opened by a tall, slim man in an expensive suit. He inclined his head as he opened the door and took a step back. "Madam is waiting for you."

Tanya greeted his formal nod with one of her own as she walked past him, pulling her bag behind her. "Thank you, Charles."

"Would you like me to take your things?" Charles stood slightly behind her, near the closed door, with his hands clasped.

"Yes, that would be lovely." She smiled at him as she handed over her bag, then took off the horrible polyester jacket she'd been wearing all day, which bore a wings pin as well as the name tag she hadn't bothered to take off yet.

Charles took her things and disappeared into another room with them. She knew she would find them in the room that was hers whenever she was in town, though she wasn't sure who slept there when she was gone, which was most of the time. Chicago was only one of her ports of call across the country.

She walked down the hallway after Charles was gone, her eyes on the double doors at the end, a smile building inside her. She lightly rapped on the door.

A brisk "Enter" came from inside.

Tanya took a deep breath and opened the doors. The room she walked into was an office that resembled an English study, with lots of dark wood and books on the walls, a large, old desk in back, and a leather sofa against one wall. Before her, on her knees, was the one she had come there to see. The woman on the floor didn't look up when she entered. Instead, she stayed where she was, her head bowed, looking at the floor, her hands behind her back, her ankles crossed. She didn't seem worried about the expensive suit she wore as she knelt there. Tanya closed the door behind her, walked up to the kneeling figure, and stood with her hands behind her back. She put steel in her spine as well as her voice when she asked, "Why am I here?"

The woman started to speak, but Tanya cut her off.

"Look at me when I talk to you."

She raised her head and met her gaze. "Because I wanted to see you."

"What do you want from me?" Tanya, hands still clasped behind her, began to circle the woman. "What could I possibly do for you that you can't do for yourself? What do you really want?"

Gaze forward, she replied, "I want to be served."

"Bullshit, you have Charles for that." Tanya faced the woman once again and leaned closer. "Why did you push my call button?" As she leaned forward, her blouse gaped open a bit, revealing a hint of what lay beneath.

The woman gulped and clearly tried not to let her gaze stray to the open buttons and down the front of Tanya's blouse. When she met Tanya's brown eyes and the smirk on her lips, she realized she had been caught and her cheeks flamed. The woman swallowed. "I need you."

Tanya took a step back. "What do you need me for? And before you answer, remember, I'm not your servant, you're mine. Now, answer carefully: *What* did you need me for?"

In a small voice, she replied, "I need you to—"

Tanya interrupted. "Louder!"

She cleared her throat and began again, this time louder. "I need you to make me come."

Tanya nodded. "I see. And how do you think I should do that?"

"Any way that pleases you."

"Oh, good answer. You've played this game before. Don't move a muscle until I say so." The woman said nothing, she just held her place while Tanya walked around her to the desk and opened a drawer. She found what she wanted and came up behind her. "Stand up. Do not turn around." She complied, and Tanya took hold of her wrists, which were still clasped behind her back, and tied them with the blue scarf she had pulled from the desk drawer. She secured them in place, tugged on them for good measure, then leaned forward to whisper in her ear, "You know how I'm going to make you wet?"

She trembled. "Hmm?"

Tanya chuckled evilly in her ear and slowly brought her arm around and cupped the woman's chin in her hand, then let her fingers slide until they had a firm grip on her throat, forcing her head back. Tanya whispered, "You're going to get back on your knees and you're going to please me as I tell you to."

The woman swallowed against Tanya's grip, but didn't resist. "Yes ma'am."

Tanya released her, then took a step back. "Stay there until I tell you otherwise." Tanya stepped out of her uniform, piling the clothes on the floor in front of the desk, and walked over to the sofa, where she sat on the edge. "Come to me." The woman did so. "Down on your knees." Tanya pointed to the floor and the woman complied. Tanya clasped both hands in the woman's close-cropped black and silver hair, pulled her forward abruptly, and shoved the woman's face in her crotch, while she thrust forward to meet it.

The woman first let her tongue graze her clit, playing with it with her tongue, then explored Tanya's lips, coming back again and again to her clit. Tanya leaned her head back on the couch, wrapping her legs around the woman's shoulders, and entwined her fingers in her hair. Tanya began to moan softly. The woman's exploring tongue found Tanya's hole and curled, until she could use it to lightly penetrate.

Tanya caught her breath, then exhaled. "Fuck!" She thrust herself into the woman's waiting, exploring mouth, relishing the hot, wet tongue as it flicked back to her clit time and time again. Her moaning grew louder and her hips began to slide around on the smooth surface of the sofa, one foot braced on the woman's shoulder, practically around her neck, the other on the floor. She took one hand off the woman's head and braced herself against the sofa as she panted to catch her breath.

Concentrating on her clit, the woman drew it into her mouth quickly and sucked on it, which elicited a loud scream from Tanya, then she slowly released it as she began to gently suck, then flick the very tip of it, which made Tanya start to shake and her breathing come in gasps. Tanya tightened her grip in the woman's hair and pulled her further into Tanya's wetness, and then Tanya let out a loud, wordless scream. As her scream subsided and as she was starting to go limp, the woman began slow, lazy licks around her lips and lightly grazed her clit. Each time she touched her clit, Tanya jerked. As she felt Tanya start to relax into the aftereffects of her orgasm, the woman suddenly pulled Tanya's clit into her mouth and sucked hard on it. Tanya gasped in surprise.

"Oh God, yes!"

Her face covered in Tanya's juices, the woman pulled back and licked her lips. She smiled at Tanya's spent form on the sofa and extricated herself from Tanya's legs, which had grown slack on her shoulders. She held her position otherwise. "Was there anything else you would like me to do for you?"

Tanya didn't reply right away. It took her a bit to regain enough energy to speak again. Finally, she said, "No. Did you come?"

The woman smiled. "Yes."

Tanya's voice held insincerity. "Aww, got that expensive suit all wet."

The woman chuckled. "It'll be okay."

With a sigh, Tanya sat forward and placed a kiss on the woman's lips, then licked her own juices off her chin. "Are you as wet as I am?"

"I believe so."

Tanya grinned. "Good. Then my job here is done." This time, when she leaned forward, it was to reach around and untie the scarf that held the woman's wrists. Once that was accomplished, Tanya leaned back and said, "You may stand."

The woman complied. Once standing, she held her hand out to Tanya, who took it and stood up from the sofa. She put her arms around Tanya's waist and Tanya encircled her arms around her neck. "How long are you here for?"

"I leave tomorrow morning. So I think we'd best make the most of it." Tanya stepped out of her embrace. "I think, Your Honor, that it's time I brought some disorder into your court."

"I concur."

"Good. Now, take that suit off."

"I think you misunderstand. The game's over. You're no longer in charge. Remember, I called you here."

"Yes, but I'm not done with you."

The woman considered her. "What did you have in mind?"

"As I said, take that suit off. Then march into my room."

"I see. All right." She untied her tie, slowly, and let it drop to the floor, then she reached up to unbutton her shirt and tossed it aside. Then she unbuckled her belt and slid down her trousers, stepping out of them and setting them aside. She stood there in her boxers and undershirt and dark socks, with her hands clasped in front of her. "Now, what else can I do for you?"

Tanya moved to stand directly in front of her. "This flight isn't over yet. I think we're about to hit some turbulence." Tanya ran her fingernail down the woman's chest, slowly and tantalizingly. "Make sure you fasten your seat belt."

Grinning, she replied, "I think I missed the safety instructions."

"Tsk, that's because you weren't paying attention. But trust me, you're not going to need an emergency exit." Tanya dropped her finger to the waistband of the woman's boxers, then hooked her finger and pulled her closer. "Come on, I'll show you some things that aren't in the safety instructions manual."

They played into the night. The next morning, Tanya awoke early, put her uniform back on, placed a kiss on the sleeping woman's forehead, then left the bedroom they sometimes shared and waved to Charles on her way out. She took the elevator back down to the street and hailed a cab and then headed back to the airport, where she caught an early morning flight to another city where another woman with another bed awaited her imminent return.

STOLEN MOMENTS

Beck Robertson

Beck is a thirty-nine-year-old erotica author currently living in London, England. Her first erotic novel, *Blood Hunger*, has been published by Bonnier Publishing, and she's had a novella published by Xcite. She's also been interviewed by the *Wall Street Journal* about her writing and has contributed to *Female First*.

Just do it.

Should she turn back? Take the plunge and do what she'd been obsessing about for the past half a year? She'd been right on the verge of leaving but something kept pulling her back, and if she was lucky, no one at work or anyone else she knew need ever know.

Suzette sighed heavily and took one last drag on her Lucky Strike, inhaling the smoke deeply before discarding the butt. Grinding it with her stiletto heel, she made the decision and pushed open the glass-fronted door that led into the upmarket boutique hotel's chic lobby.

Once inside, she gave a nod to the sweet-faced blond girl at the reception desk who greeted her with a cheerful "Welcome back." Threading her way through the lobby, she pushed open the heavy oak swing doors that were the entrance to the hotel's Art Deco style bar.

The bar was busy, which was usual for this time of the evening. Eight at night was a favored drinking time for hotel guests and random walk-ins from the city streets, and anyone else who fancied a drink in a stylish location.

She glanced up at the ornate gilt French Rococo–style clock positioned over the curved black marble of the bar as she waited for the barman's attention. He was preoccupied serving a distinguished-looking silver-haired man dressed in an expensive, light gray linen suit. As he finished, the bartender turned to Suzette, his handsome Italian looks creasing into a friendly smile.

"Hey, you came back. Changed your mind?"

Suzette nodded, giving him a shy smile as she gave him her order, a dirty martini. She waited, feeling awkward and watching while he blended it expertly. Olives deftly added at the last moment, he presented it to her with a flash of his white teeth.

Taking the drink, she made her way to an empty table she'd spotted at the side of the room. It was a great spot to people watch, and she'd be certain to see Chloe when…if…she came in, since she'd have a clear view of the entrance.

Would she show? She might be having second thoughts, too.

Nervously, Suzette toyed with the gold tennis bracelet she wore around her wrist, a gift from her mother on her last birthday.

Trying to banish her anxiety that Chloe would be a no-show, she sipped at the martini, attempting to calm her spiking nerves. She couldn't keep from glancing at the entrance periodically, hoping to spot Chloe entering, but every time she did so, she felt her complexion growing redder and redder with embarrassment.

You're a silly old fool.

Silently, she berated herself, scrubbing at an imaginary piece of dirt on the tabletop with one French manicured fingernail.

She's far too young for you. What's a twenty-five-year-old girl like her going to want with a forty-five-year-old woman anyhow?

She knew she was allowing her doubts to get the better of her, but she couldn't still the incessant chatter in her head.

As she looked up, her breath caught in her throat. There she was, tawny hair framing her heart-shaped face in bouncy, glossy waves. Chloe's lithe body seemed to undulate as she entered the bar, and Suzette could swear that just for a second, the entire room paused to watch as she walked in.

Time seemed to slow as she sashayed through the room, the white silk of her dress emphasizing her hourglass figure and the magnificent flare of her ample hips to perfection.

Hesitating, Chloe paused, her large green eyes scanning the room, her pretty face creased in consternation. Then she spied Suzette at the table, and for a blissful moment they met each other's gaze. Suzette felt a twang as Chloe smiled, a delightful expression that illuminated her whole face, her lush red pouty mouth curving up at the corners.

"Hey there!" Chloe lifted her delicate hand, waving gracefully, and Suzette found herself automatically returning the gesture. She felt like a teenager, her stomach doing butterflies, though outwardly she managed to retain her composure.

Chloe made her way to the table and Suzette stood and embraced her, leaning in to plant a kiss on the soft flesh of her cheek.

"Hi, you," she said, smiling as she flicked her eyes down appreciatively.

"Hey, hey," Chloe said, grinning at her like a goofball and showing off flawless, pearly white teeth.

God, she looks even more beautiful than usual tonight. Is that even allowed?

Suzette had always considered herself to be attractive, and at forty-five she knew she looked at least ten years younger. Time had been relatively kind, except for the fine crow's feet she'd begun to sport around her gray eyes, but overall, she'd remained largely wrinkle free, her alabaster complexion poreless. She knew she cut a chic figure with her toned, angular, statuesque frame and elegant blond crop, and she was still more than capable of eliciting admiring glances.

But Chloe was something else entirely, a truly striking beauty. Suzette couldn't quite believe that after she'd spent six months secretly crushing on her, she had finally plucked up the courage to ask her out. It had been entirely out of character, a moment of sheer madness.

Even more remarkably, she couldn't get over the fact that Chloe had agreed to meet her like this. True, the two of them had been flirting for a while at the financial research company where Suzette was manager, but she'd always chalked it up to a bit of fun on Chloe's part.

The two of them sat down again and Suzette beckoned a nearby waiter over to take their drinks order.

"I'll have another dirty martini, please," she said, pointing at her empty glass before turning to Chloe.

"What would you like, sweetheart?"

Chloe's face furrowed for a second as she considered the question.

"Uh…" She bit her lower lip. "I'll have what you're having."

Suzette nodded, then turned to the waiter again.

"Make that two, please."

Four rounds later, lubricated by the alcohol, they'd begun to flirt heavily. Suzette shivered in pleasure as Chloe's bare-soled foot slyly rubbed her naked calf, her black satin peep-toe Louboutin discarded under the table.

Reaching across the table, she slid her palm up Chloe's forearm. "You know, I'm *really* glad you agreed to meet me." She smiled warmly. "I wasn't sure if you would, you know. I thought you might change your mind."

Chloe smiled and Suzette felt her heart rate immediately start to climb.

Oh God, that smile again, I don't think I can take it.

"Oh, but I'm glad I did." Chloe caressed her arm affectionately, her foot continuing to stroke Suzette's calf.

The words seemed to purr from those maddening, red-stained lips, and Suzette could only watch mesmerized as Chloe scooted her seat closer. Her foot moved from her calf to reach up the inside of her thigh, setting off an alarming, yet entirely pleasurable, tingling feeling between Suzette's legs.

Closing her eyes momentarily, she let out a soft moan as the younger woman continued to tease her with her foot.

For God's sake, pull yourself together, you're losing all control.

Being out of control wasn't her usual style, in fact, she couldn't recall a time she had ever experienced it.

Certainly not during her marriage, pleasant though her absentminded husband had been. Part of her was incredibly disturbed by this new sensation, but another part of her, a more primal, instinctive part, wanted to embrace it, to throw all caution to the wind and just let go.

She shook her head at Chloe with a mock-cross expression, though she knew her eyes would give away the fact she wasn't serious. "Oh my God, you have to stop. We can't do this here."

Chloe grinned wickedly, arching a perfectly manicured eyebrow. "Oh, why's that?" Her tone was provocative, the way she bit into her full lower lip doubly so.

Suzette watched as the soft flesh indented, the action causing her gut to contract with lust. "Because, because…" She floundered, trying to think of something that sounded vaguely plausible, something that wouldn't make her sound like a complete square. "Because someone from work might see us?"

"So?" Chloe shrugged. "I'm enjoying myself too much right now to care."

"But what about your—"

Suzette felt Chloe's soft mouth press against hers as her sentence was smothered by the kiss. Tipping her head back, she gave herself to the sensation as Chloe's hot, wet tongue entwined with hers. Electricity fizzed through her, something she hadn't felt since her first kiss back in high school; her entire body was on edge and jangling with anticipation.

Chloe pulled back laughing, pushing back thick strands of silken russet hair, her eyes dancing in amusement as she watched Suzette scramble for her composure.

"People might talk. It's you who has more to lose than me, you know." Suzette knew she looked flustered, but her feelings were swirling madly, her senses swiftly melting together into a molten pool of lust.

Well, you're fucked now. She has you. She has you completely. There's no going back now, you silly old fool.

"I've got it handled. Don't worry about me." Chloe grinned naughtily. "Anyway, I still think it's you who's really worried. You might lose your reputation as Ms. Dependable, after all."

"Ow." Suzette jumped as Chloe gave her a playful poke in the ribs.

"Sorry. Just trying to jolt you out of your dependability."

"I'm not Ms. Dependable." She frowned at the description.

"Mm-hmm. You definitely are. Everyone depends on you at work, and you fucking love it. You thrive on it, in fact."

Maybe that was true, but was that a bad thing? She didn't want to be in control *all* the time, it was just how things had panned out. Some people were made for a life of excitement, others were more suited to responsibility and yes, dependability. That was what she'd always settled for, what she'd always managed to be satisfied with. "Hey, I can cut loose sometimes. Maybe even more so than you." She sat fully upright in the chair, feeling her cheeks begin to flame, her stomach roiling as a wave of self-doubt washed over her.

Chloe grinned, raising an eyebrow and appearing completely unfazed. Suzette's stomach settled temporarily.

"What if that's exactly what I *want* you to do?"

"What, cut loose?"

Chloe nodded, her green eyes glinting. "Show me your room?"

A wave of embarrassment swept through her, her entire body burning with shame. "I don't have a room." The lie came automatically though she wasn't sure why.

Chloe giggled. "So obviously, from that reaction you *so* do. It's okay, I'm not offended."

She sighed. "It's not like that, I always get a room." It wasn't a lie. Suzette had been divorced for five years now, but Jack, her son from her previous marriage, was only fourteen and still lived at home. Frequently, he liked to throw rowdy parties with his friends, and on those occasions, she'd rent a suite at a nice hotel in order to get some much-needed peace and quiet.

"Oh? Done this before, have you?"

Now it was getting immeasurably worse. Why did she feel so conversationally awkward right now?

"No, I mean, I come away to hotels quite often. For a break. On my own, not with anyone," Suzette added hastily, her cheeks a bright beet red. She reached for her martini, draining the glass, her hands shaking slightly as she set it on the table. "I wouldn't want you think I'd asked you here—"

"I'm only teasing. You're cute when you get nervous. It's okay, I've really enjoyed this, and you don't have to take me to your nonexistent room." Chloe smiled, reaching across the table again, the smooth warm flesh of her palm contacting with the bare skin of Suzette's arm.

Another bolt of sensation shot through her. Suzette hesitated, the words hanging on her lips. She wanted to say them, oh, how she wanted to say them.

Just do it. Just this one time. For once in your bloody boring, beige life.

"It's not nonexistent. I mean, I did get a room, and you can, we can…if you like…you don't have to." She gulped, her throat dry with nervousness as she eyed her empty glass, every silent second feeling like an agony.

Chloe chuckled throatily, her wide mouth creasing up in an amused expression.

"Thought you'd never ask. So, lead the way then, Ms. Dependable."

Ten minutes later, after a giggly ride in the elevator interspersed with a lot of touching on Chloe's part, they tumbled out, stumbling slightly as they made their way to the luxury suite.

Suzette stood outside the door to the suite, fumbling in her red satin envelope clutch purse for her key pass.

"Got it." She grinned lopsidedly as she brandished the pass, then swiped it over the electronic lock. The door swung open and she gestured to Chloe to walk inside, then followed her and shut the door behind them with a soft click.

"It's not the best, but it is a nice—"

She felt her heart race as Chloe's body pushed against hers, the heat of it setting her senses on fire. Moaning, she met her urgent kiss, her hands palming the satin that was the only thing restraining those curves, that sensual body.

"Like it?" Chloe breathed the words against Suzette's mouth, her eyes feline, her nostrils flaring with desire.

"God, you're so fucking sexy." Suzette didn't even recognize herself as she spoke. Something seemed to be taking her over, a primal instinct coming from some place she couldn't quite describe.

Chloe pulled away the flimsy fabric of Suzette's top, exposing her breasts and the hard stiffness of her nipples.

"Mm." Chloe eyed her appreciatively, then her mouth took in one of Suzette's nipples, kissing it gently.

"Oh, oh." Suzette cried out at the sensation. Cool air caressed the fire briefly as Chloe released her areola and twisted it with her fingertips before bending to suck it once again. The touch of her slick lips felt like molten silk against Suzette's aroused body.

"Please, oh God, yes." She moaned, thrusting her nipple further into Chloe's mouth, her voice sounding frantic to her own ears. Her hands moved in Chloe's hair, grabbing a fistful and pushing her head more firmly to her breast. The potent cocktail of the sensation and the sight of Chloe's voluptuous breasts spilling out of the satin gown as she pleasured her nipple were almost too much to bear.

Something stirred deep inside her. "Get on the bed." Suzette was astounded by the boldness of the instruction, but for some reason, she found she didn't feel nervous anymore.

"Oh yeah? You want me, huh?" Chloe didn't act as if she was surprised.

"Get on the bed. Take your dress off. Spread your legs. I want to see you touch yourself."

She leaned against the wall, her heart pounding. Chloe nodded and stepped back, her hands sliding to her skimpy straps, easing one down, then the other, until her large breasts sprang free, her dark areola erect.

My God, she's beautiful.

She watched, her pulse in her throat as Chloe smiled, her green eyes inviting as she stepped elegantly backward and sank onto the crisp white cotton sheets, spreading her legs as she lay on the bed.

Suzette felt her heart throb, the blood roaring in her ears, as she took a step forward. Her body was on autopilot, knowing before she did what it wanted so badly.

"Kiss me?" Chloe looked up coquettishly.

Suzette bent forward to caress Chloe's silken leg, her mouth finding Chloe's, seeking her heat, that fire.

Tongues darted in and out as hands tugged at garments, fingertips shredding clothes away from flesh in a frenzy. They were a ball of desire, a heated tangle of limbs, unclasping and grasping as they tumbled naked onto the cotton-covered bed.

"Fuck." Chloe moaned, momentarily breaking the kiss, as Suzette slid her fingers into the soft, slick flesh between her legs.

"You like that?"

"Uh, uh-huh." Chloe bit her bottom lip the way she had when they'd been in the bar and was rewarded with another digit, which elicited a little moan of pleasure.

"I've wanted you forever. You've haunted my thoughts for months. But you already knew that, you sexy little minx." The confidence Suzette heard in her own voice paired with her blatant forwardness shocked her, but she found she couldn't care less.

She ran her hands over Chloe's body as she arched beneath her touch, her tawny hair fanning out on the pillow. Her hips rolled sensuously as Suzette's fingers continued to caress between her parted thighs, stroking her expertly.

"Yes, yes oh my God oh my God," she panted as Suzette deftly worked her over.

Suzette didn't know *how* she knew exactly where to touch to bring Chloe close to the very edge of pleasure; she'd never pleasured a woman before. There had only been that one brief first kiss back in high school. Chloe seemed to like what she was doing, though, and the fires of her own lust were rising to complement the slickness she was eliciting from her, the heat between her legs increasing to almost unbearable levels.

"Fuck me, fuck me." Chloe's head tipped back, her slender throat exposed.

The words were like balm to Suzette's ragged senses.

"Beg. I want you to beg." *Where is this coming from?* She didn't even know she had it in her. But…she liked it. A lot.

Chloe pulled her closer, and unable to hold back anymore, Suzette fell upon her, her hands running over tight, smooth thighs. She gave a cry as she slid upward, her small naked breasts crushing up against Chloe's soft curves. She moaned in release as she ground herself against Chloe's slick wetness, their legs parting to enable the other to slide between. The feel of skin against skin was deliciously torturous, and Suzette's whole body was shaking, every nerve alight.

"Oh, Jesus," she moaned, her swollen clit heavy with desire as they worked a slick friction against each other, their bodies beginning to glisten with a fine sheen.

"Oh God, oh God, oh my God," Chloe breathed against her cheek. Frantically Suzette pressed her bare flesh against Chloe's sex, sitting up to ride her. She looked down and groaned at the sight of Chloe's large breasts undulating beneath her, the dark pink nipples standing out stiffly.

The air smelled of musk, perfume, and perspiration; the scent of sex. Suzette paused momentarily, one leg encircling Chloe's curvaceous hips.

"How much have you wanted this? *Tell* me." She needed to know, needed to hear how much she was desired. She'd been starving and was only now being fed, and she wanted it all, all of it, all of her.

"Don't stop, oh don't stop." Chloe reached up, her fingertips brushing Suzette's left nipple.

"Then tell me. How long have you wanted me?"

"I fantasized about you. About you taking me into your office, ordering me to bend over your desk. I thought about you telling me to take off my underwear and show myself to you."

"Oh, have you now? Naughty girl." Suzette smiled, rewarding Chloe with a small, elegant circle of her hips.

Chloe writhed, eliciting a little groan.

"Want more?" Suzette gave her a mischievous smirk as she held her pelvis away so it was mere inches from contacting with Chloe's.

"More, more." Chloe bucked, attempting to make their bodies meet again.

"Say please, then. Say 'Please fuck me, I've been a very naughty girl.'"

"Please…" Chloe faltered, her face flushing. "Please fuck me, I've been a very naughty girl."

"Oh, you have. You have." Suzette groaned as she finally relented, sinking down and allowing flesh to kiss against soft flesh once more.

She couldn't get enough pleasure as she intertwined with Chloe, searching, as if she sought to subsume her. The feeling was overwhelming.

The feel of Chloe spread out underneath her body, the sight of her nakedness, her thighs parted in lust, stirred a deep and long-buried feeling inside Suzette. A tsunami of desire roiled within, first manifesting itself in the core of her being, then spreading throughout her entire body as release edged temptingly closer, so close it was making every nerve Suzette had tingle with sensitivity.

"Oh God, oh God, please, please."

Chloe bucked and rolled her hips, calling out in pleasure, fingernails scrabbling at cotton sheets, as her head thrashed to one side then the other. The blood thumped so madly in Suzette's ears it was as if Chloe was screaming underwater, and she wanted to bring her to the point of ecstasy and beyond, but more than that, she needed to reach her own cliff edge.

She rode her hard, hips circling as she wound her body around Chloe's, her thighs gripping, hands roughly palming voluptuous flesh as she urgently sought release. Her slick heat felt as if it were on fire, and when Chloe arched up frantically to meet her, as her orgasm finally crashed upon her, Suzette found herself crying out, too, unable to contain it any longer. Digging her nails into the tops of Chloe's arms, she threw her head back, a shock wave rippling through her, every muscle twitching and pulsating.

Finally, they collapsed upon each other, their bodies a sweaty, yet satisfied tangle. Suzette stroked Chloe's hair as they lay there, her mind scrambling to make sense of things, her sensations still coming down from sensory overload. The scent of Chloe's perfume mingling with the smell of fresh perspiration was enticing, hypnotic even.

"I've wanted that from you for so long."

The sound of Chloe's voice punctuated Suzette's blissful reverie. She lifted her head to meet that fierce green gaze, and those eyes...it was as if they could see into her soul.

"I..." She paused, not knowing what to say. "I've never experienced anything like that," she finally confessed. "I've never even been with a woman before. Thought about it, though. Lots." Her cheeks reddened. "Mostly with you."

Chloe grinned, her expression feline. "Really? So, I was your first?"

She nodded. "But what about you? I mean, you're married. How does that work? Don't you feel guilty?"

"Whoa, questions." Those green eyes danced in amusement.

Suzette held her hands up in a gesture of mock surrender. "Sorry. But seriously. Don't you?"

"A bit. Sometimes. It's not how you think it is, though." The expression on Chloe's face was wistful.

"Do you love him?"

"Yes."

Not the answer she wanted to hear. Suzette's stomach sank.

"Then *why*?" She frowned, not understanding.

"It's complicated. I'm..." Chloe paused. "Hard to please. I'm greedy. I'm selfish. David knows. He knows what I'm like. I'm sorry. It's the truth." She buried her head in the crook of Suzette's arm.

"He knows you sleep with women?"

Chloe nodded.

"And he doesn't mind?"

Chloe sighed. "To be frank, he'd prefer it if it were just us two. But it isn't and it can't be because I am what I am. And I love that he still loves me for that."

"So, you love him."

"Always. I'll always love him." The answer was soft, the sincerity unquestionable.

"Do you, could you…" Suzette wanted to ask, but she couldn't form the words.

"Don't. Don't ever ask that of me. Please." Chloe planted a soft kiss on Suzette's mouth. "Please." The word was a whisper.

You're a fool. Told you, you're a fool.

"Okay. I promise."

"Thank you." Chloe's rewarded her with an expression like sunlight. When she smiled at her like that Suzette felt twenty years melt away, as if she were in her twenties again. As if it were before she'd gotten married, before she'd stuffed her own desires down for the sake of her disapproving, conservative parents.

"I wish I'd been as brave as you." She whispered the confession into Chloe's soft, auburn strands. The wrong choices she had made, the roads not taken, all through her own cowardice.

"I'm not brave." Chloe looked puzzled, a strand of hair temptingly concealing one of her large, green eyes.

"You are. You *are.* You live unapologetically. That's something I've never done. I wish I had." Suzette felt her eyes misting up and summoned the strength to push the emotion away.

"Hey. You can start now. It's never too late."

"Maybe."

The sentiment was trite. Could she? Really? After all this time?

With Chloe in her arms for a moment, she could pretend. Pretend everything was how it should have panned out before she'd entombed herself in a prison of her own making and then refused to allow herself her freedom even after it was obvious her marriage was long dead.

She'd blamed herself for the divorce. It had been her fault, after all. Was that why she'd never admitted the truth? Was that why she'd never admitted it to herself?

She let the tears come as she lay there motionless, until she heard gentle snores.

I want to live. I want to live like this forever, she thought before velvet blackness embraced her and sleep overtook her spent body.

❖

When she awoke, she realized Chloe wasn't beside her in the bed. Blinking blearily, her eyes full of morning sleep, Suzette got up and padded across the plush white carpet to peer into the little en suite bathroom.

Where the hell is she?

Puzzled, she scratched at her rumpled, bed-mussed hair. The room was entirely empty. Suzette wheeled around, frowning in consternation. Then she saw it, the small white piece of paper laid atop the dresser. She crossed the room, snatched it up, and immediately recognized Chloe's familiar, curling script.

I had the best time. Sorry I had to leave so abruptly but I had to get back. I really hope we can do it again sometime. I want to see you again. See you at the office. C x

She held the paper close to her chest before bringing it up to her nose and smelling it. She could make out faint traces of Chloe's sweetly spicy scent, vanilla notes mixed in with something more peppery, an intoxicating aroma.

Had she done something wrong? Should she feel guilty? Chloe was married, but it was complicated. She'd known Chloe was married, known for a long time, and it hadn't stopped her from wanting her or from asking her out.

Am I a terrible person?

She stood there for a moment before sighing. She knew she should feel bad, but somehow, she couldn't regret what had happened. For the first time in her life she had taken a risk, and it had paid off. For the briefest, most blissful moment she had known what it was to be alive.

I won't do it again. She belongs to someone else.

Suzette glanced in the mirror, then shook her head, smiling to herself. Her face was glowing, and she looked ten years younger.

Who was she kidding? She had never felt like this.

She crossed the room again, throwing open the heavy velvet curtains. Sunlight filtered through the flimsy, pristine white nets, filling the room in a bright burst.

Live.

The word seemed to penetrate her mind, but she wasn't sure where it came from.

She hadn't lived. She knew that. The first half of her life had been marked by self-sacrifice and she had never given herself the chance to feel. But things were different now, the world was different, people weren't so judgmental anymore. This morning, a morning where sunshine seemed to fill up everything, made her think maybe it wasn't too late, like maybe everything, *anything* might be possible.

If sleeping with Chloe was wrong, so be it. She knew she could never expect a relationship, or any kind of real love from their affair, but so what? She could let it be just for once, couldn't she, without trying to micromanage things?

Live.

Suzette glanced back at her reflection, noting the vigor that she'd thought had been sucked out of her years ago. In that moment she felt both wiser and younger, all at once.

She took a deep breath, sucking in the air before releasing it.

"Bye-bye, Ms. Dependable," she whispered to the mirror, her hand making a waving motion at the glass.

From now on, no matter what, she was determined to live.

TIED TO PLEASURE

Renee Roman

Renee Roman has lived in upstate New York her entire life and can't imagine being without a change of seasons. She works at a local college and writes in her spare time. She has three published novels, *Epicurean Delights*, *Stroke of Fate*, and *Where the Lies Hide*. Follow Renee on Facebook or her website, www.reneeromanwrites.com, or email her at reneeromanwrites@gmail.com.

I'd never been to a leather club. Mel insisted there wasn't anything like it. So far, she'd been right about experiencing parts of lesbian life I'd been missing out on, so I took her word for it. When she arrived at my door, I almost changed my mind. Her attire was a study in darkness. Black leather pants, black biker boots, and a black leather vest with a black T-shirt beneath that did nothing to hide the nipple rings that pressed against the fabric. The ensemble gave me a hint of what to expect, and I wasn't sure I was ready.

"Hi." Mel slid past me. She smiled—those brilliant white teeth of hers seemed even brighter against all that black—and her blue eyes sparkled. She held out a bag. "I bought you an initiation gift."

Excited and wary at the same time, I opened the package and pulled out a bustier. I held it up by the narrow straps, admiring the combination of soft leather cups and tapered meshlike silk that left little to the imagination.

"Mel, I can't wear this." It reminded me of halter tops young girls wore to dance clubs, meant to drive the boys crazy. I was too old for anything this daring.

Mel leaned against the counter while she popped open a can of soda, her forearms bulging. The dagger tattoo danced along her skin. "Of course you can. You'll look hot." She moved closer and kissed at the corner of my mouth. "You don't want to stand out as a newcomer, do you?" She backed up to the counter again.

That's when I noticed the bulge between Mel's muscular thighs. I couldn't help glancing first at the package in her pants, then at her face. It might not have been the most subtle thing to do, but I couldn't remember her ever packing before, and I would have. It was hard to miss. I'm sure my expression revealed my surprise, but I should have known better.

"What?" She smiled and winked.

I wanted to ask her how she could walk with that wad in her crotch but thought better of it. Knowing Mel like I did, she'd probably give me a demonstration. "Nothing." I redirected her attention to the skimpy material in my hand. She had a point about the newcomer thing. Besides, I had made her promise she'd be my date for the night, and I didn't want to embarrass her, though she'd never say anything even if I did. "Okay. I'll try it on."

"That's the spirit."

Too bad my enthusiasm didn't match hers. But once I had it on, I had to admit I looked pretty damn sexy. I'd always considered my body average, and aside from being shorter than Mel's five-foot-eight height I was also softer, with a lot of curves. My breasts weren't large, but the bustier gave me enough cleavage to make them appear tempting. The lower band of material gave the illusion my waist was narrower than it was, and I wasn't about to complain. I left the bedroom looking more confident than I felt when I went in.

Mel whistled. "Damn, baby." She gestured with her finger and I did a slow spin. "Perfect." She grabbed her keys and tossed them in the air. "Let's go."

I checked for my ID and cash card, then pulled my worn but serviceable short leather jacket from the closet. My heartbeat picked up speed we got closer to the club. Aside from women in leather, I had no idea what to expect.

"So, is there dancing?"

Mel guffawed. "Maybe. There *is* music, but it's mainly to set the mood."

I raised an eyebrow. "Mood for what?"

She looked at me sideways. "Whatever's happening on the stage."

I didn't know there'd be a show. My expression must have revealed my confusion.

"You'll just have to see for yourself." Mel parked, then she jumped out and came around to open the door when I hesitated. "Relax and have fun."

All I could do was nod. I adjusted my bustier as we approached. We stood in front of a wide black door with one of those little windows at eye level that reminded me of the ones I'd seen in speakeasy movies. Mel knocked twice and waited. The window slid back.

"Silicone," Mel said. The window closed and the sound of a huge bolt sliding echoed in the quiet before the door opened. She took my hand and led me inside while the muscular butch at the entrance greeted her.

"Nice," she said as she gawked at me.

Not sure how to respond, I smiled and kept going. The door and narrow hallway opened to a well-lit, cavernous space. The walls were a pale color that was hard to discern with the various lights overhead. The horseshoe bar gleamed and the padded leather stools looked real, not like imitation pleather. Mel found an open spot near the curve.

"Want to sit?"

I leaned in. "Not yet. There's too much to see." Soft jazz played in the background. It seemed to fit the décor but was out of place for a leather club.

Mel thumbed a twenty off a stack of bills. The bartender—a leather-clad woman with bright eyes and a snake tattoo that started at her neck, stretched along her arm, and ended with its tail wrapped around her wrist—set drinks down on the bar. She took the cash without a word and waited on another customer. Mel handed over my drink.

"So, what do you think?"

The music was calming, my drink was tasty, and the crowd was dressed in various leather goods and black jeans. I'd failed in the wardrobe department. My jeans were dark, but they weren't black. Maybe black wasn't a requirement, just a preference, so I pushed away my nerves. I didn't want to tell her it seemed a bit sedate for a leather club. It certainly wasn't anything like I'd pictured.

"It's nice." Inwardly, I winced. "Nice" wasn't a word I'd have thought of when Mel invited me to join her. I took a sip of my vodka cranberry and hoped Mel let it go. She didn't appear put off, which was a good thing. The music picked up tempo and I was about to ask if she wanted to dance when a pretty, blond-haired woman with large breasts and a studded collar walked up to her and grabbed her crotch. That got my attention.

"How's it hanging, Mel?" she asked as I stared at her a bit too long because she wasn't wearing much else in the way of clothing.

Mel laughed. "A little to the left."

I tried not to stare at their overly friendly fondling, all the while wondering if they'd slept together, or whatever it was that tops and bottoms did together. Mel's hand caressed her hip, then she pulled the woman in for an open-mouthed kiss. The demanding intensity of it shot an electric current through me and landed in my crotch. When they came up for air, the woman looked me over from head to toe before returning her attention to Mel.

"If you want to play, come find me."

Mel licked her lips. "Maybe."

The woman walked away laughing.

Mel glanced at me and my face heated. "Maybe this wasn't such a great idea after all." She swallowed the rest of her of beer.

"Why not? Just because you tickled her tonsils with your tongue?" She laughed again. "I can handle it."

"Oh, honey," Mel said. "That was nothing. I'm not sure if you're ready for the upcoming scene."

"What scene? What are you talking about?"

Mel opened her mouth to say something when the distinctive reverberation of a gong being struck drowned her out. She took my hand. "You need to be closer." She propelled us forward as the crowd closed in around the stage. A spotlight revealed shackles bolted to the floor, a detail I'd missed during my cursory observations. The gong sounded again. It was both ominous and thrilling. As my anticipation grew, I caught Mel's gaze, but all she did was tip her head toward the stage where a woman in a short leather vest and a minuscule leather thong walked to the bindings. She stood with her legs shoulder-width apart, then closed her eyes. The crowd was eerily silent. The press of bodies lent to my already warm skin. Once more the drum rang out and everyone looked at the opposite end of the stage. The house lights went down so suddenly I was momentarily blind. I sucked in air; the breath frozen in my lungs.

Mel's voice at my ear reassured me. "I've got you." She'd never let anything happen to me.

I nodded, though she likely couldn't see in the darkness. Her hand found mine and she gave it a squeeze. A second circle of light flared, and a pair of black boots trimmed in silver spikes moved across the stage as though disembodied. The ring of light expanded to show the back of a person with well-defined muscles and a tattoo of black feathered wings that rose between her shoulder blades and continued down her biceps. They rippled as though taking flight when she held her arms out, and the other woman stepped into her embrace to place her head on a winged shoulder. The display felt intimate. The stage silently rotated forty-five degrees, showing the side of the butch's face for the first time. Cheers rang out and Mel leaned in.

"If you want to leave, we have to go now."

I had no idea what was about to take place, but my body hummed with anticipation. I couldn't go now. This was what I had come for, to see the attraction this lifestyle held for the community some called darkness. "No."

Concern showed in Mel's eyes for an instant before she smiled and looked back at the stage.

A low, steady beat began to play just loud enough to be heard. The sound was primal and driving at the same time. The butch placed her hand on the femme's shoulder, and she went to her knees. A microphone was lowered above their heads, high enough not to distract from the players.

"Suck me."

I needed to know their names and whispered to Mel, who said the femme was Bree and the butch was Cole. Bree opened Cole's fly and released her black cock. The contrast of Bree's lightly tanned skin and the much darker dildo was erotic, and I briefly wondered why Cole had chosen it before the head disappeared into Bree's mouth. She slid her lips along the length while she held Cole's thighs. Cole's hips jerked. Mine responded too before Cole's eyes narrowed and she pulled away.

Murmurs spread out around me. In the dim light I saw Mel's hand on her crotch, and she gave a tug. My attention floated over the crowd before I focused back on the stage. Bree had moved over to the shackles and Cole secured her ankles in them. Another set lowered from the ceiling and Bree's wrists were restrained before they were raised. She stood spread-eagle and exposed, her eyes downcast. I couldn't be sure, but I thought I could smell pheromones in the air. Like the electrical charge before a storm. I was tuned in and incredibly turned on.

A small whip with tails of leather appeared in Cole's hand. She dragged the implement over Bree's exposed stomach, and Bree stared out at the spectators. Somehow, I knew she wasn't seeing us. Bree was elsewhere, a place between fantasy and desire. Cole unzipped her captive's vest and exposed her breasts, nudging a nipple with the handle of the whip. I watched it pucker. Bree didn't move.

"Do you want to be punished for not making me come?" Cole asked.

At first, I was upset because Cole hadn't let her finish, then realized it was part of the scene, part of the roles they were playing. Dominance and submission.

"Please, Master."

The stage rotated again, giving us a clear view of her backside. Cole stepped behind her at an angle so that we could still see. She snapped the whip and the tails grazed Bree's ass. Once. Twice. Cole rubbed her cock and smiled, then leaned closer. This time the strikes left bright red stripes on the otherwise unblemished flesh.

"Do you like being punished?" Cole asked.

Bree shivered. "Yes." A hard strike followed. "Yes, Master."

"Shall we show everyone how much you like it?"

Did she like it? I wasn't sure I understood. The stage turned until Bree faced forward again. Cole grabbed the flimsy covering from her crotch and ripped it away. Bree's mons was bare except for a minuscule strip of dark, close-cropped hair at the top of her glistening slit, and when Cole struck her again, Bree's excitement trickled along her thighs and dripped from her pussy. My sex clenched and a gush dampened my panties. Yes, she clearly liked it. Cole caressed her reddened ass cheeks. I wanted to be Bree.

"So beautiful," Cole said, then lifted Bree's chin with her

fingertips. When Bree looked up, her eyes were lust filled. "So good. So needy," Cole said.

Bree licked her lips. "Yes, Master."

I had to look away then, unsure I'd be able to contain my own growing desire. My swollen clit rubbed against the seam of my jeans and I squeezed my thighs together to still the sensations coursing through me. Several butches were rubbing their bulging crotches as they raptly watched the action on the stage. More strikes of the whip. More muffled groans from the crowd. Finally, Bree moaned and her head dropped to her chest. Cole gestured behind her, and another barely dressed femme bent to remove Bree's ankle cuffs. Cole moved behind her and wrapped her arm around Bree's waist while her wrists were freed. Bree collapsed against Cole, who scooped her up and carried her from the stage. They disappeared in the darkness before the house lights came up and the stage was cast in shadow once more. Mel's arm came around my back as the murmurs rose to the normal din of the club.

"Need a drink?"

We made eye contact. "You think?"

Mel laughed. The bartender had them ready by the time we got there. She handed mine over. "Still think this place is sedate?"

After downing half my beverage, I found my voice. "And you didn't think to warn me?"

"If I had, you wouldn't have come with me," Mel said, a knowing glint in her eyes.

I waved her off. "You make it sound like I'm a prude." My argument was feeble. We both knew she was right. But now that I *was* here, I was mesmerized. Women clad in black leather and studs. Roaming hands and possessive touches. It was beyond hot. "I don't see Cole and Bree. Have they left?" Curiosity won over decorum, and I was more than a little intrigued by their play.

Mel pointed to a staircase toward the back corner. "They went to a chamber for privacy. Cole will give Bree everything she desires…and then some."

My mind began to imagine what the couple might be doing. Was Cole fucking her with her cock? What instruments of pain and pleasure would she use? Did Bree have a say in what happened? My body reacted to the visceral images my brain was engaged in. My nipples hardened and pressed into the snug fabric of my top, and if I thought I was wet before, now I was drenched.

"I see those wheels turning. Do you want to leave?"

I swallowed my excitement. "No." I bit my lower lip. "I want what Bree wants."

For a minute I thought I was going to have to perform CPR on Mel. She'd been drinking her beer, likely in anticipation of our night coming to an end. After she stopped coughing, she faced me.

"You have no idea what you're asking."

Maybe she was right, but there was only one way to find out. "You don't know that." We stared each other down. Me, to let her know I was serious. Mel, I guessed, to try to figure out what she was going to do next. "So, how do I do—that?" I pointed toward the empty stage.

"Christ." Mel ran her hand over her face. Obviously still in shock over my request, she ordered another round. She handed me a glass and shook her head. "You're sure?"

I understood her apprehension. In all honesty, I questioned my own sanity, but in the face of how turned on I was, it was the only solution, though I could have been wrong. I was willing to take a chance to find out. "Yes." To my credit, I sounded certain.

Mel studied me while she twirled her beer, as though deciding what to do next. I thought I could help her along. "So, you can…you know?" I asked.

She took a step back. "Oh, no. That's not ever going to happen. Never."

I hadn't even considered Mel might only be an eager observer and not into the Dom/sub scene herself. "Sorry. I thought you were into it too." I gestured at the stage.

"I am, but that's not the point. It would change our relationship, and I don't want it to. Do you?"

She was right. While we were on even ground as friends, my being shackled and whipped by her would throw our effortless balance off. I stirred my drink, then sipped from the straw. I could always depend on Mel to keep me from being reckless.

"Not a bit," I said.

I looked around at the growing number of women. It was still early, and maybe there'd be another performance. If this *was* Mel's scene, then she had to know someone here who could fulfill my latest fantasy. "Then who?"

She took the seat next to me and her bulge became more noticeable. Again, I wondered what it felt like. "Butch or femme?"

The words cut through me. I was actually going to do this. I didn't take long to answer. "Butch. Definitely butch." Mel moved closer while scanning the area. She pointed to a woman, and I checked her out. She wore the right clothes but couldn't pull off the attitude. "No. More confident."

She looked around some more, then abruptly stopped. A small smile played on her lips. She drained her bottle as she stood. "Since you're sure…" Mel grabbed my hair, exposing my throat, and bit down hard enough I knew there'd be a mark. "That's to keep other women away. Don't go with anyone. I'll be back."

I was still in shock as she walked away. I ran my fingertips over the spot and felt the raised flesh. An unexplainable electricity ran through me. Mel's bite had hurt for an instant, but the resulting rush of excitement had been worth it. I sipped while I waited. Before long, Mel returned.

"Okay. When you finish that, head upstairs." Mel ordered a tonic water. I wondered who she'd talked to.

"Then what?"

"First door on your right. I'll be here when you're done."

My skin tingled. I stood on trembling legs. Excitement coursed through me. "What do I do…" I wasn't sure how to say what I was thinking. Bless Mel's soul, she must have guessed my dilemma.

"The only thing you have to remember is that a submissive is always in control."

I nodded. I should have googled expectations while she was gone.

"She'll ask for your safe word."

Safe word. What the hell was that? "A little help, Mel."

"It should be unique," Mel said. "A word you wouldn't normally use in conversation."

I racked my brain. It wasn't functioning at the moment. "Orchid?"

"Is that a word you'll remember?"

It was my favorite flower. "Yes."

Mel's smile reassured me she wasn't worried about where I was going. "Good. See you later."

I downed my drink, took a breath, then headed upstairs. The higher I climbed, the faster my pulse beat, and my heart felt like it would burst through my chest at any minute. The darkness receded and the walls of the hallway lightened, shimmering with pale purple and soft white lights. The door I was supposed to go through loomed in front of me. For a moment I considered leaving, but I wasn't going to let a little apprehension keep me from feeling alive, the way I had when I'd been watching the scene below. I pressed the handle and stepped into the semidark room. The walls were a soft gray, the lighting dim, but I could make out all the details. One wall was covered with whips, objects made of leather, and other play instruments I couldn't name. Some looked like they were made for pleasure, others for pain. I tried to swallow, but my mouth had gone dry when I spotted her. I was fascinated by the woman whose back was to me. She raised her arms and pulled her shirt off her shoulders, revealing the tattoo I'd admired earlier.

Cole turned around. "Jill. I understand you've requested a scene."

I nodded, focused on her small, high breasts and the ripple of muscle as she moved. She closed the space between us and touched my face, her fingers surprisingly soft.

"It's been ages since I've worked on a novice. Especially one so young. So…" Cole fingered my wavy hair. Even her voice was erotic. "Beautiful and unafraid."

I stopped breathing in that moment. Was I unafraid? It didn't matter. I wanted her to want me. To take care of me as I'd imagined she'd done for Bree.

"What is your safe word?"

"Orchid." It came out as a whisper.

"You'll need to be sure I hear you if needed, but I want you to know you can take much more of what I can give than you may think you can. Relax into it, but know I'll stop if you say the word."

Shivering at her words, I had no idea what to do next.

Her eyes softened. "I'm Cole, but you will call me Master whenever we're together."

She had no way of knowing if this would happen again, but I liked her confidence and the way her eyes undressed me. She took my hand and we moved farther into the room. She stepped behind me and held on to my hips, then pressed herself against me. I felt the ridge of her cock and couldn't help hoping it wasn't the same one she'd displayed earlier. Her hands closed on my breasts and she squeezed them firmly. Just enough to let me know she was capable of giving the right amount of pain and pleasure. I sucked in a breath.

"What are you into? What do you like?" She was taller than me, and her lips were at my ear, then her teeth at my throat.

"I don't know. I…"

Cole's hand cupped my crotch and she grabbed my sensitive, swollen flesh. "Are you wet?"

"Very." Moisture soaked my panties.

"Do you trust me?"

I didn't know her. "I trust Mel." I trusted Mel with my life and was confident she wouldn't have selected Cole as my first if *she* didn't trust her. Apparently, that answer was good enough.

"Shall we begin?" Cole turned me around. "Watch what I'm doing."

She pulled on the zipper of my top and revealed my chest. She palmed my nipples until they were tight knots, then roughly yanked each one. I jerked in response.

"Very nice," she said. "But you didn't seek me out because you want nice. You came to me to be pushed, to find your boundaries."

God help me, she was right, and I was about to find out how much I needed to be pushed, along with how talented she was. She knelt to remove my shoes, then stripped me naked. I reached to cover my exposed mound. Cole slapped my hand away with a quick, hard strike.

"Never hide yourself from me." She unzipped her pants and pulled out a purple cock sheathed in a rubber. Her boots were gone, and she stood barefoot and magnificent. From the nearby wall she selected a riding crop and lightly tapped it against my sex. Liquid heat trickled from my folds, and Cole noticed. I didn't think she missed much. She gathered my juices on her fingers and held them up.

"Clean them."

I opened my mouth and she shoved them in just shy of gagging me. When I was done, she used the crop to nudge my thighs into a wider stance before moving behind me again.

"Lean over."

My breasts hung heavy, like weighted pendulums. I kept my hands on my thighs for balance. The crop strike stole my breath, and my head came up. Her warm hand smoothed my heated flesh. Cole repeated the action a dozen times, and when she'd finished, I was dripping, the floor beneath me pooled with moisture. She pushed me over the back of a black leather armchair.

"I'm going to fuck you and make you come."

"Please, Master."

Cole's cock filled me. She rode me hard, circling inside me while she hung on to my hips and I hung on to the chair. Need rose in me, coursing through my veins and making my body tingle. This was the kind of orgasm I'd been longing for. She pulled out and I groaned. Cole slapped my ass hard.

"Did I say you could make a sound?" Her voice was rough as she slammed inside my pussy.

Somehow, I managed to answer. "No, Master."

By the fourth time she'd brought me to the brink, I could barely see through the haze of lust. I wasn't even sure if I wanted to come anymore. The state I was in was the closest thing to pure ecstasy I'd ever felt, and now I knew what the attraction was for this kind of sex. The kind of trust in a sexual liaison so intimate there weren't words to describe it. Just when I'd given up all hope of climaxing, Cole replaced her cock with her hand and buried it deep inside me. I took all of her, feeling the knuckles of her fist against my walls. One more thrust and she blew my mind and body with the most explosive orgasm I'd ever had. I screamed and bucked, feeling the climax in my soul. My legs went numb. This kind of pleasure could be addictive. Before I stopped shaking, she took me in her arms and cradled me in her lap. My skin was flushed, my ass tender to the touch, and my nipples rock hard.

"Such a good girl." Cole was tender with me for the first time since she'd touched me.

She'd given me exactly what I wanted, reading my body like a map and playing with my mind. She was a gifted top who I appreciated on a whole different level. She pulled back my hair and gently kissed my neck. The first and only kiss between us.

"I hope I performed to your satisfaction."

Cole had pushed me beyond the limits I'd dreamt of so many times I'd lost track, and I wished I could keep her for my own, but that wasn't possible in this type of play. Taboo or not, I wanted to thank her for accepting the role, welcoming me into her world, and making me feel alive. I brushed my lips over her cheek. Before I asked for more, I stood.

"Thank you, Master." I didn't look at her while I dressed, still unsure of our boundaries, if there were any, but I was willing to learn.

Mel was standing over a woman, pinning her against the wall when I descended from the upper rooms. My legs were still rubbery. My ass chafed beneath my clothes. I went to the bar and ordered a seltzer and shots of tequila. It didn't take her long to find me. She studied me for a beat.

"You okay?"

I handed her a shot and raised the other. Without a word, we threw them back and I smiled before taking her hand. We got in her car and she turned the key, then looked at me.

"So?"

I looked at the nondescript building and the blacked-out windows of the upper floors that housed the rooms. I thought about Cole and wondered if she ever got off, then studied Mel.

"I need to go shopping."

The smile was slow to appear on Mel's expressive mouth, and as we headed home, I couldn't help but wonder what else life had in store for me. Whatever it was, I would keep an open mind and remember tonight, and the ones that would follow, knowing it was only a matter of time before I'd be ready for my stage debut.

Playing with Fire

Lacie Ray

Lacie Ray writes erotic short fiction about women who love women. She loves reading and making up stories, happy endings, chocolate, and summer nights.

This was the third time in a month that I needed to call the fire department. High-pitched beeps were coming from the fire alarm panel in the front lobby of the library. Josephine, the circulation manager, arched her brows and gave me the hairy eyeball each time I walked past her desk to the lobby. There was a disagreement between Cityside Alarm Company and the Marshfield Fire Department as to who was responsible for the alarm panel. It's up to me to get to the bottom of it. I'm the new library director at Marshfield Public Library, and it's just one of the seventeen small calamities I've dealt with in my first five months in my new position. I was upstairs in my office when my phone rang.

"Andrea, there's someone here from the fire department."

"Thanks, send them up."

I stood up, took a deep breath, and blew it out slowly. My hands smoothed the back of my skirt. I heard heavy boots coming up the stairway.

"Good morning, ma'am, we got a call about the alarm panel? I'm Firefighter Taylor Briggs, new to the department."

This wasn't one of the guys. Taylor stood in the doorway and extended her hand. My heart raced as I looked into her warm brown eyes. I seemed to have forgotten my name. A beautiful woman in uniform does that and more to me. But only in my head. The closest I've been to having sex with a gorgeous woman in uniform is in my imagination.

"I'm...um...Andrea. Yes, we called, well, I called, about the alarm. Welcome to Marshfield. I'm new here too, about five months. Let me show you where it is," I said. My hands started to sweat.

"I know where it is, ma'am, but you can show me if you want," Taylor said.

Taylor grinned and looked me over. Oh God, she had a hint of a Southern accent too. As Taylor's eyes traveled over me, warmth followed and lingered between my legs. The thought of listening to Taylor's heavy leather boots behind me as she watched me descend the stairs drove the heat between my legs higher. Oh yeah, I wanted to show her where the panel was. My pussy did too. I looked up at Taylor.

"Follow me," I said, and walked out of my office to the stairway.

I could feel Taylor's eyes on me as I started down the stairs. My silk underwear rubbed against the inside of my skirt with every step I took. The sound of her boots on the stairs and her equipment belt jingling made my nipples tingle. Their hard points rubbed against the inside of my bra. I took an unsteady breath when we reached the landing. Taylor continued to walk behind me as we passed the circulation desk. The pulse between my legs matched the thunder of my heart. I pushed open the door to the front lobby a little too vigorously, and it hit the bricks on the lobby wall.

"Easy there," Taylor said. She grabbed the door on its rebound trip.

"Here it is," I said.

I turned to face her. My cheeks felt warm. She was younger than I first thought. Probably a good ten years younger than me. I licked my dry lips and swallowed. The wetness between my legs was distracting. Hell, Taylor was distracting. She stood there with one hip cocked and a big smile on her face. I looked at her hands, then back up at her beautiful, smiling face. Her eyes traveled over me again and I watched them stop at my breasts, just for a second, before they moved to meet my eyes. Enough time to cause my nipples to tighten even more. I felt swollen and wet and ready for sex. Not good at ten in the morning at work in a public library.

"I'll take a look at it and then should I come…back to your office?" Taylor asked. She paused after the word "come" and she looked into my eyes as she said it. She seemed to know the effect she was having on me, and I hoped it wasn't visible to anyone else.

"Okay," I said. I licked my lips again and saw Taylor's gaze shift to my mouth. I needed to get back to my office. My body didn't like being ignored for five months, and it had decided that this morning it would take full advantage of all those years of firefighter fantasies. Taylor caught my mind and body completely off guard. In fact, the guards seem to have disappeared altogether. The gate was open. I walked on wobbly legs back to my office.

On my way there, two patrons asked me for help, a staff person wanted to know if she could leave early, and Josephine shoved three message slips into my hand. When I finally got back to my office my heart rate was close to normal and my head had cleared. I just needed to keep distracting myself and not think about Taylor downstairs in her firefighter uniform, leather boots, wicked smile, gorgeous hands, and toned forearms. *Damn.* Strong forearms that probably never got tired. *Damn.* I made a promise to my neglected body that I would satisfy her tonight.

There were piles of financial reports left undone by the former library director that were due to the library board in two weeks. I poured what little focus I had into them. I brought up one of the reports that I had almost finished yesterday, opened the new spreadsheet on one monitor and the old report on my second monitor, and began to peck away at the updates. After about twenty minutes I clicked save, then print, and nothing happened. The printer was from the nineties, and every so often it needed to be unplugged and plugged in again to work. I hated to call Jenny, our reference librarian and IT person, every time I needed to do it, but it was a pain in the ass to crawl under my desk, especially if I had a skirt on like today. Still, I got down on my hands and knees, scooted under the desk, and grabbed the power strip with one hand.

"Please don't get up on my account, ma'am."

I jumped at Taylor's soft voice behind me and at the same time felt my pussy tingle and open. With a soft, low groan, I backed out on my hands and knees and reached up for my desk. Taylor's hand grasped mine and she helped me to my feet. I stood and pulled my hand away, making a show of brushing off my skirt while I regained some piece of my composure. I looked up at Taylor, and her eyes held mine. The thought of Taylor standing in my doorway looking at my ass while I was on my hands and knees made me swell with desire.

I tried to clear my head and looked at the painting behind Taylor. Why had I never noticed it was a Georgia O'Keeffe? Great, a great big open pussy on my wall. I bit the inside of my cheek to keep from making any noise. Maybe there was something hormonal going on with my body, because I had never felt this horny in my life. Not when I was a teenager, not when I was with Kendall, whom my friends had nicknamed the Sex Olympian. But right now, the thought of Taylor touching me, kissing me, reaching her hand up under my skirt and feeling how wet and open I was for her... I tried to breathe normally.

Taylor took a step closer. I realized my lips were parted and soft panting noises were coming from my mouth. My lips felt large and swollen. I closed them. My nipples were hard and tight, and Taylor's gaze traveled to them after she stared at my lips. Her gaze drew my nipples out even more, and they ached to be touched. I dug my fingernails into the palms of my hands. She took a step backward and cleared her throat.

"I think I figured out your panel issue. The heat from the sun might be tripping a sensor in there. I've done a temporary fix until we can figure out what to do next. I'll let the captain know, but I'm real glad I was the one who was called out to the library today. I hope you don't mind me saying that you look nothing like what I pictured a librarian would look like. You're...you're..."

I smiled and took a step toward her to let her know that I didn't mind at all where this conversation was headed.

"Yes?"

"You're younger and more...um..."

"And more...?"

"I'm getting a little warm with all my gear on. If you know what I mean." Taylor smiled at me.

"I do." I beamed a smile right back.

"I get off tonight at seven, and I'd be happy to come by and just make sure that temp fix will hold for tomorrow." Taylor's eyes went to my nipples then back up to my face. "That is, if you'd like me to, ma'am."

She shifted her weight to her other foot and leaned her hip against the doorframe of my office. The flashlight on her tool belt shifted and the carabiners clicked against each other.

I wasn't sure I could speak. I felt a small trickle of wetness run down the inside of my left thigh. I crossed one foot over the other, trying to look nonchalant. I bet she could see the pulse in my neck.

"The library closes at six, but I'll be here working late. You could stop by then," I said softly.

"Are you sure you want me to stop by after hours? I just want to make sure that's okay."

My heart raced. "Just call the library and I'll let you in."

I locked the doors in the front lobby after the last employee left and walked one more time around the building to double-check that all staff and patrons were gone. Plus, I couldn't sit still. The library was busy today, but every minute I wasn't doing something, my mind formed images of Taylor touching me, licking me, putting her fingers inside me, and my body responded. The phone on the reference desk rang just as I walked by.

"Marshfield Library, this is Andrea."

"Hi Andrea, it's Taylor. Do you still want me to come and check on things?"

I heard her voice and I think my pussy started moving of its own accord.

"Yes, I definitely want you to come," I said. *Two can play at this word game*, I thought.

I'd never done anything like what I hoped was going to happen here tonight. I followed the rules. I've never even had a speeding ticket. That was part of the reason my last girlfriend and I broke up. She said that I tried to plan every minute of our life and life can't be planned. But right now, my mind and my body wanted the same thing, and that interplay was driving my desire to a place I never knew existed. All my senses were heightened.

My skirt felt tight as I walked, and my ass felt full and round. My back arched involuntarily as I thought about Taylor's hands, and I stopped mid-stride. My heart raced as I walked down the stairs to the front lobby. I was so wet. Taylor stood just outside the glass doors. She wasn't in full gear, but still in uniform. I unlocked the door and almost forgot we were standing in a very well-lit area. Not many cars went by, but I didn't want to take a chance anyone would see or hear us. There was still a small part of my logical brain that worked.

We didn't speak. Taylor followed me. I didn't dare touch her. There was only one place in the library where we wouldn't be seen. The media room had blackout curtains and soundproof panels on the walls for library movie nights. I had pulled the curtains down earlier in the day and was happy to see they were still down. I turned the lights on, then dimmed them to the lowest setting. Taylor closed the door behind us.

"I parked around back," she whispered and stepped toward me.

I was panting. One wet line traced down the inside of my thigh, then another. My breasts pushed against the silk fabric of my bra.

"I've been thinking about you all afternoon," I said, my voice raw and husky.

Taylor wrapped one arm around my waist and pulled me to her. She bit her lip and cocked her head.

"Are you as wet as I've imagined all day?" she said.

A soft moan came out of my mouth and I pressed my breasts against her jacket. Her kisses moved down my neck. She slid her tongue over my collarbone, and then she began to unbutton my blouse. My legs melted and she backed me up against the soft wall of the media room. Her lips were on my neck. Then over my ear. Her tongue traced the outside of my ear while her hands slid my blouse off my shoulders. I reached to unbutton her shirt and she gently pushed my hands away.

"Not yet, ma'am. Not yet," she whispered in my ear. Then she reached around my back and unhooked my bra with one hand while she used the forefinger of her other hand to trace a line under the waistband of my skirt. My hips pressed forward.

"You are so beautiful. You want me to touch you, Andrea?" Taylor said.

"Yes."

She leaned the length of herself against me. My clit throbbed in anticipation and my legs opened as wide as they could with my skirt still in place. I wiggled my ass and reached behind to unzip my skirt.

My body had been denied pleasure for so long, and it wasn't going to wait much longer.

"You're going to come for me so many times tonight," Taylor whispered in my ear.

A low, deep groan moved from somewhere deep inside my throat and across my lips.

She backed away but kept her lips by my ear. "I'm going to reach up under that skirt right now and pull your underwear down."

I groaned and my pussy clenched; my nipples stung with desire, and her uniform brushed against them, making my back arch. The only part of me against the wall was my upper back. The rest of me arched toward Taylor. I grabbed at her hips. She brushed my hands away and stepped to the side.

"Please, now, please," I said.

I felt her fingers brush the inside of my thigh as they climbed higher and higher. My moans matched the rhythm of my breathing. She reached under my skirt and I felt the tips of her fingers brush along the wetness of my lips, then she reached a little higher and pulled my underwear down in one quick motion.

"I'm going to play with you now, and I want you to focus on my fingers, okay? Will you do that?" Taylor's voice was low and husky with desire.

I whimpered and rocked my hips.

Her fingers moved just inside my pussy lips. I threw my head back and bent my knees to lower myself onto those fingers I needed deep inside me. My skirt hiked up around my waist as I lowered myself down the wall. Taylor grabbed one side of the skirt and I grabbed the other and we got it out of the way. She never stopped moving her fingers in and out of me, then curled them and somehow turned them. I don't know what she was doing but it felt like her fingers were twirling, dancing. I was going to come. Hard.

"Oh…Taylor…I…"

"Yes, right now, ma'am. Right now," she said.

My hips bucked hard against her hand. My arms flew back up against the wall and I felt myself clench and release with each wave of my orgasm. A line of sweat trickled down my spine. I rolled my head from side to side. She slowed her movements.

"More." I breathed into her neck.

"Oh yes, there's lots more. Do you want more of me inside you?"

I nodded and grabbed her shirt and pulled it out of her pants. My fingers fiddled with the buttons.

"Let me, it'll be faster."

She unbuttoned her shirt, slid it off her shoulders, and put it carefully over the back of a nearby chair. She was beautiful.

Taylor steadied herself against the wall with one arm next to me as she leaned against me. She gently slid one finger into me, then another. Her fingers pumped inside me, in and out, and in and out. Each time she withdrew her fingers, her thumb circled my clit. I reached blindly for her. I reached to unbuckle her leather belt, but she turned away and never stopped her fingers going deeper and deeper with each entry. I felt her fingers slow, and my hips jerked and pumped to make them go faster. I bent my knees to get more of her inside me. The she started twirling and pumping me at the same time. Her thumb pressed my clit again and again. I reached down, pulled her hand out of me, and put it on my clit.

"There," I groaned. My body bucked and I moaned with every out breath.

"If you look at me like that again I'll come," she said.

Her fingertips swirled and rubbed and teased my clit, and it grew larger and harder. Then the world collapsed and there was only Taylor's fingers and my clit. My clit was attached to every fiber of every nerve in my body. I came in an explosive body wave. I yelled out. Smaller waves followed. I clenched around her fingers.

"More," I said, looking into her eyes.

"Yes." She groaned and her body tensed, then relaxed.

I grabbed her shoulders and felt the buckle of her leather belt press against my stomach. My thighs were wet. I kissed her, and her tongue met mine with promises of what she would do to my clit. Her tongue circled and probed my lips with its stiff tip, then softened and explored my mouth.

Usually my body hit a nice plateau after I came. But there was no plateau now. I could feel my body racing toward another orgasm. I reached for Taylor in a frenzy and pulled her undershirt over her head. I tried to unbuckle her pants, but my hands fumbled with her belt. I wanted to feel her skin against mine. Her tongue grew more demanding as she reached down to help me with her belt. Together we slid her pants over her ass, and when her flat stomach and warm breasts touched me, I came again. My head thrown back, I yelled the names of twenty gods or so.

"Taylor, Taylor, I need to catch my breath," I said.

Taylor rolled off me and leaned on her side next to me. She traced my hairline with her finger.

"Wow, Andrea," she said.

She ran her finger down my jaw and neck and chest to my belly. My hips started jerking involuntarily. I took her hand away. I tried to move away from the wall, but my legs were too shaky. Now that my breathing was starting to slow down and my eyes could focus again, I got my first good look at the woman beside me. Taylor didn't forget to go to the gym. It took dedication to get a body to look like hers. I ran my hand down her side and over her ass. My stomach muscles clenched. I couldn't believe my body's reaction to this woman, and I'd barely touched her.

"You look like your legs might not be holding their own," she said.

"I want this skirt off," I said. I yanked my skirt back down to its original location and reached behind me once again to take it off.

"Please don't take it off yet. Could I ask you something?" Taylor asked.

She started to trace circles around my right breast. I moaned and felt wetness gather once again. My mouth was dry. I licked my swollen lips. Then Andrea licked my lips.

"Yes?" I said.

"When I walked up to your office and I saw you bent over under your desk...oh my God, Andrea. All I could think about all afternoon was how I wanted to lift that skirt up and bury my face in you and make you come. That's all I've been thinking about."

I could feel my heartbeat between my legs. I took a deep breath and gathered the one scrap of willpower I had left. I wanted to touch this woman, but I didn't want to come. I wanted her to lose a bit of her self-control.

"So that's why you didn't want me to take my skirt off?" I said.

I moved my hand down her side and stroked her hip, then I ran my hand down her belly and groaned when I felt how wet and open she was. I spread her lips with two fingers and dipped the tip of the third finger into her. She gasped.

"Do you want me to bend over in this skirt, right now?" I asked. I curved my middle finger and stroked her in short, even strokes.

Taylor nodded and a long, low moan rose out of her chest. A small rush of liquid poured over my hand and I dragged my finger slowly out of her until it reached her clit and I teased her with the tip of my finger, making small circles. Taylor started panting.

"I want my mouth on you," she said. "Now."

I withdrew my hand and slowly lowered myself to the floor onto my hands and knees. I heard Taylor groan behind me.

"Oh my God, Andrea, you have the most gorgeous ass," she said.

Taylor got on the floor and slid my skirt up and over my bare ass. She moved my legs apart and slid a finger slowly into my swollen pussy. I moaned and lowered my head onto my arms to push my ass higher. I felt the tip of her tongue on the inside of my thighs, licking and pushing the soft flesh. I moved my legs apart even farther. Then she moved away. I felt nothing but cold air on my ass and pussy.

"You are so fucking gorgeous. I want to look at you like this," she said. Her voice was thick and low.

No one had ever asked to look at me this way before. I was vulnerable and ached with desire. My pussy was expanding and opening to meet her gaze. The gaze of desire, just like the Georgia O'Keeffe painting. I groaned and my hips began to rock.

"Taylor?"

"Yes, ma'am?" she whispered.

I heard her shift, and all at once her tongue was on me. She spread my lips and started lapping and licking me. I moved my hand to reach for my clit. She moved my hand away and I felt tip of her tongue touch my swollen clit. I came and rocked faster and faster. Taylor buried her face between my legs and swirled her tongue in and out of me. I ground my hips into her face and came again. My hips were jerking and she tried to steady them while she continued to lick every bit of my pussy. She slowed for a second and I felt her moan. I screamed and she flipped me over and spread herself on top of me, kissing my face and neck and hair. I held on to her as our bodies vibrated with the energy of our orgasms.

She rolled to the side but kept one arm wrapped around my middle.

I tried to catch my breath as we kissed. I smoothed her wet hair away from her forehead. She traced a line down my arm to my fingers. We held hands.

"I think that alarm panel might need a few more adjustments," Taylor said softly into my neck.

"If that's your professional opinion, then I guess you'll need to come back until I'm satisfied with the results," I replied.

WITH PLEASURE

Nicole Stiling

Nicole Stiling lives in New England with her wife, two children, and a menagerie of dogs, cats, and fish. When she's not working at her day job or pounding away at the keyboard, she enjoys video games, comic books, clearing out the DVR, and the occasional amusement park. Nicole is a strict vegetarian who does not like vegetables, and a staunch advocate for anything with four legs.

The clock on the nightstand was nearing six o'clock. I sighed heavily and walked into the bathroom to freshen up. This wasn't my idea of a good time. Sure, the hotel was nice, and the lake was amazing. I wished Carrie and Marissa had just planned an evening boat ride or something like that for their bachelorette party. Instead, we had to sit in humiliation for an hour and a half. But as I constantly tried to remind myself, this wasn't about me.

Being the only single on the trip didn't help matters much. Everyone else was coupled off and giggling about what exciting things were going to be taught and how they were going to use their newfound knowledge. They joked with me that I'd have to find a one-night stand at the hotel to practice on. Because yeah, that's the kind of thing I usually do. I still struggle with asking for extra ketchup packets at my local fast-food joint.

I've been friends with Marissa since high school, and I couldn't be happier that she found love. It was no surprise when she came out to me at seventeen—I think it was seventeen, might have been eighteen—because I'd known for a lot longer than that that she was into women. She thought she was all elusive and mysterious, but it was so obvious. And no one cared. We just waited for her to find the right time to tell us. When she finally did, I think she was met with more shrugs than gasps.

She'd been trying to set me up since we graduated. First with men, then with women. I'd been so entrenched in schoolwork and college prep that I just assumed my lack of interest in boys was because of my laser-focus on academia. Turns out, it was just that I didn't want to date boys. I've dated a few girls over the years, mostly in college, but I never had that gut-punch-face-slapping-stars-in-the-eyes kind of feeling. We were intimate, and we did stuff, but secretly I still don't see what all the hype is about. I mean, it's nice, and it feels good, but so does a back massage. Marissa told me that the fact that I feel that way at twenty-six years old makes her want to weep. She talks a lot about the "right one" and the "force of the pull" and even "mind-blowing sex." But honestly? Sounds like bullshit to me.

I forced myself to apply a touch of lip gloss and ran a brush through my hair. The light in the hotel bathroom made my natural waves look exotically auburn, but it was really just brown. I looked down and decided that the black jeans and gray V-neck T-shirt I had on were good enough. I threw on a pair of strappy sandals to show that I tried.

"Oh good, you're ready," Marissa said as I walked out into the hallway.

I closed the door behind me and felt my pocket to make sure the keycard was there. All set. We got onto the elevator and I sighed heavily. "Can't we just have a few drinks and hang out by the fire pit? Doesn't that sound *so* much better than this?" I asked as the elevator doors opened, waving my hand toward the conference room at the end of the hallway.

"No! Stop being such a Debbie Downer, it'll be fun. Most of the girls are already in there. I'm just waiting for Carrie to finish plucking her eyebrows," Marissa said with an eye roll.

"Fine. You owe me. I'm only doing this because I love you and I don't want to be *that* girl at your bachelorette party." I cast a weary glance at the closed beige door.

"I know, and I appreciate you peeking out of your comfort zone for me. Honestly, we'll have a few laughs, a few drinks, and then we can hit the pool or something. Sound good?"

I nodded. "Yeah, it does. Now don't make me walk in there alone."

Carrie joined us in the hallway moments later. She had her long blond hair tied up in a strategically messy ponytail that looked thrown together but probably took an hour to perfect. "She's here, I think she's outside getting the stuff," she said.

We walked into the conference room together, which was set up like a lecture hall. It was named the Lakeview Room, which seemed odd, considering there were no windows. There were folding chairs in two lines of five, although there were only nine of us. A table at the front of the room looked like either a massage table or an embalming table. Could have gone either way.

I was talking to Laura about hitting the beach bar after the class when the side door opened. Everyone mostly kept talking, but I felt my breath catch in my throat for a second.

A woman with longish deep brown hair, brown lipstick, and sunglasses pushed up onto the top of her head walked in, pulling a large suitcase on wheels behind her. She looked down at a business card and then looked up at us. "Samantha?" she asked.

Sam, Marissa's maid of honor and coordinator of the bachelorette weekend, stood up and greeted her. Laura was still talking about the array of fruity drinks they served at the tiki bar, but I couldn't pull my eyes away from the woman at the front of the room. I had no idea how old she was, maybe thirty-five, maybe forty, but I did know that she was breathtakingly beautiful. I'm not sure what I expected. A pinched-looking woman who'd be annoyed with anyone talking and not paying attention? Basically, my third-grade teacher, I guess. Not that it mattered, but it sort of *did* matter. I cleared my throat to snap myself back to reality and listen to Laura, who was still speaking.

"Really, Paige? Really?" Laura was looking at me with amusement in her eyes.

Ugh, was I that obvious? "Really what?"

"Oh, please. Put your tongue back in your mouth, it's unbecoming."

"Stop, I wasn't even looking at her."

Laura rolled her eyes and turned around in her chair. The woman up front was emptying out her suitcase onto the table. She then taped a small banner to the front of it. It read: *With Pleasure*. She assembled the torso and legs of a lifelike mannequin and placed it on the table. She took her sunglasses from the top of her head and put them into the top pouch of the suitcase. Then she straightened the collar of her silk blouse and faced all of us.

"If you're all ready to begin, I'd love to get started."

Everyone turned to her and quieted down like we were in a real classroom. She leaned against the table with her legs crossed at the ankle. I shifted a little in my seat.

"My name is Vivian and I'm here to share with you a few techniques that will enhance your sex lives, both physically and mentally. I have a few different courses that I offer, but for this evening Sam has selected one of my very favorites. 'How to Make Love to a Woman,'" Vivian said, smiling.

Our group smirked and laughed softly, as I'm sure most do at the beginning of one of these things. I was equal parts horrified and turned on. Marissa looked back at me and gave me an exaggerated wink.

"First, I'd like to congratulate Carrie and Marissa on their upcoming wedding. Hopefully, you'll find a few things to add to your repertoire for your honeymoon," Vivian said. Marissa smiled and Carrie blushed. "I'm sure most of you are skilled in this area, but the first thing I always like to focus on is, in my opinion, the most important. The kiss."

Vivian licked her lips and I prepared for death. Never in my life had I been this attracted to a person. This stranger was stirring something inside me I didn't know existed. I was sure she got that kind of attention all the time in her line of work, so my chances with her were pretty much nil. Add that to the fact that I'd never asked anyone out in my life. That fear-of-rejection struggle is real. And pretty limiting when it comes to dating.

"The key to making your partner weak in the knees isn't your experience level or your ability to perform a cavity search with your tongue. It's one thing and one thing only. Confidence."

I swallowed.

"It doesn't matter if you've been dating a week, a month, a year, or if you're just meeting for the first time. Kissing is an art. There is always room to improve your technique, and practice makes perfect. Don't go into it nervously, or your partner will sense it. Speaking of partners, do we have any couples here?"

Eight hands shot into the air. I closed my eyes, hoping the floor would miraculously open and devour me whole.

"Perfect. We're all adults here, so there shouldn't be any reason to be embarrassed or shy. We all have sex. And we should all be enjoying every part of it. Physical demonstration is usually best."

I tore my eyes from the ground for a split second and saw Vivian looking at me. Oh goody, maybe she'd send me out for snacks.

"What's your name?" she asked.

I cleared my throat. "Paige."

"I don't normally use live subjects in my demonstrations, but if you're open to it, I'd like to use you as a model. If you're uncomfortable in any way, it's perfectly fine. I can use Molly the Mannequin just as easily." She seemed amused at my lack of response.

I forgot how to speak.

"She'll totally do it," Laura said, turning back to look at me.

I glared at her. "Uh, sure," I said. "Anything for education." Yes, I actually said that. Out loud.

"Wonderful. Come here, then." Vivian curled her finger, beckoning me. I ran a hand through my hair nervously.

"Okay," she said, authoritatively. "Face each other."

Vivian turned toward me, pushing her hair behind her ear. She raised her eyebrows at me seductively and smiled. I briefly thought about running screaming from the room, since being on display in front of people, friends or not, was a fate worse than death, but then I saw the most adorable crinkle at the sides of her eyes when she smiled. Fuck it. What's the worst that could happen?

"Place your hand on your partner's neck. If they have long hair, make sure it's skin on skin. Pull slightly, but with purpose. Let them know in that tiny tug that you want them, completely."

She came closer and put her hand on the back of my neck. Her hand had the slightest chill, but the warmth I felt spread throughout me negated it.

"Ease into it. No rushing. No jumping. If you rush it, your mouths could be at odds, and that would make it awkward. Look into her eyes. It's a cliché for a reason, my friends."

While she spoke, she stared directly into my eyes. I almost looked away out of habit, but I was mesmerized. The deep brown staring back at me oozed sensuality. I swallowed again, thankful I had eaten a handful of Tic Tacs right before I left my room.

"Again, no rush. Start with soft, sweet kisses. Kiss her top lip, her bottom lip, the sides of her lips. Make her feel as sexy and as wanted as *you* know she is. Make her yearn. If you take one thing away from this class today, let it be that *yearning* is crucial. And it's up to you to make it happen."

I looked at the group and saw that they were doing what Vivian had said to do. Laura and Sam were giggly about it, but everyone else seemed serious and kind of into it. I looked back at Vivian and wondered what the hell I was doing up there.

"I won't kiss you if you don't want me to," she whispered into my ear. The heat from her breath sent shivers everywhere.

"It's up to you," I said. Did I want her to kiss me? Fuck yes. But I couldn't answer honestly because there was a sea of people out there. Paying absolutely no attention to me, granted, but my brain didn't catch that. I didn't want to say yes and then have her laugh and say that she didn't do that sort of thing.

"I don't do this sort of thing," she said.

Ah, of course. "That's fine, I didn't expect you—"

She pulled me forward, bringing our faces less than an inch apart. She kissed my top lip lightly, her lips so soft and tender I almost fainted dead away. I wanted to disregard everything she had just said and push her down and kiss her with ferocity. I wanted her *badly.* That was an entirely new sensation, and I can't say that I didn't like it.

Vivian kissed my bottom lip, and then each side of my mouth. I found my mouth opening slowly, begging her for more. She pulled away and faced the group again. My body was electrified.

"Once you have her where you want her, graze her lips lightly with your tongue, showing her that you want to enter, but let her know that you're not being forceful. This is a dance, and you both need to participate. When she reciprocates, you can begin to increase the intensity and passion. Chase her tongue. Let her chase yours. Pay attention to her and make sure you're keeping the pace that she's signaling she wants."

She turned back toward me, resumed her position with her hand on the back of my neck, and kissed me lightly again. Without thinking, I put my hands on her hips. I had to resist the urge to pull her into me. She danced her tongue on the outside of my mouth, and I wasted no time inviting her in. When the tips of our tongues touched, I felt a jolt between my thighs. I moaned unintentionally and pulled away, embarrassed.

"I'm sorry," I whispered.

She looked into my eyes again. "Don't be."

Vivian pecked me lightly on the lips and once more turned back to the group. I wanted to tell them all to fuck off and get out.

"Obviously, every situation will be different, but the basics remain the same. No rushing. React to *her* reaction to you. Next, we'll move onto the breasts." Vivian looked at me and smirked. I must have looked terrified because she laughed. "Thank you, Paige. You've been an amazing assistant."

"You're welcome," I said stupidly. I walked back to my seat where everyone was staring at me with giant grins on their faces. Sometimes I really hate my friends.

I watched, rapt, as Vivian glided her hands over the mannequin's plastic breasts, caressing the plastic nipples with the tips of her fingers. I could nearly feel her fingers on my own body, and I had to shift in my seat again. I was on fire. I was going to have to ditch the beach bar and go back to my room.

Vivian continued to make her way down the mannequin's body, using her hands and tongue with expert precision. Everyone was watching her, like I was, but I was just about ready to explode. She caught my eye right before she dipped her head between the thighs of the mannequin and licked slowly and languidly, her tongue dancing over the mannequin's plastic sex. I looked at the clock to see how much time was left in the class. That must have been the grand finale because there were only a few minutes left. When she reached up to cup the breasts while still working her tongue below, I jumped out of my seat. Laura and Marissa turned back to see what was happening.

"I'm not feeling so good," I lied, and walked quickly toward the door. I know Vivian stopped what she was doing to ask if everything was okay, but I didn't turn back. I was so filled with sexual tension that I was physically in pain. I wanted to take Vivian upstairs and ravish every inch of her, inexperienced or not. I didn't even care.

I pressed the up button for the elevator about twelve times, like those impatient, rushed people always do. I usually judged them for being ridiculous, because slamming the button doesn't make the elevator come any faster. Yet there I was.

It didn't come, so I decided to take the stairs instead. I was only on the third floor, and maybe the exercise would snap me out of it. I'd have to make up some excuse about why I was abruptly feeling well again when I showed up at the beach bar later. Hopefully, no one planned to come and check on me. I was on the third stair when I heard the heavy door open behind me.

"Are you okay?" Vivian asked, looking concerned. "I'm so sorry if I made you uncomfortable back there. I never involve the participants, because that's not the type of business I run, but you were so cute, just sitting there like that, and it was totally unprofessional. Please forgive me."

I was stunned for a second. She couldn't have been more wrong. Although it did make me feel good to know that she thought I was cute and that's why she pulled me up there and that it wasn't something she did with every class.

Wait, she thought I was cute? This beautiful woman who could have anyone she wanted, any time, any place, thought I was cute? Wow. Talk about an ego boost.

"No, it's not that at all. It's the opposite, actually. I was, uh, having a tough time watching you."

She looked puzzled.

"It was too...intense?" I said.

She smiled. "My classes aren't for everyone. I know they're pretty graphic."

Vivian misunderstood again. I didn't want to come right out and tell her she'd made me so wet that I needed to go upstairs and change.

"You..." I paused. There was no right word. "Excited me. A lot. So, I just needed to get out of there for a minute. Sorry."

She cocked her head and then nodded slowly. I watched her turn and flip the deadbolt on the door marked TWO. It happened so fast I didn't really comprehend what was happening. She came toward me and placed her hand on the back of my neck, like she'd done in class. My heart began to race, threatening to break right through my chest.

"Don't be," she said, echoing her sentiment from earlier. She leaned forward and kissed me with purpose, her tongue requesting entrance. There was no delay. I opened my mouth eagerly and let our tongues touch, lightly and slowly. I wasn't going to make it. I wrapped my arms around her waist and pushed our lower bodies together. Not exactly subtle, but I needed to feel her. I didn't know what her endgame was, but my body was moving of its own accord. The only way I'd be able to stop was if she told me to.

She didn't. She lifted my shirt above my bra line with one swift motion. I instinctively covered myself. "Vivian, there's a window," I said, pointing to the rectangular window with the crisscrossed lines. "And there might be another door upstairs? That isn't locked?"

"There's not," she said, reaching around to the clasp on my bra.

"How do you know?"

"I don't," she said, shrugging. She pulled my bra forward, exposing me in the gray cement stairwell. I'd never been so mortified or so turned on in my life.

"Maybe we should..." I trailed off as her tongue glided over my nipple, hardening it immediately. It sent a signal of electricity between my legs and I nearly doubled over. She guided me gently toward the stairs, where I hit the cold cement.

"I don't want to wait," she said, between gently sucking each of my breasts. "I knew I had to have you as soon as I walked into that room." She unbuttoned my jeans and yanked them down to my ankles, lifting me slightly so she could pull them down over my ass. I was sitting on a cement stairwell with a small window eight feet from me, completely exposed, with a beautiful woman kneeling in front of me. Mental overload. I couldn't even bring myself to care that someone could walk in at any moment. If Vivian had asked me to run through the hallway naked, I would have done it.

I reached above my head and gripped the steel railing, trying to find purchase on the slippery step. Vivian ravished me with her mouth, kissing my stomach, my breasts, my sides. I needed her and she knew it. My body was heaving with want, and I could see the sweat glistening on my skin. She looked up at me before pulling my knees apart. "You're really beautiful," she said, sliding her middle finger up the length of me, but barely touching me. I shuddered on contact, so ready for her.

She smiled playfully and leaned into me. I felt her lips caress each of my thighs, her tongue making tiny circles in anticipation of what she was about to do. I moaned and had to stop myself from begging.

Vivian knew. She moved toward my center, dancing her tongue

like silk through my wetness. She landed exactly where I needed her, and I clapped a hand over my mouth to muffle the cry that escaped. She licked lightly at first, flicking up and down, driving me to a wild place that I didn't know was real. I felt like I was floating above myself. I tangled my hands in her hair, pulling and tugging, not even sure where I was anymore. She reached up and began stroking my nipple to the same rhythm of her tongue, in soft, tight circles.

My breath hastened and my pulse quickened. Intense heat began down inside my abdomen and then spread throughout my body. I teetered on the edge, my hands tightening in Vivian's hair. She gripped my thigh with one hand, steadying me. It was happening. I closed my eyes and saw flashes of light behind my eyelids. The tension began deep within my sex and then washed over me in a tidal wave, radiating pleasure from the center of my body to the tips of my fingers. I moaned her name, which seemed to incite her even more. She continued her movement throughout my convulsions, only slowing when my body finally relaxed. I was pretty certain I had never felt so high, so relieved, so spent, and so adored in my entire life.

"I don't even know what to say right now," I said as she straightened up. She pulled my shirt down over my bare chest, as I seemed to be unable to move. She leaned forward and placed feather-light kisses on my lips.

"You don't have to say anything. I'm sorry I had to rush. Goes against everything I teach," she said, smiling.

"Can you come up to my room?" I said, sitting up with urgency. I touched her arm, the flames reigniting even though I was completely spent.

"I can't. I have another class in," she checked her watch, "twenty minutes."

Clearly noting my crestfallen look, she handed me a business card from her pocket. "That doesn't mean I don't want to see you again. My class tomorrow night at six is 'The Art of Shibari.' I have a job I think you'll be perfect for."

I was about to ask her what the hell Shibari was, but she kissed me again and left through the same door she'd come through. I sat on the cement, my pants askew and my bra lying in a pool on the ground. What had just happened? I watched about ten different people walk by the window, none of them giving a second thought to the second-floor stairwell. I tucked the card in my back pocket, then stood up and ruffled my hair a little, attempting to look like I had a modicum of composure. There was no way I'd be able to walk up a flight of stairs. My legs were like jelly. I opened the door warily, hoping I wasn't going to confront a police officer who was ready to arrest me for lewd and lascivious behavior.

"There you are!" Marissa yelled, stomping over to me with Carrie watching from a distance. "I've been looking everywhere for you! It was my fault; I never should have made you come to that. You're too shy and reserved for that kind of thing. And you don't even particularly like sex. So, really, that was shitty of me. I'm so sorry. I'm a terrible friend. When we leave tomorrow, maybe we can stop off for an ice cream or something? Just the two of us?"

"Seriously, don't even worry about it. In all honesty, I even enjoyed the class a little. But I can't do tomorrow. I'm staying a little later. I have to learn what Shibari is first, though." I shrugged and then jogged slowly toward the elevator, leaving my friend staring after me. I brought my fingertips to my face and inhaled the scent of Vivian's shampoo. My schedule was about to become a lot more hectic with all the courses I found myself needing to take. With pleasure.

LEARNING TO ASK

Butch Indeep

Butch Indeep is a commercial transactions attorney by profession and an avid consumer of lesbian erotica, trying their hand at writing and blogging as an escape from the corporate treadmill in the middle of Flyover Country, USA.

They're late tonight. Usually Damian is here and seated by eight, but it's already nine thirty and I'm starting to worry they won't show. That happens sometimes, when they're under a deadline or have a big case they're working on for their company. Damian is a corporate lawyer, super smart and in a prominent position. I like that about them: employed, intelligent, energetic, and invested in their work. They have so much going for them. And *gorgeous*. I like their style so much. It's unconventional and unique. Although at first glance it's a very masculine look, Damian has an enticing energy about them that is both masculine and feminine, which undercuts the binary and makes it something new, something all their own.

When the door finally opens just before closing time to reveal them hesitantly looking around, I breathe a sigh of relief. I'd been working up to this night for a long time, and I was beginning to think I'd miss my opportunity and my courage would fail me on another night. Damian had been encouraging me to be bolder, to learn to ask for what I want, to put myself first. I've been working on it and had decided I'd do exactly that tonight. So, when their eye caught mine and they smiled a little, I could feel the flush fill my cheeks, and my lips curled in an answering smile.

"Hi there. You're just in time," I said, trying not to sound too breathless.

"Oh, hi. I'm afraid it's too close to closing time to order dinner."

"Not at all. Come have a seat and I'll let the cook know there'll be one more order." I led them to the back table they usually preferred, pulling out the chair in the corner that let them see the entire dining room and the front door. "Be right back," I said, lightly touching their shoulder as I stepped away.

After popping into the kitchen to let the cook staff know that Damian had arrived and would be ordering dinner, I gathered a glass of ice water and a lemonade and went back to their table.

"Here you are. I've let the cook know and he's on standby, ready to cook whatever you'd like." I could hear the breathiness in my voice and silently cursed myself for a fool. If I was this worked up over taking their order, how on earth was I going to get the nerve to ask them on a date?

Damian surprised me by clasping my wrist and looking me in the eye. "Are you all right, Ellie? You seem a little out of sorts tonight." Their expression was concerned, their voice solicitous, and their touch on my arm was intoxicating.

I stared into their smoky gray eyes for a long moment, my breath coming in small puffs, as I dreamt of Damian sliding that hand up the back of my thigh and under my skirt as I ran my fingers through their short salt-and-pepper curls. Before I could embarrass myself, Damian rose from their chair and guided me quickly into the chair next to theirs, frowning slightly in concern. "Ellie? You're flushed and not breathing right. What's wrong?"

As soon as I sat and found myself eye-to-eye with them, I came back to my senses. Smiling faintly, I said, "Oh, I'm so sorry. How silly of me. Yes, of course I'm okay. Just a little…" I didn't finish my sentence as I got lost in the depths of those intriguing gray eyes.

"What has you so distracted, beautiful, hmm?" Damian's voice had dropped and their eyes, always intense, had darkened as their gaze searched my face.

"I…I, um, wanted to ask…" I was stammering, close to losing my nerve, and breathing heavily. Their proximity, the woodsy, earthy cologne they wore, the intensity of their gaze, were making it hard for my brain and mouth to work together effectively.

Leaning forward so their lips were right next to my ear, their breath softly caressing the sensitive skin on my neck, they whispered, "Ask. Ask me and I might say yes." Their lips brushed the shell of my ear so lightly I may have imagined it. I shuddered at the contact and at the warmth of Damian's breath. So intoxicating was the mixture of stimuli that my brain must have short-circuited because what came out of my mouth was far from what I'd intended to ask.

"Come home with me." It came out in a whisper I wasn't certain either of us heard correctly, but I knew the moment the words were out that they were the deepest truth I had within me at that precise moment.

Damian stared into my eyes for a long moment, seeming to search for a sign of regret or insincerity. Before they could respond, I took my courage in my hands and repeated, "Come home with me…and stay for breakfast."

Although heat suffused my face and my heart was hammering in my chest, I was wildly proud of myself for finally voicing my desire. I wanted this gorgeous, genderqueer person and I said it out loud. It was rather a monumental moment for me. The next moment was even more momentous.

"Yes," Damian said in a low, sultry breath. And then they leaned forward and kissed my neck with a hot, open-mouthed kiss that made my whole body quiver. "I'm proud of you, Ellie. You finally asked for what you want. I've been waiting for you to do exactly that." Their lips and tongue on the sensitive skin just below my ear sent shivers down my spine even as flames seemed to lick every inch of my skin.

Sitting back and breaking contact between us, Damian looked me up and down and said, "I would like to have my dinner before we go, though. Would you join me?" Unable to speak, I simply nodded and stood to take their order. "Good. My usual, then. You may bring it and sit with me."

I jumped to obey as they turned their eyes away from mine. I strode directly to the kitchen where I was happy to see the chef already preparing Damian's plate. They ordered the same thing every visit, so it wasn't much of a risk to assume that was on order tonight. As the plating was completed, I began to tremble, wondering how this meal was going to go and what they had in store for our night together.

Back at their table, I placed the plate in front of them carefully and then sat as directed. Damian looked at the plate with satisfaction and turned an indulgent smile on me. "You knew what I would order and had them working on it before I asked. Thank you. That was very thoughtful of you." They leaned forward and placed a chaste kiss on my lips as reward. Then, almost automatically, as if we sat intimately together all the time, they placed their left hand on my knee and started to stroke my thigh absently as they took a forkful of the cheesy pasta and vegetables. But instead of taking it themselves, they raised the fork to my lips and lightly squeezed my thigh as a signal to open my mouth.

Feeding me two bites for every one they took, they continued to stroke my thigh, a little higher each time. On the fifth bite, their fingertips reached under my skirt, and they leaned in and kissed my neck again. "Open your legs a little for me, Ellie…good girl."

My legs fell open as they placed the fork in my mouth and slowly drew it out between my lips. Kissing a drop of sauce from my lips as I chewed, their fingertips brushed lightly over the soft, damp skin of my inner thigh. As I finished the bite, I tilted my head back, arching my neck as their hand lightly stroked the skimpy panties covering my mound. There was a pronounced dampness to the fabric, and my mouth fell open as their finger stroked rhythmically over the cotton covering my slit.

"Are you ready to go home?" Their low growl in my ear immediately before their teeth grazed my earlobe nearly shot me out of my chair.

"Oh, yes!" I practically shouted it. Then, looking quickly around the dining room, was relieved to see that we were quite alone. "Yes," I said again in a more sedate tone. "Are you finished eating?"

"Not even remotely." They gave a firm squeeze of my mound. "But I'm finished with this food, yes." Their grin was wicked and held a promise of a decadent night to come.

"I'll just clear the table and then I'll be ready to go." I was a tiny bit unsteady on my feet as I rose, and their hand on the back of my thigh, under my skirt as I gathered the dishes from the table, made me tremble even more. Looking down into their stormy eyes for only a moment, I stepped away with a sway in my hips that I could feel them watching as I strode to the kitchen.

Dumping the dishes into the bus bins and telling the cook to lock-up as he left, I yanked the apron off over my head and grabbed my bag from the hook in the cloakroom. Not giving the restaurant another thought, I let Damian lead me out the door.

"Which way?" they asked as we stepped onto the street. Before I could answer, they pushed me roughly against the side of the building and pressed a hard thigh between my legs as their tongue demanded access to my mouth. The searing kiss made me moan into Damian's mouth, begging for more. But they pulled back and asked again, "Which way to your house?"

It was the longest six-block walk of my life. Though I was anxious to get Damian into my bed, I was enjoying the frequent and sudden stops they made to kiss me and feel me up. I felt so desired and desirable in those moments. Damian's dark eyes, full of lust and promises of pleasure, seemed to see into my very soul. Their firm, clever hands stoked flaming heat over my skin. Their low, growling voice whispering filthy promises and asking daring questions intensified the passion consuming us both.

As soon as we stepped through the door of my brownstone and shut the door behind us, Damian pushed me hard against the door, kicked my feet wide apart, and shoved my skirt up over my ass, pulling my hips toward them and pressing my face into the curtained glass panel. Exposing my wet panties over my swollen sex, they growled their appreciation. But instead of taking me hard right in the doorway as I expected, Damian simply massaged and caressed my ass cheeks, humming their pleasure.

Finally, with a sharp slap to my ass, they commanded, "Strip. Now." And they stepped back, crossing their arms over their chest, feet planted wide apart, expecting my obedience. Damian wasn't disappointed. Maintaining my ass-out position, I watched over my shoulder as I stripped my wet panties off, slowly revealing my bald, wet pussy. Satisfied with the intensity of their look of desire, I pushed the thong down over my knees and stepped out of it before I unzipped the skirt bunched at my waist and slid it quickly over my ass and onto the floor. Straightening and turning around slowly, I began to unbutton the white shirt I wore, looking them directly in the eye. I loved the heat in Damian's stare as their eyes tracked my fingers over the buttons and then over my skin as I stroked inside the opening before moving to the next button. When the shirt was finally open, I stroked my stomach and gripped my breasts before slipping the shirt off over my shoulders and letting it fall to the floor. Since I hadn't worn a bra over my small breasts, I now stood naked but for my sheer black stockings and black pumps.

"No, leave them on," they commanded as I reached to roll one of the stockings down my leg. "Follow me."

Damian strode confidently into my home, as if they owned it. I followed quickly, eager to know what they would do with me next. They walked past the living room entry on the right and directly to the dining room table visible through the open doorway ahead. Picking up the dining chair at the end of the long oval dining table and setting it in the corner to the left of the doorway, they pointed at the open end of the table. "Bend over."

Obeying immediately, I silently stepped to the table and took up the requested position. "Mm, very good girl." They softly stroked my ass. Squeezing my ass cheek before giving it a sharp slap, they said, "You seem very pliant, Ellie. That pleases me."

I didn't say anything, not knowing if Damian was expecting a reply or simply making a statement. This was the right move, as they praised me again. "So quiet and obedient. Such a good little girl."

I felt their hot breath on my ass as Damian talked to me. Then their hand moved between my legs, stroking a long, thick finger over the length of my slit as they again praised me. "Good, good girl." Damian paused. "You asked me to come home with you and stay for breakfast, Ellie. What do you want me to do while I'm here?"

"I want you to touch me, fuck me, make me come over and over again. And then I want you to tell me how to pleasure you."

"Very good, Ellie. You're learning to ask for what you want. I'm glad." As Damian spoke, they stroked their thick finger up and down my wet slit lightly, sending sparks of desire through my core. "Be explicit. What do you want me to do first?"

My inhibitions were gone, and the words came tumbling out. "I want you to fuck me on this table with your whole hand until I come, screaming your name. I want you to lick my pussy from behind as you stroke my clit and then I want you to finger fuck me deep and hard until I'm coming so hard I can't hold myself up anymore and your hand is so wet you can't grip me securely."

"Oh, Ellie, that's very good." They were already stroking me, using my wetness to circle my clit. When I finished speaking, Damian thrust two thick fingers into my pussy and began to do as I asked. Then, dropping to their knees behind me, they thrust their tongue into my pussy as deeply as it would go while rubbing my hard, throbbing clit slick with my pussy juices. Sucking my pussy and stroking my clit for what seemed like hours but was only a few long minutes, Damian brought me to a shattering orgasm.

"Damian, oh yes, yes!" I screamed loudly as the first orgasm crashed over me. Then, as they shoved a third finger into me, filling me completely and banging hard into my G-spot with every forward thrust, I came a second time with a guttural, incoherent shout.

Not bothering to ask me what I wanted next, Damian stood and grabbed me by the waist, yanking me upright and turning me around to face them. Then, grabbing a fistful of my hair and shoving me to my knees, they opened their belt and fly with one hand. Pulling out the realistically shaped and textured phallus they habitually wore, Damian pressed it to my lips. Breath still ragged from my orgasms and body still quivering, I opened my mouth to receive their member. I could taste their desire on the shaft, as it had been pressed tightly between their legs for hours.

With their fist in my hair guiding my head to where they wanted it, Damian used my mouth hard. Thrusting their hips, gyrating slightly, they pressed the silicone shaft into my mouth and let its base press firmly against their swollen clit. I did my best to suck and lick and provide the right kind of pressure and suction as Damian fucked my mouth with their cock. I was growing aroused again, knowing that they were taking their pleasure from my mouth. When their groans deepened and their breath began to falter, I opened my throat as much as I could and sucked them as deep as I could. Damian's hips spasmed with their thrusts and I grabbed their ass to help steady them and prevent them from choking me. Squeezing their ass just as they growled and thrust their cock forward, I felt Damian come. Their juices splashed slightly out from under the base of the cock and onto my cheeks. I was inordinately smug at that moment, even as I continued to suck their silicone cock, that I was able to pleasure them to orgasm.

I didn't have long to gloat over my achievement. Damian quickly pulled out of my mouth and tugged me up to a standing position. Whirling me back around and bending me over the end of the table again, Damian growled fiercely as they shoved their cock into my dripping pussy from behind. "Think you're something, huh? Sucking my cock till I come down your throat? Well, now I'm gonna fuck your pussy until I come inside you. Is that what you want?"

"Please, Damian! Fuck me hard. Make me come." I panted as they were already moving deep inside my wet pussy. It felt incredible, thick, and warm first from their body and then my mouth, their cock felt real—soft skin over firm, muscle-like silicone.

"You're gagging for it, Ellie. You want my cock in your pussy?"

"Yes, I love your cock inside me, Damian. Please fuck me hard with your big, butch cock." I begged with abandon, not caring how it sounded.

They began to slam into me full force. Pulling back until they almost pulled out altogether, they gripped my hips and slammed forward, bottoming the cock into my pussy, hitting my G-spot on every thrust. I was lost in the rhythm, shoving my ass back as they snapped their hips forward, feeling their shaft fill me. I was shuddering and a continuous, breathy whimper was keening from my throat as they slammed into me over and over. Finally, the impact to their clit too much to bear, they gave an almighty thrust and held fast as we both came with screams of ecstasy. Holding still inside me while my walls convulsed around them and both of our clits throbbed, I felt Damian tremble as I was lost to waves of pleasure.

Finally, slowly, and carefully so that they wouldn't hurt my oversensitized flesh, they pulled out and then lifted me in their arms. Carrying me down the hall to my bedroom, Damian kissed my forehead tenderly and whispered soft endearments I could barely hear. I felt so safe and cherished in their arms, even as the delicious throbbing, burning of our rough sex continued between my exhausted legs.

Laying me carefully on the bed, Damian lovingly removed my heels and caressed my legs as they rolled the stockings down. Then they slipped my legs under the comforter and stood. I was afraid for a moment that Damian would leave, but I needn't have worried. They stood by the bed and watched me with warm eyes full of tenderness as they stripped off their shirt, kicked off their shoes, removed their now damp jeans, and pulled off their socks. Then they carefully, reverently, removed the harness that held their cock, laying it neatly on top of the jeans and shirt they had folded onto the chair beside my bed. Leaving their tank top and boxer briefs on, Damian then slipped into the bed beside me, turning out the lamp.

Pulling me close, laying my head in the hollow of their shoulder and slipping their arm around me, Damian gently stroked my hair and cheek. "Thank you, Ellie. That was a beautiful experience," they whispered in the dark.

"Damian, won't you take these things off and let me hold you, skin to skin? I want to make you feel as good as you've made me feel tonight."

Damian was quiet for so long, I feared I had angered them and that they would reject me. But after long moments in which I felt their muscles tense, they sat up and pulled off the tank top. As I sat up with them, Damian cupped my face in both their hands and looked deeply into my eyes. "I don't normally allow this, Ellie. But because you've come so far and have learned to ask for what you want, I'll honor your courage. Please don't make me regret it."

I could feel their vulnerability in the tremor in their hands and hear it in the tentative note in their voice. I was so proud of Damian for facing their fear and was so honored. "You're safe with me, Damian. I won't dishonor this trust." My voice was hushed as I lightly stroked my lips over theirs and my hand slid over their neck and shoulder. I felt the tremble in the muscles of their stomach as Damian lay back on the bed and I leaned over, kissing them. With my hand stroking the smooth skin up their side, I slipped my tongue over their lips in a kiss that I hoped would convey all the emotion I held inside my chest.

When their hand closed over my wrist as I was about to cup their small, flat breast, I stilled and sought their eyes. Seeing the fear there, I moved my hand away and kissed their neck, whispering, "It's okay. I won't touch you in any way you don't want. Please, teach me how to please you."

Cupping my face in their hands, Damian's gaze lingered for a long moment, searching my eyes for any sign of deception. Finally satisfied that they could trust me, they pulled my face down with one hand to kiss me deeply, and grasped my hand with their free hand, guiding it carefully and slowly to their breast. As they kissed me, their fingers slipped between mine, tutoring my hand on how to hold and stroke and tease them. It wasn't so different from how they fondled my own breasts, but I sensed their need to control this exploration.

Soon, they were guiding my hand down their stomach, until our joined fingers reached the waistband of their boxer briefs. Damian stilled and pulled back from our kiss. Looking me in the eye the whole time, they slowly released me and reached down to push the boxers off their hips.

Unable to resist, I cupped Damian's face and whispered, "Thank you for trusting me," against their lips as I kissed them deeply. Sucking their tongue into my mouth and surrendering myself to their need, I slipped my arms around their neck and rolled to my back, pulling them on top of me. Disengaging the kiss momentarily, I breathed, "Make love to me, Damian. Use me to pleasure yourself. Teach me how to please you."

Damian kissed me hard then, thrusting their tongue deeply into my mouth and holding me hard around the waist as they knelt between my legs. Then, pulling back from the kiss, Damian stroked the entire length of my body. Looking into my eyes in the faint light from the hallway, they leaned forward as they stroked up the inside of my thighs, pushing them wider apart and lying between my open legs, pressing their waist to my mound. Stretching their hands up to cup my breasts, Damian said in a low growl, "You make me want to break all my rules. Your body is gorgeous. Your face and your spirit are beautiful. You ask me to give you what you want. Now you've asked me to take my body's pleasure from yours." Leaning forward and placing a series of hot, wet, open-mouthed kisses on my stomach just above my mound, they moaned. "I can't *not* give you what you ask for."

And with that confession, they gripped my hips and dragged their firm, smooth body over mine, pressing their skin to my pelvis and thighs, until their mound came to rest against mine. The sensation was electrifying. I was stunned to feel their pussy was waxed smooth and their lips, pressing firmly on my own, were wet and puffy and hot to the touch. As Damian closed their lips over one of my erect nipples, they ground their pussy into mine and I was lost. Moaning into Damian's mouth, pulling their bottom lip with my teeth, dragging my short nails up their back firmly, I began to beg once again. "Fuck me, Damian. Fuck me with your wet pussy."

"Oh God, Ellie. You make me insane." Damian began to gyrate their hips hard into me. As we kissed in a frenzy, sucking, and licking and nipping each other's mouths and necks, Damian bucked, grinding their clit against mine rhythmically. As the friction built, along with the wetness and pleasure, the volume and desperation of Damian's moans of pleasure increased.

Soon, they pressed their arms into the mattress, lifting their head and arching their back. I felt their clit swell, pressing into my folds as they rocked their pussy into me. Just as my spread legs began to quiver with the beginning of my orgasm, a primal cry ripped from Damian's throat as hot, wet come gushed out of their pussy, bathing my lips and clit in wetness. They shook for long minutes, their mound pressed to mine, a guttural moan rolling out from their lips before Damian collapsed onto my chest.

Cupping my breast instinctively and snuggling into my body, they lay on me, recovering from their ecstasy for a long, deliriously perfect moment. Then Damian moved up my body and kissed me deeply before settling back onto the bed, pulling me tightly to their side.

"I know I promised I wasn't done eating, but I'm spent. I think I'll have you for breakfast instead of a midnight snack, okay?" Damian chuckled weakly.

I laughed. "That's a promise I'll hold you to, stud."

As we drifted to sleep, I couldn't help but dream of the delicacies I'd ask for in the morning.

ABSINTHE KISS

Tina Michele

Tina Michele was raised on Florida's warm and sunny Space Coast. An eternal daydreamer and procrastinator, she often sets aside her notebooks and sketchpads to indulge her insatiable wanderlust. If she's lucky, she returns home with a few minor abrasions, several hundred photos, and a genuinely awkward story to tell.

Shea adjusted the bulge between her legs, lunging and pulling on her black denim jeans until everything was tucked in and hung the way she liked. She didn't pack every day, just on those days she felt rough and ready. She liked the extra swagger and confidence it gave her when she was on the prowl. Shea wasn't looking for a fight or a fuck, though she would never turn down the latter if the opportunity came calling. She was on the hunt for inspiration for her next piece.

Shea slipped on a black tank top to match her pants, without bothering with a bra. If anyone was interested in staring at her small, tight tits they were welcome to it. New Orleans was too humid for unnecessary clothing, especially once she decided on adding a little extra heat in her pants.

She snuck out the back door into the courtyard to avoid disturbing anyone else in the house. Her large, soft-side portfolio hung across her body. The thick canvas strap pressed between her breasts, all but smashing her right one flat against her chest. The scent of Southern jasmine was strong as it hung in the air, clinging to the thick fog that had rolled in off the bayou. She latched the ornate metal gate behind her, careful not to slam the heavy door as she left.

In the French Quarter, predawn was the quietest time of day. It was the golden hour between the end of one party and the beginning of the next. Shea waved and nodded as she passed familiar shop owners and bar managers as they sprayed down the sidewalks to wash away the revelry from the night before.

Shea's footsteps on the cobbled streets echoed off the façades of the grand residences layered with wrought iron balconies and grand windows. The city seeped with culture, history, art, and booze, and Shea loved every bit of it. Although at this time of day, she loved nothing more than coffee from her favorite corner bistro, Café La Laurent. The beautiful, open-air patio sat along the busiest street in the Quarter that bustled day and night with tourists and locals alike.

She floated into the shop on the delicious scent of coffee and fresh beignets and gave the barista a wink before sitting down at her favorite table in the corner. Shea had arrived just minutes after they opened, though several other regulars had already taken their usual seats and were contentedly sipping away at their steaming beverages. A few people peered over their newspapers or looked up from their tablets to give her a friendly, welcoming nod, which she returned in kind.

Shea adjusted herself to relieve the pressure that the base of her dildo was putting on her clit after she sat down. Once comfortable, she pulled out her Moleskine sketchbook and waxed canvas roll that held her pens and pencils. She set them on the table and leaned back in her chair, arching backward over the seat back. The fog had begun to lift above the wet streets when Pete brought over her coffee. The ear-piercing sound of heavy cast iron being dragged across the concrete startled her, and everyone else, out of their peaceful morning reflections.

All eyes were on the woman with the wild red hair who noisily moved a chair. A vision flashed into Shea's imagination of a black velvet chaise draped with emerald satin, flaming hair flowing down a delicately arched back. Shea adjusted herself in her seat, pulling down at the knee of her pant leg to ease the sudden increase of pressure between her legs. It seemed the Muses had chosen to bless her with a most captivating and arousing inspiration after all.

The fire-haired nymph shied away from Shea's gaze, her face blushing crimson. Shea rolled open her case and flipped over to a clean page in her sketchbook. Studying the soft and innocent features of the woman's face, from the perfect arch of her full brows to the subtle curve of her jaw, Shea tried to capture the way the wisps and curls of her hair mimicked a midnight bonfire as they blew around in the light morning breeze. Yet as hard as she tried, she couldn't seem to recreate the true uniqueness of her appearance with the neutral tones of dusty black charcoal. Her vibrant energy could only be truly captured in full color.

Shea stood and strode over to her. She set her hands on the back of an empty chair and peered down at the job listings of the local *Thrifty Nickel* classifieds. "You'd have better luck walking from shop to shop to find work," Shea said.

The vibrant green of the woman's eyes shot through her when she looked up from the paper. "Thanks, but I've already tried that." Her curt response surprised Shea and intrigued her all the same.

"What line of work are you in? I know the area fairly well, maybe I can help." Shea wouldn't have thought the woman could've been more alluring until her face lit up with a rosy glow.

"Really?"

"Sure. Whaddya do?" Shea didn't want to assume her interest was an invitation to sit, so she motioned to the seat and asked, "May I?"

"Of course," she said, shuffling papers and moving them out of the way. "I…I don't really know. What I do, that is. All sorts of things, I suppose. Cashier, Uber driver, and I was a receptionist at an insurance agency up until a few weeks ago."

"What happened with that?" Shea leaned back in her seat and stretched out her legs.

Her gaze flashed down between Shea's legs and quickly back up. "Um…I…Well."

Shea couldn't help but grin at the complete loss of words when the woman had spotted the package between her thighs. There was a confident throb pulsing against the harness, and Shea was glad she'd made the decision to wear it. She sat up straight, reached out, and said, "Let's start over. I'm Shea."

The glow in her plump cheeks deepened, and it darkened the freckles on her nose. "Charlotte," she said, sliding her hand into Shea's.

Her hand was soft and smooth against Shea's rough, dry ones. She turned it over and traced her fingers along the deep lines of her palm. Charlotte's fingers were long, with short nails painted black. She could be a musician. A pianist, maybe? Shea felt like a palm reader as she studied the details of her delicate hand. She felt Charlotte give it little tug, and Shea released her. "So, what brings you to New Orleans, Charlotte?"

"I needed a change," she said.

Shea set her elbow on the table and rested her chin on her fist. "Of heart, or scenery?"

"B...both." Charlotte stuttered and cleared her throat, and Shea smiled.

It had been a while since she'd encountered anyone so easily riled. Charlotte was gorgeous, alluring, and responsive. It seemed that Shea might just be able to help her after all. "Seeing as you're not having much luck with the job hunt, I have a proposition for you to consider." Shea sat back in her chair again.

Charlotte's mouth dropped open. "Excuse me? I'm not..." She looked around and lowered her voice. "A prostitute."

Shea bellowed with laughter, drawing the attention of everyone in the cafe. Charlotte blushed, and she sank lower in her seat.

"While I've paid plenty of women for their various services, I can assure you I've never paid for sex." After that reaction, Shea doubted Charlotte would be eager to accept the opportunity she was going to offer.

"I didn't mean...I'm sorry."

Shea reached out and took Charlotte's hand. She would need to change tack. "No worries. It's my fault. I'm afraid sometimes I come off a bit intimidating when I see something I want." Shea watched Charlotte swallow hard, but she didn't pull away.

"Oh?"

Shea let her go and reached into her pocket for her wallet. She pulled out a business card and handed it to Charlotte. "I have a studio a couple blocks over. I'd love it if you'd model for me."

"Me? Model?" Charlotte took the card, turning it over in her hand and rubbing her thumb across the raised letters. "Nice card."

The smooth, soft strokes of her thumb could have been upon her own skin by the way it sent chills rippling down her spine. She cleared her throat. "Verté, like the color of your eyes."

"Ah. So, you're a what? A photographer?"

"No, an artist. Oil portraits mostly, but I dabble in a little of everything." Shea rose and stepped over to her table to grab her Moleskine book. "This is my sketchbook. Would you like to see?"

Charlotte's eyes lit up. "Yes, please." Shea flipped through to the last page she'd been working on, and Charlotte gasped. "That's me," she said, before covering her mouth with her hand.

"Yes, but it doesn't do you justice in the least." Shea knew Charlotte was far more vibrant in color than she could ever be in a charcoal sketch.

Charlotte blushed and gave her a shy smile. "You're very talented, Shea. What else do you have in there?"

Shea turned the book around and handed it to Charlotte to peruse. She flipped to the beginning and thumbed slowly through the pages. Shea watched the flush of red climb up her neck and into her cheeks with each turn. With each breath Charlotte took, Shea watched her full breasts strain against the fabric of her shirt. She felt a light throbbing between her legs thrum against her harness as she witnessed how Charlotte's body reacted to her work. "Do you like?"

"Yes, but...um...they're all naked."

"They are."

"Is this...am I...Will I be naked?" Charlotte whispered.

Shea raised an eyebrow and smiled. Her response was as hushed as Charlotte's question. "Do you want to be?"

"Oh. I've never done anything like that before. Certainly not in front of someone I don't know." Charlotte bit down on her plump bottom lip and gently set the book down on the table.

"You don't have to do anything you don't want to do. Come by later and see the studio. No pressure." Shea pointed to the address on the back of the card she'd given Charlotte. "I'm going to get in a few more sketches and finish my coffee. But come by any time after noon, and I'll be there."

Shea got up to leave, and Charlotte grabbed her hand to stop her. Her hand was soft against her skin, but her grip was tight. "You didn't say how much this position offered."

"No, I didn't. We can discuss that when you stop by," Shea said as she winked and walked away.

❖

Charlotte paced back and forth between the bed and the door. She'd tried at least three times to leave her room. She couldn't believe she was considering taking Shea up on the offer to model for her. Not only considering it—she'd come back to her room to shower and change into her sexiest bra and panties. Her body was thrumming with anxiety and anticipation. She could feel the steady pulse of arousal pumping between her legs at the thought of exposing herself to Shea and letting her steel-gray eyes rake over every detail of her body. She was almost more afraid of Shea recognizing her obvious attraction than seeing any of her perceived imperfections.

Charlotte had felt almost as vulnerable in the café under her penetrating gaze, and she'd been fully clothed. The stiff and noticeable bulge between Shea's legs had surprised her and ignited her desire the instant it caught her eye. Shea's sexuality was as mysterious and seductive as the Crescent City itself. She could only wonder if both had cast a spell upon her in the most sensual way.

Charlotte pulled the card from the back pocket of her shorts and flicked her fingernail against the edge of the stiff paper. The green foil sparkled against the matte black card. Verté; the accent above the letter *e* had been replaced with a tiny green fairy. She brought the card to her nose hoping to catch any scent that Shea might have left on the card. She could barely make out a musky aroma that hinted of licorice, a scent that had lingered in the air long after she had walked away. She closed her eyes and drifted back to those moments in the café where Shea had sat beside her.

Though the air was thick and warm, Shea's nipples were hard. Her small, pert breasts strained against the thin fabric of her black tank, just as the erection between Shea's legs had against her dark, fitted jeans. Charlotte had never been approached by anyone so brazen and confident in attitude or in appearance. Even the smudge of charcoal over her right eye added to her allure. The heat of the moment mixed with the atmosphere had set Charlotte on fire. Her clit throbbed as she squeezed her legs together and felt her wet heat build. The tension and anticipation were unlike anything she'd experienced before, and all for this tempting dark-haired woman named Shea.

Before she could turn back once again, Charlotte charged out the door and out onto the street. It was full of midday tourists recovering from their previous evening of debauchery and starting anew. It was a warm afternoon with the sun in the cloudless sky streaming light into the narrow streets and alleyways. The city's unique scents wafted on the light breeze as Charlotte made her way along the sidewalks beneath the ornate balconies that decorated the million-dollar mansions of the Quarter.

Large mahogany doors greeted her when she arrived at the address Shea had given her. The le Fee Verté gallery wasn't at all what she'd expected, and she felt significantly underdressed just standing in the doorway. She tugged at the hem of her casual summer shorts, hoping for an extra inch or two. Charlotte had been more concerned about what she wouldn't be wearing than what she was. Before she could turn and bolt, the doors opened, and a finely dressed gentleman welcomed her in by name.

Charlotte crossed her arms and rubbed her hands over her exposed biceps. She very well could've been as nude as the women in the paintings that hung on the walls; the beautiful, vibrant, and very, *very* naked women. Not only had she underdressed, but she'd also underestimated Shea's talent. The man excused himself and allowed Charlotte to roam around the gallery while she waited. Each portrait was deep, intimate, and raw; full of color and movement. Shea had managed to capture much more than bare skin and delicately folded fabrics. Charlotte could feel the joy, the sadness, and the lust in each sensual image. Her ears warmed and her pulse quickened as she moved along through the collection. Would Shea portray her in the same provocative and arousing way as she had these women?

The thought that Shea would look upon her body with such reverence and sexuality sent a rush of heat through her. The light scent of licorice caught her attention, and she knew Shea was near. Charlotte's pulse quickened and her knees trembled. She closed her eyes.

She heard the slow, steady steps of Shea's heavy boots as she came up behind her. Her voice was deep and hushed as she leaned over her shoulder and whispered into her ear. "I hoped you'd come."

Shea's breath on her neck threatened to buckle Charlotte's legs. Her mind flashed back to the café and what she was packing in those tight jeans. Before she could press her ass back into Shea and find out if she was still hard and ready, Charlotte turned around. "Sorry I'm late." Her voice trembled and all other words stuck in her throat as her eyes met Shea's.

"Better late than never," she said with a wink.

The scent of licorice was heavy on her breath, and Charlotte licked her own lips trying to taste it.

"Absinthe," Shea said.

"What?"

"The green fairy, le Fee Verté." Shea turned over her wrist to show her a small, green fairy tattoo indelibly inked on her skin and identical to the one from her business card. It seemed such a delicate image for an otherwise handsome and sinewy woman.

Charlotte reached out and took her hand, running her fingers over the permanent art. Her hand was strong, rough, and stained with a rainbow remnant of hues. The steady pulse in her wrist beat against Charlotte's fingertips in a quick cadence to match Charlotte's.

Charlotte swallowed hard around the pounding knot in her throat. "What is absinthe?"

"Liquor. Come on, I'll show you," Shea said, taking her by the hand and leading her out of the gallery.

❖

Charlotte's hand was soft and supple. Shea held it as she led her from the gallery and into her studio. The space was bright yet intimate and was a stark contrast to the elegance and order of the gallery. Despite having two floors of living space upstairs, Shea spent most of her days and nights in a room as hectic and colorful as her mind.

She liked the openness of the space, with the floor to ceiling windows leading to the courtyard that flooded the room with light even on cloudy days. Stacks of paintings in various stages of completion lined the walls, and bolts of luscious fabrics in every shade leaned in each corner of the room. Shea had gathered several rolls of various greens, trying to match Charlotte's eyes, and laid them out on the platform in the center of the room.

"Is that a bed?" Charlotte asked with the slightest tremble in her voice.

It was, in fact, just a mattress, dressed in fresh white sheets and piled with pillows, but it wasn't there for sleeping. "Technically, I suppose. But I like to think of it more as a stage. It sets the scene, so to speak."

As Charlotte sauntered toward the bed, a particularly vivid scene flashed into Shea's mind of her bare and creamy flesh basking in the afterglow of climax; the light perspiration on her skin glistening in the rays of afternoon sunlight. Shea's pussy throbbed and swelled against the leather straps of her harness, and she groaned in pleasurable pain.

Charlotte ran her slender fingers along the green silks and white sheets on the bed, and Shea's skin tingled. *Fuck.* She took a few steps closer, drawn to the toned legs stretching up to a fine, full ass. Her mouth watered, and her blood quickened through her veins. Another step closer and the fresh scent of spring rain overwhelmed and intoxicated her. Shea was close enough to touch her, to reach out and take her, kiss her, fuck her. It was more than her cock that was hard and ready for Charlotte. She was wet, hot, and swollen with need.

When Charlotte turned and gazed over her shoulder at Shea, she thought she'd come right there. Her eyes were dark, and Shea's breath caught in her chest. *Fuck is right.* Charlotte turned around and stepped forward, leaving little room to breathe without their breasts brushing against each other with each breath they took. Every inch of Shea's body burned, and her clit pounded between her legs.

When Charlotte spoke, her voice was thick and smooth. "So, how about some of that absinthe?"

Shea had all but forgotten that she'd offered her a beverage. "Oh, right," she said, starting to turn away.

Before she could take a step, Charlotte grabbed her by the arm to pull her back, pressing their bodies together. "That's okay. I'll get it." That was all she said before threading her fingers through Shea's hair, pulling her head down, and claiming her mouth.

Charlotte slipped her tongue deep into Shea's mouth and she moaned. Their tongues moved together as Charlotte sucked at the sweet flavor of the liquor on her tongue. A flood of wet heat soaked through her jeans, and she pulled back from Charlotte to look down at the rosy blush of her cheeks. Shea was breathless with desire, and her heart hammered in her heaving chest.

She was struck speechless when Charlotte dropped to her knees and flicked open the button of Shea's jeans before pulling down the zipper to release her cock. Charlotte gripped the shaft and stared up into her eyes. When she licked the tip, Shea's legs quivered. Charlotte hooked her fingers into her waistband and slid her pants to her ankles.

Shea stood there exposed as Charlotte fondled her, pressing the base into her turgid erection, and she gasped. When she took the dildo into her mouth Shea's breath caught in her lungs.

The leather straps dug into the back of her thighs as Charlotte sucked and stroked her hard, coaxing her to come. When Charlotte slid her fingers between Shea's wet lips, she called out. "Fuck!"

In all the years she'd worn the strap-on beneath her clothes, never had anyone tried to please her this way. Charlotte dipped her fingers into Shea, plunging in and out of her with each mouthful of her cock. Shea's body began to tremble as she teetered on the cusp of ecstasy. She was going to come and come hard. When Charlotte dug her nails into her ass cheek and the base pressed into her clit, she tumbled over the edge. She growled and gripped Charlotte's loose hair as she came in her hand. Her pussy pulsed around Charlotte's fingers as she squeezed every last ounce of pleasure from the moment.

Shea curled her fingers beneath Charlotte's chin and gently pulled her up from the floor. She brushed her thumb across her lips, plump and red from pleasing her, and kissed them. Shea slid her hands from Charlotte's shoulders to her soft, full breasts. A few quick flicks brought her nipples to attention, and Shea's mouth watered. She hooked her fingers under the hem of Charlotte's shirt and pulled it up over her head. The delicate lace covering did little to deter Shea as she leaned down and took a tight peak into her mouth, sucking it hard through the fabric. As she kissed and licked her way over to the other nipple, her fingers worked quickly at the buttons of Charlotte's linen shorts.

She pushed them over her hips to the floor, where she removed her own boots and pants from around her ankles. Charlotte's bra dropped onto the pile of clothes they had created, and Shea smiled. Finally, she slipped off her own shirt, which left nothing at all between them except her steadfast hard-on. She walked Charlotte back toward the bed and laid her down on the soft, silken fabrics, her hair splaying out in a fiery contrast to the shimmering field of green beneath her.

She slipped her fingers through Charlotte's wet folds and coated her hand with her slick heat before sliding it up and down the length of her cock. She teased Charlotte open with the tip, and she hissed. When Shea plunged deep inside her, Charlotte cried out, her mouth and eyes wide with an unbidden yet welcome awakening. There was a carnal need in Charlotte's darkened eyes that Shea wanted to fulfill. Shea pulled out, and she whimpered.

"Roll over," Shea said, pushing herself up onto her knees, and Charlotte obeyed.

She grabbed her hips, pulled her ass back tight against her, and rammed into her. Charlotte screamed out as Shea filled every inch of her with her cock, thrusting and pulsing in and out, their skin slapping together with sharp stings of delicious desire. Charlotte's fingers gripped at the silks and sheets, her fists twisting into the fabric as she called out for more. Beads of sweat formed in the dips and curves of Charlotte's back, and Shea ran her hand over the slick surface of her skin. She could all but taste the salty bite on her tongue.

Shea reached around and slid her fingers along Charlotte's full folds, sliding her hard clit between two fingers. With each thrust of her hips, she circled the rigid peak, drawing her closer to climax with each stroke. Charlotte grew tighter around her, and she knew she was close. Her back arched and bowed as she slammed herself harder and faster against Shea's hips. When her body began to shudder, Shea held on, her breasts brushing against Charlotte's wet back. Shea stroked her up and over the edge until Charlotte's body grew rigid and she cried out as she came for her.

Sated and breathless, they collapsed onto the wrinkled and rumpled fabric on the bed. Shea ran her fingers up and down the length of her wet and slippery belly. Her tits heaved and her heart pounded in her chest as she lay there in the warm sun, content with the silence between them. Shea turned toward Charlotte and in that moment was captivated by the ethereal vision beside her. The sun, the light, and the colors combined for a phantasm she'd tried her entire life to capture. Shea slipped from the bed and took her place behind the canvas. Naked and inspired, she began to paint the absinthe nymph of her dreams.

Excitement Awaits

Amelia Thorpe

Amelia is an LGBT romance and erotica writer. She enjoys discovering new places with her characters, pushing them out of their comfort zones, and exploring how they react. She has had one novel published, one self-published, and one short story published.

Excitement awaits. Come and play.

Jenna hovered her finger over her phone screen. The caption on the Sanctuary's photo was enticing, the picture even more so.

Two women stood with their backs to the camera in heels, garter belts, and tiny black thongs. One of them held a black riding crop.

Fuck it. She was free now. She was going to do it.

❖

She didn't feel as confident as she stepped out into the dark London night in her tiny dress, leather jacket, and heels. Insecurities about her thighs aside, it was bloody cold.

She frowned as she walked up to the building, number forty-seven, that's what the website had said. Number forty-seven didn't have a queue of women outside, a bouncer, or a neon sign above the door. All it had was a small intercom. In blue ink someone had written The Sanctuary—Members Only.

She took a deep breath and put her finger over the plastic button.

She pictured her ex-girlfriend's condescending expression and pushed the button, jumping at the shrill shriek it emitted.

One stomach-churning minute later the lock clicked. Jenna fought the temptation to run for her life.

"Come in!" A middle-aged woman in a white suit ushered her through the door.

It looked more like a hotel lobby than a sex club. Jenna felt out of place in her tiny dress and fought the urge to pull it down a few more inches.

"Have you been here before?"

"No, I joined online." Jenna was pleasantly surprised to find that her voice still worked.

"I'll give one of the girls a call and she'll come and show you around." The woman picked up the phone. "Hello? Emma, I've got a newbie, could you come and give her the grand tour, please?"

Emma came through the double doors wearing nothing but black lace underwear, garter belt, and heels, and Jenna didn't feel overdressed anymore. She didn't think she'd ever seen anyone that beautiful wearing that little clothing outside of a lingerie magazine.

"Hi, I'm Emma. Do you have a phone?"

"Yeah?"

"You'll have to put it in one of our lockers, no phones are allowed in the club."

Alarm bells rang in Jenna's ears.

"It's because they've all got cameras in these days, that's all. We'll put it in a locker. You're free to come and check it whenever you like."

"Yeah, sure."

Jenna slipped the locker key in her jacket pocket, feeling far more naked without her phone than she did in her tiny dress.

"This way."

She followed Emma along a corridor and up a flight of velvet-lined stairs. The thud of bass hummed through Jenna's feet and she was reassured that she was going to a club and not some sort of chanting sex cult.

"Now." Emma stopped her before they went through the next set of double doors. "Our only rules are no means no, no drugs, and you can have sex anywhere you want in the club, apart from on the bar." She shrugged. "Health and safety don't like it."

Jenna's eyes widened, wondering what she was going to find on the other side of the door. Emma pushed it open. It wasn't nearly as dark as Jenna hoped it would be. She took a generous gulp of her champagne and looked around at the sparkling, confident women populating the dance floor. She spied the brown leather sofas in the corner as a safe place to hide. At first it looked much like any other club: the dance floor, the relaxing area with the sofas where the music was quieter, the outdoor smoking balcony.

"And then down here we have the playrooms and the dungeon area." Emma gestured to it as they walked through the area that, with all its wooden benches, leather, and metal hooks, reminded Jenna more of a workshop that anything remotely sexy.

She nodded, like she explored places like this all the time.

"Then we have our little spa area through here. There's lockers on the side."

The smell of chlorine filled Jenna's nostrils and she thought, quite inappropriately, of childhood swimming lessons. Jenna panicked that she'd forgotten her swimsuit when she realized that the current occupants of the jacuzzi were all naked. Jenna looked away and followed Emma back to the main room, embarrassed by the warmth between her legs.

"I think that's everywhere. The acts start at midnight. Have fun!"

She left Jenna stranded on the dance floor, so she went to the bar for some familiarity and glanced around as she waited to be served. She'd never imagined it was possible to feel overdressed in something that only just covered her butt. The pale redhead behind the bar turned to her with a grin. She wore a black leather dress and bright red lipstick, and made Jenna's mouth go dry.

"What can I get you?"

Jenna wished she had the courage to say something flirtatious.

"Margarita, please."

The woman nodded and whipped a bottle of tequila down from the shelf, running a line of salt round the rim of the glass.

"Nine pounds, please."

Jesus. London prices. Jenna handed the money over.

"Thank you! Have a good night." The woman winked at her and Jenna wished she had the balls to take a seat at the bar and ask the woman her name.

Instead, she fled to the sofas in the corner, nursing her drink and watching the other women dance, laugh, and exchange lavish kisses on the dance floor. The music throbbed and the blue and green lights danced over the walls and one song turned into another. Jenna was back at school, at the school disco, her back pressed hard against the wall, praying someone wanted to dance with her. She didn't even want to go back to the bar to get another drink because she knew the redhead bartender was probably thinking how socially challenged she was.

Jenna sighed. Her ex-girlfriend had been right. This had been a terrible idea. She was far too old for this. And definitely too old to be doing it alone. She was awful at starting conversations at business conferences, let alone at a sex club.

What time was it? She had no way of knowing. She'd given up her phone and there were no clocks in the place. She tipped the glass all the way up, draining the last tiny drop of liquid, flicking her tongue round the salted rim. She put her glass on the table and got up to leave.

It was then that the music dropped, the lights went out, and a voice came over the speaker.

"Ladies, please welcome our first act of the evening, our beautiful aerial artiste, Alexa Starling."

Jenna sat back down as a hoop lowered from the high ceiling. An awed hush came over the room. A woman sat inside the hoop with her legs crossed, her hands on her knees. A dark purple top hat balanced at an angle on her head, covering one eye. Black curls peeked out from under the hat and her gemmed eyelashes glinted as they caught the light. Her skin was milky white, contrasting against her dazzling blue corset, black garter belt, and heels.

She put her hands out to the sides and the room broke into cheers. The music kicked in and she dropped, hanging from the glittering hoop by her crossed ankles. She was a goddess. The woman flung herself back up onto the hoop, flipping and spinning around it with elegant grace. She balanced on top of the hoop in a handstand, her legs stretched above her, perfectly vertical.

Jenna stared.

The woman swung down and sat back in her hoop, crossed her ankles, and leaned casually to one side. She looked out across her captive audience as her hoop slowly spun. She looked straight at Jenna and Jenna had the sudden, horrifying realization that she was staring at the woman with her mouth open. The woman gave her a small smile, unpinned the hat from her head, and threw it across to her. It landed in her lap. The woman winked at her and the girls around her giggled. Jenna's stomach flipped and she looked down at the hat. She ran her fingers across the smooth velvet rim and looked back up, but the woman had looked away.

Then she began to sing. Her deep voice made the hair on the back of Jenna's neck stand up. It reverberated around the room, stunning it into silence again, before the women began to sing along. Jenna didn't know how long she sang for, but for those precious minutes, Jenna didn't care that she was too timid to talk to any of these women. It didn't matter. All her anxiety faded, and she relaxed into the sofa.

The woman finished with a flourish of spins and balances, sat back in her hoop, and was lifted back into the shadows.

The spell broke. Too many people. Too many people laughing, joking, and all far drunker than she was. A group of younger girls sat down on the sofas next to her, shrieking at something one of them had said. Jenna fled to the bar, the woman's hat still in hand. The bar was two people deep in women waiting, tapping their feet, leaning forward and scrabbling for the grip on the gold bar that meant they might be next. The redhead who had given her a smile was now far too busy for such exchanges as she poured with one hand and ran the prices up on the till with the other. Jenna turned for the door but found it blocked by a flock of girls coming in.

She decided on fresh air instead of fighting her way through the crowd and headed to the smoking area. The cold air on her face was a relief. Several dark blue velvet chaise lounges and matching armchairs were arranged along the paving, with blankets thrown over the backs. Stone ashtrays sat on glass tables, and for a moment Jenna could forget her failed outing.

She walked to the edge of the balcony and leaned on the cold metal railing. The neon London night glowed below her and she rested her chin on her hand. She looked down the three stories to the ground, wishing there was a fire escape to flee down. Her teeth chattered.

She turned the velvet hat in her hands, wondering who she was meant to give it to. She was sure the woman would want it back.

"Hey."

Jenna jumped at the voice behind her and the blanket lightly draped around her shoulders. She realized the one thing more terrifying than no one talking to you at a club was someone talking to you *and* expecting you to reply. The rush of warmth from the blanket was matched by the rush of warmth to her cheeks as she turned to see Alexa Starling standing next to her.

"Hi."

Jenna was horrified to find that the woman was even more attractive close-up, and even more glittery.

"Alexa." The woman put out her hand.

"Jenna."

Alexa's hand was small in hers. How on earth did she hold herself up on that hoop?

"You weren't planning on throwing yourself over, were you?" Alexa peered over the balcony.

"Do I look that miserable?"

"You didn't earlier."

"Your show has been the highlight of my night so far."

"Have you been here before?"

Jenna shook her head.

"Ever been like a club like this?"

"No."

"And you came on your own?"

"Yeah." Jenna cringed.

"That's brave!"

"I don't think anyone else is here on their own."

"They're obviously not as brave as you," Alexa said.

"Did you want your hat back?"

"Oh yeah, that was supposed to be my opening line." Alexa winked at her, took the hat, and put it back on her head.

Jenna's stomach flipped at the idea that this woman could be hitting on her.

"What do you do?" Alexa asked.

"Oh, it's boring, I work in an office."

"Yeah, me too."

"Isn't that your job?" Jenna said, pointing back inside.

Alexa laughed. "Oh, no. Doesn't really pay the bills, especially round here." She looked out at the London lights accusingly. "It's more of an evening and Saturday job."

"But you're so good!"

"I'm average, in the grand scheme of things. Cabaret nights are all I aspire to."

They turned at the sound of heels clicking over the balcony. The redhead from the bar walked over with a tray of three margaritas.

"Did I guess right?" Alexa asked.

The redhead rolled her eyes. "She didn't guess, I told her what you ordered before."

Alexa hit her lightly on the arm. "Spoilsport!"

"And I thought your act had finished," the redhead teased. "I'm Jax."

"Jenna."

"Can I share your blanket?" Jax asked Jenna.

Jenna held up a corner and Jax slipped under next to her, lacing her arm round Jenna's waist. Her skin was freezing. Jenna put her arm around her, wondering why on earth these two stunning women were interested in the shy little girl in the corner.

"Find your own date for the night." Alexa tutted at Jax as she put her cigarette out on the metal bar of the balcony.

"I'm just keeping yours warm."

Alexa threw her cigarette butt over the balcony and onto the street.

"Come on, let's go back inside."

The initial warm relief as Jenna walked inside fled, replaced by a tight chest at how crowded the place had become whilst they'd been outside.

"It's always like this on a Saturday night." Jax apparently sensed Jenna's unease. "Meat market."

They led her through a door Jenna hadn't noticed before that read Staff Only.

"I thought we were going to the Jacuzzi?" Jenna asked.

"Oh God, no, it'll be rammed."

They took her into a changing room and Jenna blinked as the two gorgeous women started taking off their clothes.

Alexa turned her back to Jenna.

"Could you undo me, please?"

Jenna's hands trembled as she undid the black ribbon and loosened Alexa's sparkling corset, revealing her pale skin underneath. She reminded herself that she'd had sex with women before. She didn't need to have these fumbling hands.

"Thanks, hon."

Alexa put it down with a heavy thud on the bench. "Ah fuck, that's better." She stretched her arms above her head, showing the lean muscles of her back. Her skin showed red lines from the corset.

"I don't know how you wear that fucking thing," Jax said, walking past them both to the mirror.

Jax was completely naked. She casually stood by the sinks and pinned her red hair on top of her head.

Jenna realized she was still standing there fully dressed and quickly pulled her dress over her head, trying to undress as gracefully as they had and not end up with it wrapped round her neck.

"Would you like a hand?" Alexa grabbed the dress and pulled it off.

Jenna hoped she didn't look as flushed as she felt.

Alexa reached around her and unhooked her bra, and Jenna looked down at Alexa's delicate breasts. Steel bars decorated both her nipples. Alexa dropped her bra on the bench and moved her hands to trace Jenna's breasts.

Jenna forgot how to breathe.

"You'd better not be starting without me," Jax said, her voice muffled by the pins she was holding between her lips.

"No?"

"Liar." Jax slapped Alexa on the butt as she walked past. She moved behind Jenna and ran her hand down her back.

"Let's get this hair up."

Jax ran her hands through Jenna's hair, twisting it up and pinning it on top of her head. She traced her fingers down Jenna's neck, leaving a trail of goosepimples.

"How wet are you?" Alexa whispered in Jenna's ear.

Jenna gasped as Jax slipped her hand into her panties.

"Fuck!"

Alexa laughed in her ear. "How wet is she, Jax?"

"Dripping." Jax bit down lightly on Jenna's shoulder.

"I'd hope so." She grabbed the back of Jenna's hair and kissed her hard.

Jenna gasped into Alexa's mouth as Jax moved her fingers in circles round her clit. Alexa coaxed Jenna's lips open and slid her tongue against hers. She tasted like cigarettes and tequila. Jax pulled Jenna's panties down with her spare hand and leaned in to whisper in Jenna's ear.

"Come on, let's get out there before someone nicks it." Jax took Jenna's hand, pulling her away from Alexa and out the door.

Jenna shrieked at the cold and looked around in alarm. She was standing on the rooftop, naked in the London night. Jax walked over to the hot tub and slid into the steaming water.

Alexa ran past Jenna, shrieking with laugher, and threw herself in the bubbles.

Jenna tiptoed over the freezing decking and dipped her foot in the water. She sighed at the heat and sat on the edge before lowering herself into the warmth.

"It's gorgeous out here, right?" Jax took out some beers from the little fridge on the side and handed them out.

Jenna looked up at the cloudy sky lit by the city lights.

"It's gorgeous. So, are you two…?"

"What?" Jax teased.

"Girlfriends? Partners?"

Jax looked at Alexa and burst out laughing.

"Oh thanks, bitch!" Alex splashed water at her.

"I wouldn't date her, she's crazy."

"You're so rude."

"We're open-minded friends."

"Do you have a girlfriend?" Alexa asked her.

"Just broke up."

"Thought you might say that."

"I always wanted to come somewhere like this, but she told me I was too old."

"She sounds awful. When did you break up?"

"Three months ago."

"Well, come here then, sweetie, let's break that dry spell." Alexa patted her lap.

Jenna finished her beer, plucked up her courage, and climbed onto Alexa's lap.

Alexa grinned, running her hands up the backs of Jenna's thighs, grabbing her butt hard. "Good girl."

Alexa took a handful of Jenna's hair and pulled Jenna's mouth down to her lips. The water sloshed behind her and Jax claimed her waist with her hands. She slid them between her legs and Jenna moaned. Alexa played with Jenna's breasts, rolling her nipples between her fingers.

"Let go, baby, it's good for you."

Jenna slid her fingers over Alexa's glistening skin. She tried to forget she was naked on a rooftop with two strangers. This beautiful dancer's body was hers to explore. She spun Alexa's nipple bar, and Alexa responded by jerking her hips and moaning into Jenna's mouth.

Jax giggled.

"Hey, Lexa, I think she discovered your weak spot."

Alexa laughed against Jenna's lips. Jenna moved her hands lower, and Alexa spread her legs so Jenna could feel the slightest stubble between her legs.

Jenna raised her eyebrows as she discovered another metal ball between Alexa's legs, just above her clit. She turned it experimentally and elicited a squeak.

She lost concentration as Jax moved her other hand down her back, unashamedly between her cheeks to tease her tight hole.

It was Jenna's turn to squeak. Jax pulled on her earlobe with her teeth. "You like that, dirty girl?"

Words like that would usually have made Jenna cringe, but they sounded right on Jax's lips. Jax slid her fingers over her hole and slid slowly inside her.

Jenna gasped and grabbed onto Alexa's arm. Alexa smirked at her until Jenna pushed her fingers inside Alexa and she sighed, her mouth slightly open and her head tilted back.

They moved against each other, Jenna sliding between them both. The sound of breath and moans mingled and became one dirty mumble in the London night.

Alexa grabbed Jenna's waist and spun her round in her lap, so she was facing Jax. A stray red curl had fallen across her eyes. Jenna caught it between her fingers and moved it behind her ear. Jax kissed her, softer than Alexa. Slow. It left Jenna completely unprepared as both their fingers slid inside her wetness.

"Oh, fuck!"

Alexa held her hips tight with her free hand and Jax twisted one of Jenna's nipples between her fingers.

"You a little whore for us, Jenna?" she purred in her ear.

Jenna whimpered at the onslaught of sensation.

"Don't scare the poor thing." Jax stroked Jenna's hair, her fingers slow inside her, her thumb pushing on her clit.

"I think we should take her to the playroom," Alexa said.

Jenna groaned, rocking against their fingers. "No, I'm comfy here."

Jax laughed.

"Oh, honey, we can get you much more comfortable in there." Alexa twisted her fingers inside her.

"It's only across the hall," Jax whispered in her ear.

Jenna groaned as they both pulled away. She watched them emerge from the water, their wet skin glinting in the light. She would probably follow these girls anywhere, and she climbed out of the hot tub.

She took a towel off the side and wrapped it round herself, shivering.

Jax grabbed a towel and threw another one to Alexa.

"Come on, honey, it's much warmer in the playroom."

They guided her across the corridor to an unmarked door. Jax tried the handle and found it locked.

"Ah, shit."

"You got a key?"

"No. Crap. I'll go get it."

Jax ran off down the corridor in her towel.

"We'll just have to amuse ourselves for a minute." Alexa let her towel drop to the floor. She reached for Jenna's towel.

Jenna panicked. She put her hands over Alexa's to stop her. Anyone could come past.

"Come on, I'm cold. You could at least let me share your towel."

Jenna gave another glance up and down the corridor and opened her towel.

Alexa pounced, pushing Jenna hard against the wall and kissing her, moving her hand between Jenna's legs, stroking her clit.

Jenna groaned, trying to do the sensible thing and push Alexa back before anyone showed up for a show. Then she closed her eyes and gave up. It was too good. Her hot skin against hers, the waves of pleasure her fingers sent through her, and that tongue stud catching against Jenna's skin as she licked her neck…it was all so, so good.

Footsteps. Jenna snapped her eyes back open.

Alexa chuckled in her ear.

"Hey! No fair having fun without me," Jax said.

Jax squeezed past them, turned the key in the lock, and pushed it open.

"After you," Alexa said to Jenna.

Jenna was glad to get out of the public space and stepped into the dark room. It was warmer and lit with a soft purple light. She could hear the music coming through from the club below.

The room was small, only just big enough to fit all of them in.

"Who wants to go first?" Alexa asked.

"First?" Jenna asked.

"Obviously, our guest should go first," Jax said.

They guided Jenna against the wall and pulled her arms up on either side of her head. Leather cuffs closed round her wrists.

"Oh, God."

Jax kissed her forehead. "Don't worry, honey, we take good care of our guests."

"Now spread your legs." Alexa knelt in front of her and swatted her legs apart.

Jenna's breath was coming in short bursts. She could finally feel herself letting go, and as the leather closed around her ankles, she gave herself over to them completely.

"Good girl." Alexa seemingly sensed a shift in her. Then she grabbed Jenna's ass and pushed her face between Jenna's legs. She licked her hard, and Jenna reached out in vain for something to hold on to but was held fast.

"Fuck!"

Alexa's tongue stud kept catching in all the right places.

"That's it. You get nice and loud for us." Jax kissed Jenna, her hand on her throat, holding her hard against the wall.

Jenna was so close already. They'd already played with her,

ramping up her desire. Even if they hadn't, having these two beautiful women naked on top of her would have gotten her halfway there.

"What shall we play with?" Jax took her hand off Jenna's neck and walked over to a box in the corner.

"How about a wand?" Alexa suggested.

"How about a strap-on?"

"How about both?" Alexa laughed.

Jenna squirmed. Anything. Whatever they wanted to use, if only they wouldn't stop.

"So, Jenna, you see those curtains on the opposite wall?"

Jenna heard a toy in Jax's hand start to buzz. "Yeah?"

"They give a lovely view over the dance floor."

"And everyone can see what a delicious little slut you're being for us. Would you like that?"

Jenna's breath caught in her throat and she couldn't respond.

"Really, baby, I think everyone deserves to see how good you look all tied up like this," Alexa said, "And I'm sure you'd put on a lovely little show."

"What do you think?" Jax asked.

Jenna moaned as Jax pushed the wand vibrator against her clit.

Alexa rested her head against Jenna's hip and pushed two fingers inside her. Jax kissed Jenna's neck. Alexa pulled her dripping fingers out and put them in her mouth, sucking them dry. "You're so wet, baby. Are you right on the edge?"

Jenna nodded.

"Well, we're not quite done with you yet, sweetie, and you won't come till we tell you to, will you?"

Jenna groaned.

Jax bit down on her neck. "Say yes, I promise not to come till you tell me to."

"I promise," Jenna said, breathlessly.

"Good girl. Now then, shall we open those curtains?"

Jenna stared at the curtains. What the hell.

"Yes."

Alexa whooped. "Yes, girl! Open 'em, Jax." Alexa took the wand off Jax, moving it up to Jenna's breasts as she delved her tongue between Jenna's legs again.

Jenna's head dropped back, and she forgot all about the curtains being opened. All she could do was feel.

Jax pulled on the beaded string at the side and they slowly opened. The glass-fronted booth was about a floor up from the dance floor. "There we are. Now everyone can see how lovely you look when you're getting off."

"Oh, God."

Jax took back the wand, running it over her body as Alexa continued to fuck her with her mouth and fingers.

"Oh fuck, you're getting me so close." Jenna squirmed in her cuffs.

"Not yet, sweetie," Jax said. "I wanna fuck you."

Jax came up beside her and stroked the pink silicone strap-on against her leg.

"Please," Jenna gasped.

"She's getting very obedient, Jax. You haven't even started spanking her yet."

Jax chuckled in her ear. She undid the straps on Jenna's wrists, and Jenna teetered off balance.

"Hands and knees, there's a good girl." Jax guided her to the floor. "You can go down there too, Alexa."

Alexa giggled and got on her hands and knees next to Jenna.

Jenna moaned as Jax pushed the silicone strap-on inside her, her hands on her shoulders as she began to fuck her.

She grabbed Alexa's hand.

"Fuck."

Alexa turned and kissed her, pushing the wand over her clit again.

Jenna moaned. The strap-on filled her perfectly, pushing in just the right places. Jax's fingers dug into her shoulders as she rode her hard. Jenna could see Jax's grinning reflection in the glass, her breasts bouncing, her hair falling in curls over her chest.

"Can I come?" Jenna gasped.

"Wait," Jax said as she fucked her harder.

Jenna groaned and dropped her head. Her eyes met a woman's on the dance floor. She was looking at Jenna with a half-smile and her eyes wide. Alexa put a hand on Jenna's cheek and turned her face back toward her. She kissed her softly, then whispered in her ear.

"Come for me."

Jenna's world exploded.

She cried out into Alexa's mouth as she came, her nails digging into Alexa's wrist.

"Yes, baby." Jax ran her hand through her hair, holding her with her other arm as she shook beneath her.

Jenna managed to breathe again, and the world came back to her. She dropped her face to the floor.

Alexa laughed and ruffled her hair. "You okay, sweetie?"

"Mm-hmm."

"Your turn, darling," Jax said to Alexa. "Get on your back."

Alexa turned onto her back. Jenna watched, dazed, from the floor as they moved against each other, obviously attuned to each other's bodies, knowing exactly where to touch. They were stunning together, and Jenna wondered if she'd imagined having sex with them both.

They cried out and arched against each other at nearly the same moment. Jenna looked away and blushed, despite everything.

Eventually, Jax stood up and ran her hands through her hair. She looked over the dance floor and laughed at the women looking up at her. She took a dramatic bow and received cheers from below.

Alexa laughed from where she was lying on her back, her hair splayed across the floor. She rolled toward Jenna and smiled, running her hand down her cheek.

"Have fun?"

Jenna was dazed. Speechless. She nodded.

Jax laughed. "Judging by that grin on her face, I'd say so."

Jenna hadn't even been aware she was smiling.

Jax offered her a hand to help her up and gestured to the crowd. "Congratulations, you're officially a Sanctuary performer."

THE KEY TO HAPPINESS

Jeannie Levig

Jeannie Levig is an award-winning author of lesbian fiction. She is an avid reader; loves writing, movies, time with her family and friends, and her four-legged best friend, Jackson; and lives in Central California. Visit her and say hi at her website at JeannieLevig.com.

I sit at my desk in my plush high-rise office, the helm of the corporation. I've been editor-in chief at *Global Forum Magazine* for four years, and the job is thrilling, but today…

I rifle through the pages of the annual budget and grit my teeth until my jaw aches. "*This* is all you have, Jeffery?"

The chief financial officer stares at me with rounded eyes from one of the leather and chrome chairs across from me.

"If I want to run this exclusive, I have to be able to pay for it. And I *do* want to run it. Am I clear on that?"

Jeffery shifts in his seat. "Yes, Kendall. But I might need—"

"What *I* need," I say stonily, "are *real* cuts for this month, not the elimination of donuts from the staff writers' room." Of course, that isn't what he's proposed, but in my state, his offerings seem insufficient. "I'm not asking for the moon." It isn't his fault, this mood I'm in. It isn't even the budget issues. I squirm slightly. It's this damned—

"Ms. Warren?" Amy's voice is soft from the doorway, but I hear the edge in it. "I'm leaving for lunch. Is there anything you need before I go?"

I don't dare look at her. I *shouldn't*, for my own sake. As this week has passed, being with her at work has become more torturous with each day. I know what she's wearing—a black pin-striped pencil skirt that hugs her shapely hips and ass like a lover's caress; a crisp, white silk blouse, somehow at once professional and alluring; and...my God, those shoes, with enough of a spiked heel to accentuate her toned calves and those thin, sexy little straps, crisscrossing over and around her slender feet, painted toenails, and delicate ankles. I don't have to look. I know it all from the furtive glance I stole as I passed her desk this morning. And underneath? *Christ.* Underneath, her stockings are held up by a black lace garter belt. I know from experience. The ache that's been trapped in my clit for days deepens. "No. Thank you, Amy. I'm fine."

"All right then." She turns to leave.

I keep my focus fixed on Jeffery.

He fidgets.

"Oh..." Amy pauses. "Did you see the lunch appointment I added to your schedule?"

My breath catches. This time, I can't help but look. My eyes meet hers. "I didn't."

She smiles sweetly, but something mildly wicked flashes in her vibrant green gaze. "The details are in your calendar." Then with a swish of her long, lush brown hair, she's gone.

I toss the budget toward Jeffery. "Have some more realistic suggestions by this afternoon's production meeting, or I'll be tempted to use your salary to finance my exclusive." I'm being a bitch, and I'm sure to pay, but I want Jeffery out of my office. When I'm alone, I check the information on the appointment Amy added and am out the door in seconds.

I let myself into my penthouse apartment, and I know she's already there. I don't know how I know, but I always do. And, as always, I stop just inside the foyer and undress, stripping down to nothing but the leather chastity belt that's kept me under her total control for eight long days. I fold my clothes neatly and place them on the table beside the door, my shoes in their place beneath it. My breathing is shallow, my pulse racing. The need between my legs grows more demanding with every second. I hurry into position, lest she catch me unprepared, and kneel, thighs spread, my ass resting on my heels; my hands linked behind my back; my gaze riveted to the floor directly in front of me. I wait.

I'm always embarrassed at this stage, in that shift from my outside world persona as the top executive of an international news magazine—accomplished, successful, in charge—to my intrinsic nature as a sexual submissive—waiting to serve, to be used, to be taken by my Mistress. After all this time, though, it only takes something simple, like a whispered word from her lips, her warm breath on my skin, a kiss, gentle or cruel. Or as now, the clicking of those spiked heels on the tile floor as she comes to claim me. I plunge into subspace.

She stops in front of me.

I keep my head bowed, my focus locked on those shoes, her feet, her ankles. I don't dare move or lift my eyes. I'm desperate for this punishment to end. I can't take another day.

She's silent, studying me, watching so closely for disobedience. Finally, she strokes my hair, then slides my blindfold over my head, covering my eyes. She cups my chin and lifts my face. Her lips press to mine, warm, soft, possessive. "Hello, pet," she whispers.

I moan quietly as I sink deeper into her command. "Hello, Ma'am." My voice is husky with desperation.

She slips my collar around my throat and buckles it at the back of my neck. Her fingers graze my skin, and she hooks one through the D-ring, then coaxes me to my feet.

My hands still at the small of my back, I follow her lead. I wish I could see her. Is she still fully dressed, or only in her garter belt, stockings, and bra? Are her nipples as hard as mine, her arousal as evident, even though she used my mouth for her pleasure just this morning, before my early breakfast meeting?

She stops, bringing me to a halt as well, the thickness of my bedroom carpet cushioning my bare feet.

"First things first," she says, her tone efficient. She could be sitting at her desk, going over my weekly schedule, except that her hand is at the back of my neck, and she's bending me over the foot of my bed. "You've been very cranky at work these past several days, sniping at people and being unnecessarily critical." She hooks the D-ring on my collar to the long chain always connected to the headboard, along with the restraints attached to the four bedposts, to hold me in whatever position she wants me in at any given time. "And did you think I wouldn't hear your threat to Jeffery's salary as I was leaving? Shame on you. You know he's scared of you." There's a smile underlying the threat in her voice as she runs her fingernails over my bare ass cheeks.

I clench my eyes shut beneath my blindfold. I know what's coming. More punishment. But at least it isn't another day in chastity, like last weekend when I was distracted by the throb in my clit and burned our popcorn. "I'm sorry, Ma'am."

She brings her hand down hard on my ass. "What?"

I yelp. "I'm sorry, Ma'am," I say loudly.

"Much better." She rubs my stinging flesh, then trails her finger down the strap of the chastity belt that runs between my cheeks. "Just because you're a horny little slut that's gotten herself into a predicament doesn't mean you don't still have responsibilities to fulfill. Does it?" She taps her nail firmly against the hard leather covering my clit, punctuating the last two words.

The vibration draws a low moan from me. I want to squirm, but I don't. "No, Ma'am."

"Okay. Let's get this out of the way quickly, then." She rubs the crotch of the belt hard, pushing cruelly against my trapped clit. "I have other things I want to do with our time."

I feel her move away. Then it comes, the sting of her favorite strap, a three-layered number, worn soft from use over the years. Without the blindfold, I'm sure I would've noticed it first thing, on the bed beside me. It's never far from her. I manage to keep quiet under the first stroke, but the second pulls a cry from my throat.

"Are you going to be nicer when you get back to the office?" she asks pleasantly.

Another thwack.

I suck in a breath. "Yes, Ma'am."

She spanks me again. Harder. Then harder still.

My heart pounds. I twist my hips, trying to ease the impact.

She presses her free hand to my lower back to hold me in place. Her strength has always surprised me. "Hold still and take your spanking so we can move on."

The pause allows me to catch my breath. "Yes, Ma'am."

Then she rains down ten hard, fast ones, leaving no time in between for me to recover.

When she stops, I am panting and go limp on the bed. My ass

burns, and I feel the rising welts. She's always known exactly when to stop. She's my safe place, where I can be what I am and let go.

She drags her nails over my angry flesh and moans. "So pretty," she whispers. "I'm going to fuck this reddened ass later tonight." She unhooks the chain from my collar and pulls me from the bed. "For now, though, we're going to have a different kind of fun." She turns me around and covers my mouth with hers.

Her kiss is soothing, her tongue tenderly probing. The contrast between that and the harshness of her strap scrambles my brain. I press against her and whimper at the soft caress of her silk blouse on my bare breasts and stiff nipples.

She withdraws her tongue, her kiss, her warmth and pushes me to my knees. "Show me your devotion, slut. Show me again how sorry you are for your disobedience."

I inhale her scent. In my darkness, it makes me dizzy with want. I lean forward. My nose brushes her soft thatch of curls. I reach for her with my tongue and find her clit engorged and ready.

She sighs and presses her hand to the back of my head.

I want to touch her so badly, to hold her hips, caress her ass, slip my fingers inside her, but I can't. Part of my punishment is the denial of any use of my hands. *Until I'm convinced you've learned not to touch things that don't belong to you*, she'd said. It's almost over. I have to be good. I dip my tongue into her hot, wet slit, savoring her. I lick her clit.

She makes a guttural sound deep in her throat. Her hands are in my hair, twisting and pulling my mouth hard against her. "Don't tease me, slut. Eat my pussy and make me come."

I open and suck her clit between my lips. It's so swollen. I graze my teeth over the tip.

She lets out a loud groan and tightens her grip in my hair, commanding my pace and movements. "Yes. So good," she whispers. "That's my good girl. My sweet girl." She grinds against my face.

Her tone and words of praise and affection combined with her rough handling of me remind me I'm owned, cared for, protected. I can be who I am here with her. No matter who or what I have to be in the world, I am always loved and accepted for this part of me, too.

She shifts, and I feel her lift one foot to the edge of the bed, opening herself fully to me.

I bury my face in her swollen, soaked pussy, my focus completely on her pleasure. I'm her servant, her slut, her slave.

We met when she interviewed for the position as my new admin assistant eight years ago. I immediately liked her and knew we'd work well together. I wasn't wrong.

A year later at an exclusive play party, I looked across the room, and there she was. Not in her professional attire as I was accustomed to seeing her, but in black leather pants, spiked heels, and a cream-colored satin corset. She stood behind a bound submissive, wielding a multitailed suede flogger like she was born with it in her hand. When she was finished, she returned the whip to the sub's Domme, who smiled and thanked her. She turned.

Our eyes met.

She stilled, but her dominant demeanor never wavered.

In that moment, I knew I belonged to her.

But she made me wait. She walked toward me, holding my gaze with hers until I finally lowered mine to the floor in open submission.

I held my breath when she stopped in front of me. The seconds crawled onto one another, stretched, and writhed. They served her as though she controlled time itself. I felt the intense heat of her gaze searing me everywhere it touched; my bare breasts supported by a half-cup bra that presented my nipples for teasing and torment, my leather G-string that covered little to nothing, the silver bands at my wrists and throat that indicated I was available for the use and entertainment of any of the vetted Dominants personally invited by our hostess.

My skin burned. A hot blush spread over my chest and up my neck into my face.

Then she walked away—without a word, without a second glance.

I had no idea what to expect the next morning as I stepped through the doorway of my office suite. My gait caught at the sight of her, already at her desk, dressed appropriately for her position as my assistant, handling her duties with customary efficiency.

She looked up and smiled—that sweet smile that I've learned holds so much more. "Good morning, Ms. Warren."

I remembered her with that whip in her hand, the dark red lash marks across the sub's back, and the need for her command surged through me.

Long days that flowed into weeks blurred together, though, and she never made the slightest reference to that night, never addressed me in any way other than professionally as her superior. But there was always something else. The knowledge of my true nature…and hers. It drove me mad with need.

Then one day, a new appointment appeared on my calendar, cryptic in nature. All it said was *Lunch*, along with an address familiar to me. It was the leather club.

And now, here I am years later…on my knees, serving her, my face deep in her succulent pussy, her moans of pleasure washing over me, my ass burning, my cunt—*her* cunt—locked away and at her mercy.

"Harder, slut," she says, her jaw clenched. "Give me your tongue." She's close, right on the edge.

I angle my head and push into her, slipping inside.

She cries out and fucks my face, gripping my head to keep me exactly where she wants me.

In that moment, I'm nothing but a sex toy, to be used, then put away. The demeaning thought threatens my control of my own arousal.

She pumps faster on my tongue, her clit hardening even more. She comes with a rush. Her orgasm floods my mouth.

I drink it in, savoring every drop. She crushes me against her, quivering and jerking as I bring her down. Her legs begin to shake, and she lowers herself onto my bed. She strokes my hair. "Such a good little slut," she whispers. She still holds my face to her pulsing pussy, but she loosens her grip.

I run my tongue through her still hot folds, gentle in my ministration, focused in my attention. It's an instant of pure obedience, compliance, fulfillment—a moment of sublime surrender in which everything and everyone but her has vanished. There's no career, no responsibilities, no burning desire between my legs, no ache for my own release. There's only her.

Then she pushes me away, and the spell is broken.

My rampant need rages back in like a violent storm. My body and its demands usurp the serenity of the previous instant. I fold to my knees and double over with the pounding throb in my clit.

But she's back in charge, on her feet, pulling me up. "Now that we've taken the edge off," she says, as though nothing else is happening, as though my body isn't consumed in flames, "let's see how your punishment is doing." She pushes my ass against the end of the bed and sets to work. When I'm standing, hands secured in the cuffs that dangle from the tops of the posts, ankles attached to a spreader bar and legs open wide, she steps back.

I know she's looking at me. I know *her*. I feel her gaze, simultaneously predatory and adoring, cruel and loving.

"You look so hot, all bound up like that." Her fingertips trace the sides of my breasts, her thumbs grazing my stiffened nipples. Her mouth is on mine, sucking the remnants of her climax from my lips, licking her juices from my cheeks and chin. "I like the way I taste on you. Do you like the way I taste, slut?" She trails her tongue along my jaw and down my neck. She nips at my collarbone as she squeezes and rolls my nipples. "Do you like the way I taste, when you're buried in my pussy?"

Her words, the memory, the heat of her breath, the taunt of her fingers combined to steal my ability to speak. I can only gasp, then moan.

She moves away. "Are you not going to talk to me?"

A tinkling sound, metal on metal, draws my attention, giving me a chance to recover. "Yes, Ma'am." My voice is shaky.

"Yes, Ma'am...what?" She waits.

"Yes, Ma'am, I'm going to talk to you."

"And..."

"And..." I struggle to remember what she asked me. "Yes, Ma'am, I like the way you taste." It all comes back in a rush. "I always *love* the way you taste, Ma'am."

"Better," she says, sounding smug. "I like the way you look in your chastity belt, too." She cups my cunt, pressing lightly against the thick leather covering it.

I ache to be able to feel her soft hand cradling my pussy lips, her slender fingers slipping into my folds. I crave something inside me, to be taken, to be filled. I want to thrust my hips, force more contact, but I'm afraid of the consequences. I hold still, but it takes everything in me.

She laughs sympathetically. "My poor sweet slut." She rubs the leather between my legs. "How do you like being in chastity?"

I whimper. "I hate it." I want to clench my thighs tight around her hand.

She glides her fingertips along the edges, brushing the sensitive flesh where the very tops of my inner thighs would meet my outer lips…if the horrible belt weren't in the way. "I suppose that's fair," she says, her tone thoughtful. "It *is* a punishment, after all. You aren't supposed to like it. In fact, that's exactly why I had to buy this belt for you. You've learned to like my strap a little too much for it to be a harsh discipline when you need it." She steps close and reaches around me with her other hand. She pinches one of my welts. "Isn't that right?"

I lurch forward, my breasts pressing hard into hers, my captive cunt igniting with need. "Yes, Ma'am."

"Oh, this could be fun." She tweaks another welt, making me twist and writhe against her. She lets out a wicked chuckle. "But we don't have time for it right now. Someone…" She moves away. "Has to get back to her office to run a production meeting. Maybe I should just leave you locked up."

Her words hit me like a full body slam. "No!" My objection comes out as a whine. "Please, Ma'am. You promised."

"I promised?"

In my mind, I see the indignant arch of her eyebrow. I call myself into check. "I'm sorry. I mean, you said this would be my last day of punishment."

A long pause heightens my panic.

"I did say that," she says finally. She runs her fingernails up my arm and teases the sensitive spot behind my earlobe. She knows *all* my weaknesses.

Instantly entranced, I lean into her caress.

"But there are still almost eleven hours left in this *last* day of your punishment."

I groan in disappointment and frustration. "Please?"

"Do you even remember what you're being punished for?" she whispers, her breath hot in my ear.

The throb in my clit quickens. "Yes." My answer is barely audible. "Yes, Ma'am," I say more convincingly.

"Tell me." Her hand leaves my cunt, and she begins toying with my nipple.

I arch into her touch and moan.

"Tell me," she says with more command as she tightens her grip.

"For masturbating for my own pleasure, Ma'am," I say quickly.

"You do remember." She moves away, leaving me breathless. "Which is why I had to lock that greedy little pussy away."

I sway slightly in the absence of her support.

"So why should I let it out now? It's been kind of a fun week, don't you think?"

I hear that tinkle again. A key...maybe...on a chain? My heart leaps in anticipation. "No," I answer. "Not fun."

She hesitates. "Well, maybe not for you." She's close again. "I don't suppose it was much fun for someone so important and respected to have to ask to be unlocked every time she needed to use the restroom, then be monitored by her lowly assistant because she can't be trusted to keep her fingers out of her dirty little pussy. Or have that same assistant unlock her every morning only to wash her and put her away again." Her mouth claims mine in a kiss of ownership, deep, hard, and demanding. She leaves me panting and glides her body down mine as she lowers herself in front of me. "And it probably wasn't that much fun meeting all of my needs all week, while your own went completely ignored." There's a light tug on the belt and the sound of a key slipping into a lock.

"No, Ma'am," I manage, but all I can think is, *she's letting me out.* Then, *Please! Please touch me.*

But she doesn't. Instead she's silent and motionless.

I'm drawn toward her, my back arching, my hips tilting, my need seeking her out. Her fingers, her mouth, her breath...anything at all.

Then she's opening me.

My knees weaken.

"My, my. What a mess." She dips her fingers into my folds, teasing and taunting.

I begin to tremble.

"Is my little slut that close to coming for me?"

"Yes, Ma'am." My voice breaks.

She stands and presses her coated fingers to my lips. "Suck."

I obey hungrily.

"I don't believe for a second that you deserve to come this soon," she says as she probes my mouth. "I'm not convinced you've learned your lesson."

I want to answer, to convince her she's wrong. I want her back inside me. Not in my mouth but in my cunt. I want her stroking my clit, fucking me. I want...

"But I also know for a fact that you can't run a meeting in this state. Your horny, slutty pussy has taken you over, and that's *all* you can think about, isn't it?"

I nod frantically, no longer able to speak. I suck harder.

"I thought so." She pulls her fingers from my mouth, then slips them between my cunt lips once more.

I gasp. My knees buckle.

She catches me around the waist and pulls me to her. Her other hand remains between my legs.

My breathing is rapid, my senses on overload. I clench my eyes shut against the myriad sensations assaulting my body and the warring thoughts overwhelming my brain.

"Are you listening, slut?"

I can only nod again.

"Here's what I'm going to do." She pauses, as though waiting for her words to sink in. "I'm going to take just enough of this orgasm from you—"

I release a cry of relief.

"Shh. Listen," she whispers. "Just enough so you can function, and so you can be nice to your staff. Then tonight, you'll prove to me that you've learned your lesson about whose pleasure this pussy is for, and I'll take care of my good little pet generously. How does that sound?"

I groan so deeply my whole body vibrates. "Yes, Ma'am. Please, Ma'am. Thank you, Ma'am."

She chuckles quietly. "There are rules, though." She increases the pressure on my clit.

I jerk my hips. *Fuck!* There are always rules. "Yes, Ma'am?"

"You're not allowed to move," she says, stilling her fingers. "I won't count those little jumps and jerks because I know a horny little slut like you can't help those. But if you start thrusting those hips and trying to fuck my hand, I'll stop, and we'll be done. Do you understand?"

"Yes, Ma'am." Merely talking about my long-denied orgasm threatens my control. Can I really not move once she starts?

"And you're not allowed to speak," she continues. "No asking or begging to come or to get it faster. This orgasm belongs to me, and I'll take it when *I* want it. You can make those dirty little gasps and whimpers, but no words. Am I clear?"

"Yes, Ma'am," I say, following it up with one of those whimpers.

"All right, then. Let's see if you can behave yourself long enough for a little release." She slowly slides her fingers along the full length of my soaked slit, then presses the tips into me, only enough to tease my hungry hole.

I cry out, but no words form. I ache to lurch against her and pump my hips wildly, as she knew I'd want so badly to do, but I clench the muscles in my legs and ass to hold still.

"Very good," she says in my ear. Her voice is a seductive croon. She still holds me with one arm tightly around my waist.

I lean into her as best I can in my restraints.

She kisses my forehead. Her hand is moving, stroking, caressing. She glides two fingers around the sides of my clit and squeezes.

I gasp. The orgasm straining for release charges forward.

She withdraws, then is back, then withdraws again.

I scream, *please, please, please* in my head but keep the words as trapped as my release. My Mistress doesn't make idle threats. She *will* leave me like this.

"You're being so good." Her breath fans my face. "I think it's time."

I grit my teeth, biting back anything but a loud keen.

She pushes her fingers into me, deeply but gently. The heel of her hand rubs my clit.

I start to come immediately, a cry of pleasure and relief tearing from my throat. My knees buckle.

She tightens her grip on me, holding me up. Then her hand is gone, leaving my clit throbbing against air, the orgasm receding after only a beginning rush. Tears of frustration and desperation wet my cheeks. A sob escapes my lips.

"Shh. I'll take care of my pet." She slides her fingers over my clit. Once, twice, three times.

Another wave of ecstasy crests between my legs, and I'm screaming again.

Once more, she removes her touch.

Whimpering and trembling, I try to close my thighs, give my

pulsing clit the pressure it needs to finish, but my legs are bound too securely. I'm frantic to beg, but if I can hold back, maybe she'll return.

She does…three times. With each, she takes a bit more, allowing me a small release. Little by little, the pressure in my cunt lessens, but there is no burst of pleasure, no full-on climax.

She holds me close against her. Her touch leaves my cunt.

Through shallow breaths, I clean her fingers with my tongue as she whispers in my ear what a good slut I am and how proud of me she is. Her words soothe the remaining ache still held captive between my thighs. I've pleased her. That's all that ever matters.

She runs her hand down my back, her comforting touch calming me further. Then she releases my wrists from the cuffs. When my ankles are free as well, she lowers me to the bed.

I can't even protest when she locks the belt back into place and leaves me to regain my composure.

At the front door, she pushes me to my knees once more. The fabric of her skirt brushes my face. She cups my chin and kisses me, just as she did when I arrived. "Don't be late," she murmurs against my lips. "I've cleared the rest of your afternoon, so as soon as we're finished with the meeting, I'll bring you back here, take the rest of that orgasm, and spend the remainder of the evening reminding you how much better it is to be my good little pet than a disobedient slut."

I moan and rub my cheek against her palm. "Thank you, Ma'am."

She removes my blindfold. Then she's gone.

When I enter the conference room, my production team is already assembled. With each step, my clit is caressed by my still soaked cunt lips, but the partial release she allowed me has quelled the raging need of the past week.

She sits in her spot to the right of my seat at the head of the table. She offers that sweet smile. "Good afternoon, Ms. Warren. Did you enjoy your lunch?"

"Yes, thank you, Amy. Are we ready to get started?"

"Whenever you are."

As I sit gingerly, I notice the key at the end of its chain, nestled in her cleavage. I remember her words. *I've cleared your afternoon…as soon as the meeting's over…* I smile at my staff seated around the table. "Thank you, everyone, for your hard work on this month's issue. Let's see what we have, shall we?"

NICOLETTE

C.A. Hutchinson

C. A. Hutchinson lives in the UK, writing as often as she can in her busy lifestyle. She discovered her love for writing after discovering fanfiction. She now avidly reviews books in the women-loving-women category and only aspires to be as good as those who inspire her dreams.

I wonder if she's a screamer.

"Rosie?"

The sound of my name had me crashing back to reality. When had I drifted? Swallowing hard, I straightened in my chair, looking to the front of the room and focusing on the screen.

"Sorry, could you repeat the question?"

My voice croaked awkwardly. Reaching for my glass, I took a sip of water, still looking at the information displayed. Heat crept up my neck, and I knew everyone's gaze was on me. So yeah, I'd stopped paying attention, but it was her fault.

She looked hot in her floaty cream blouse unbuttoned to the point that it showed just a hint of cleavage, tucked into a tight black pencil skirt. She was wearing tights or stockings; either way it didn't matter, but the latter was what I was imagining. The whole outfit was set off by those heels. Damn! They were easily six inches, higher than I'd seen anyone actually wear. Then there was her immaculate makeup, her long red hair, and her sultry voice. It was the accent. Russian, with broken but still fantastic English. Yep, Nicolette Black was the ultimate distraction.

"So, Rosie…your thoughts?"

She'd had to pull me back from distraction once more. The way she said my name had heat pooling between my thighs. I'd missed the question again. I stared blankly at her, cleared my throat, and sat forward a little.

"Yeah. Looks good to me."

"Lost profit looks good to you?"

Shit!

"Well, no. I meant the reasons for it. Like, why you are saying it's happening. Yeah. Sounds right."

It was a pathetic attempt to cover my ass. I finished with a smile, falling confidently back into my chair. My gaze didn't leave hers, and her expression screamed unimpressed.

The room was silent. Nicolette just stared at me, her expression unreadable. Then suddenly, as if the moment of me making a complete fool of myself hadn't happened, she carried on with her presentation. To my left, a bloke whose name escaped me made notes; to my right, Sophia scribbled notes with an unnatural amount of enthusiasm. But she adored Nicolette. You could tell from the idolized stare she always had when looking at our boss. Not like me; my staring was a little more intense and a whole lot less innocent.

I'd had a dream about her once. Then it had happened again. And again. And now it didn't just occur at night. Nicolette was on my mind every hour of every day.

I rested my elbow on the desk, my chin on my hand, listening to the sound of Nicolette's sexy voice but not comprehending a word she said. Until I heard my name again.

"Rosie? A word."

She caught me off guard. I realized my colleagues were vacating the meeting room, so somewhere along the line I'd drifted back into my fantasies and missed the end of the meeting. I stood up, acknowledging her, and wondered if my face betrayed how anxious I was feeling.

Nicolette went first, strutting from the meeting room with a confidence I could only wish to possess. Her hips swayed as she crossed through the maze of desks toward her office, with me hot on her heels just trying not to trip over my own feet.

"Sit."

God, that voice did funny things to me. Nicolette's authoritative tone had me jumping to attention. I sank into one of the large leather chairs she pointed to and focused my gaze on my feet. I'd never been pulled into her office before, but it was as I had imagined it would be. My palms were sweating and the heat I could feel in my cheeks was burning. So much for the brazen cockiness my fantasy self had when talking to her. Every time I got her alone, it abandoned me.

She crossed the room, disappearing somewhere behind me, and I heard the click of a lock. So, we weren't going to be disturbed. How much trouble was I really in? Okay, I hadn't been paying attention in the meeting, but only because I didn't understand all that corporate stuff. And did it really matter? Everyone knew why I had this job, and it wasn't because I was smart.

"Do you know why you are here, Rosie?" Nicolette asked as she returned to me and took a seat in the opposite chair.

I shrugged.

"I know what you were thinking," she continued.

Now *that* got my attention. There was no way in hell she knew what I'd been thinking during that meeting. I felt myself flush at the memory. I glanced down, catching a glimpse of the tops of her creamy breasts on show.

"Stop biting your lip."

My head snapped up, and I met her sparkling, unbelievably green eyes. But it didn't stop me biting my lip. Nicolette stood up slowly and my eyes traveled the length of her body. She perched on the arm of my chair as the side split in her skirt answered my earlier question. *Stockings.*

I felt a light tickle on my skin. My hair was gently being pushed behind my ear. A light scratch followed. Those blood red nails were trailing my jaw, resting under my chin, tilting my head up to look at her—only I didn't meet her eyes. Her blouse gaped, showing two swells of full breasts, not so safely nestled in black lace. The appreciative moan escaped my lips before I even had a chance to stop it.

"Rosie," she said softly.

I glanced up to find a smile gracing those perfect, plump lips of hers. My red face had to match their pigmented color. I wanted so badly to feel her smooth skin against mine. My heart pounded as I just stared, captivated by that dangerous twinkle in her eye. She might know what I was thinking, but I sure wished I knew what was on her mind.

My whole body tensed as her fingers fell away from under my chin, landing lightly on my shoulder, then trailing down my bare arm. An involuntary shiver ran down my spine. This woman was unbelievable. She leaned in, giving me an even better view down her blouse, and she was so close I could feel the warmth of her breath on my skin.

"I've heard things about you, Rosie."

I swallowed hard. *What things?* I wanted to ask, but my voice broke when I went to speak, and words continued to abandon me. Hopefully, she'd elaborate. Her fingers traced every inch of my arm, teasing as she stayed close. If she wasn't careful, she was about to tumble right off the arm of the chair, straight into my lap. Not that I'd complain.

"Show me," she whispered in my ear.

Somehow, she had moved even closer, and I had been oblivious. I reached out, placed my hand over hers, resting against her thigh. I hoped she wouldn't notice how hot and clammy my hand was. After all, it was her fault I was hot and bothered all over.

I shifted slightly, blatantly looking back down her blouse again, and swallowed hard. This was gonna happen. I was going to… Wait, what was I going to do with Nicolette Black? If I misread this situation, got it wrong, then that was me; I'd be unemployed. I had to try and think clearly. What was happening? Was I reading too much into this? Were we on the same page? But how could I be wrong, with Nicolette practically draping herself over me as she was?

Her fingertip brushed lightly down my neck, toward my own hint of cleavage at the top of my dress. I squeezed her hand and shifted forward. Pressing my thighs together, I tried hard to ignore the warmth spreading between my legs.

Take control, Rosie. Come on, you can do this. You want this.

I cleared my throat again.

"Sit over there." I pointed to the chair opposite.

Nicolette smiled. She inclined her head and rose. I instantly missed her touch. The slight distance was an instant relief though, giving me a chance to compose myself. She sank into the chair, adopting a confident pose as she relaxed. Her arms rested on either side of her and she crossed her legs.

I got up slowly, hesitating before stepping forward to approach her, faltering over the way she eyed me with a hunger I'd only ever seen in the movies. This still felt so surreal. It was going to take every ounce of my confidence, which, like my words, always disappeared around her. I glanced down and matched her bewitching smile with one of my own. There was no way I looked anywhere near as sexy as she did, though.

"What are you waiting for?" Nicolette challenged.

It was a good question. What was I waiting for? Any doubt about what was happening here was clearly all in my mind, right? Nicolette wanted me. She wanted me to touch her. To make her feel good. No pressure, then.

I gulped.

Nicolette's perfectly manicured hand reached toward me. She took my hand and pulled, hard, and I tumbled straight down onto her. For a moment I was frightened to move, but I couldn't stay in this awkward position, even if it was nice to feel the heat of her body against mine and her thigh brushing between my legs. She still had a tight grip on my hand. As I squirmed, I felt it tighten further.

"Where are you going?" she whispered in my ear.

I felt my insides clench. If she kept this up, I was going to explode, and given our current position, she'd feel it.

Her other hand found its way into my hair, tangling in my curls, caressing lightly as she kept me close. I adjusted my position as carefully as I could, kneeling awkwardly upon the chair where my knees sank into the soft padding, and my dress rose dangerously high as I straddled her lap. If this wasn't a compromising position to be in with the boss, I didn't know what was. I looked down at her now, getting a better view of her exquisite body every time she moved. Nicolette released my hand and began unbuttoning her blouse. Slowly. I was going to die. I'd only had a glimpse, but I bit my lip so hard to stop myself grinning, I thought I'd draw blood.

"Damn," I whispered.

"Damn, indeed," she murmured back as she grabbed my wrists and placed my hands on her breasts.

I squeezed, gently of course, which elicited the most amazing moan from her lips. She drew me in closer, our lips brushing. Then we kissed. And Nicolette kissed amazingly. She had so much passion as she pushed her lips lightly against mine at first, then gradually increased the pressure, giving me just a taste. She had taken my breath away, and when we finally broke apart, she lightly bit my bottom lip. I just couldn't bring myself to look away, and as I leaned in to kiss her again, I felt her hand gliding over my hip, then against the warmth between my legs.

"You are very wet."

I swear she spoke slowly on purpose. She knew what it did to me. Usually, I'd thank someone for stating the obvious, but I was still unable to form more than a single verb.

She took my hand from her breast, trailing it over her blouse. I gripped hard, pulling it from the waistband of her skirt, exposing her toned form. I couldn't see her face, but I bet she was smiling. The skirt wasn't going to be as easy, but I sank my fingers below the waistband and was rewarded with the feel of more lace. I stroked over it, pressing firmly against her as my hand cupped against her sex. I wasn't the only one showing signs of desire.

The mix of floral and wood that made up the scent of her perfume invaded my senses, overwhelming me as the heat of our bodies mingled. God, Nicolette Black really was something else, and I was the one lucky enough to be having this moment with her. She moaned deeply as my fingers worked gently against her, teasing as I tried desperately to compose myself and focus on the task she'd set for me. I needed to satisfy us both somehow so that I'd survive the rest of the day, although I wasn't sure I would after this high.

Trailing my fingers over the lace of her underwear, I slipped them under and against her bare, silky skin. Not what I'd expected to find, and I continued slipping my fingers lower, where I kept up my teasing. Nicolette tightened her grip on my hair. Pulling my head back, she threw her own back against the chair, then pushed my face against her chest, hard, almost suffocating me in her cushiony bosom. Not that I cared. Peppering light kisses against her breasts, I moved toward a lace-clad nipple, taking it in my mouth and sucking hard.

It felt so good to feel her push back against my light touch, trying to get more from me than I was willing to give yet. I had dreamed about this long enough; what was her rush? Savoring every second was my intention, and nothing would make me give that up.

"Rosie!" she groaned through gritted teeth.

Frustrated, Nicolette?

I smirked, grazing my teeth over her nipple, and was rewarded with a guttural moan. Okay, so I sucked at my job and paying attention, but this I could do. My fingers slipped into her wetness, curling against her as I worked them in slow, small strokes. Navigating from this angle wasn't something I'd attempted before, but given the delicious sounds Nicolette was making, I'd say I had it mastered. She tugged on my hair, but I wasn't giving up that nipple for anything.

A knock at the door startled us both. I kept my hand in place but stilled and pulled back from her nipple to glance at the door.

"Not now!" she called out. "Don't stop." The command was softer but no less demanding.

My fingers twitched but I ignored her instruction. Whoever was outside tried the handle, noisily rattling it, but of course the locked door wasn't going to budge. We waited a moment, just the sound of our erratic breathing out of sync filling the space between us. Looking up, I was just in time to see Nicolette's eyes fly open and her head raise, twisting to glare at the door as if it had just insulted her. A look of murderous rage crossed her face.

"Nicolette?" the male voice called.

"Damn it! I said *not now*!"

I'd never heard her shouting so up close and personal before. I mean, we'd all heard her temper from a distance, but this was something else. We waited a heartbeat, just to make sure Dave from Accounts had buggered off, and then we returned to our activities.

Taking her nipple back into my mouth, I sucked gently, slowly moving my fingers again. Nicolette's head fell back again, and she moaned, as if on cue, but it was muffled. Her other hand gripped hard at my backside, her nails digging in painfully despite the protective layers of my dress and underwear. Those talons were practically lethal. Still, I wasn't complaining. If I had to live with a ripped dress and raised red welts on my backside to get this moment, it was worth it. Her hand trailed lower, and her thigh rose, pressing hard against my heated, wet core. I gasped, releasing her nipple, and she took advantage of my distraction to pull me up so our lips met. She kissed me furiously, pushing her tongue against mine as she began working her thigh against me.

Her hands moved across my hips as I felt her moving beneath me, more than the writhing of my actions should allow for. She gripped me tightly, pressing her thigh harder against my burning apex, and shifted position, biting my lip as she broke our kiss. Catching me completely off guard, she pushed me back. I stumbled out of the chair, pulling her up with me, and almost tumbled over. We would have landed in a heap on the floor, but by way of a miracle I managed to keep my balance and kept my hand planted firmly against her sex.

My back slammed against a wall. She moved so fast it was almost inhuman. I hissed with the pain reverberating through my body, but it was soon forgotten when I felt her kissing my neck, working the same spot, before grazing her teeth against my delicate skin.

"Rosie…"

It came out desperate sounding; not begging, necessarily, but authoritative.

She pressed her body against mine. Her fingers scrabbled at the front of my dress, grabbing and squeezing my breasts hard, before I heard a rip. My eyes opened and I glanced down to see the front of my dress torn, my chest fully on display, and I was quite proud of the fact I'd deliberately chosen to go without a bra. Not that Nicolette noticed.

"Fuck. Me." She wasn't vague about what she wanted.

My breathing turned ragged as my heart beat erratically. My fingers pumped hard against her, adding pressure against a spot I knew would undo her frustration. She pinned her thigh again between my legs, deliberately pressing it against my wetness. Grinding against her thigh, I felt myself building up to my own rewarding release, and if I timed it just right, we'd…

A strangled scream escaped Nicolette as she stopped breathing for just a second upon finding sweet release. I was more the silent type, but I felt it too. So, in sync, I fell forward against her, gasping for breath as my lips searched for hers again.

Nicolette's grip on my hair loosened as she held me, keeping me as close to her as possible as we calmed. We'd just fucked and somehow, she still looked perfectly put together. I probably looked like I had been dragged through a hedge backward before going ten rounds with a punching bag that had kicked my ass. I was exhausted. Resting against Nicolette was a dream. Her smooth skin felt warm against mine, which was all clammy and sweat-drenched. Her fingers trailed gently down my neck, to my shoulders, as she continued to hold me.

"Rosie?"

Why did her voice suddenly seem so distant? I heard my name again, a little clearer now, sharper. A sharp whacking sound caught my attention, as my eyes fluttered opened to see Nicolette. She was fully dressed, just as she had been before our little escapade, makeup and hair perfectly in place, and she wasn't smiling.

"Yes?" I croaked.

"Care to enlighten us?"

Nicolette quirked a perfectly shaped eyebrow, gesturing to our surroundings. I looked around to see our colleagues staring at me.

Seriously?

I groaned and dropped my head onto the meeting table as Nicolette called the meeting to a close. All I could hope was that none of them had been aware of the intimate scene that had played out so perfectly in my head. There was a loud dragging of chairs collectively over carpet as my colleagues vacated the meeting room. I lifted my head slowly, intending to do the same. The afternoon would go quickly if I just hid in my cubicle.

Nicolette had returned to the front of the room, closing down her laptop and disconnecting it from the presentation screen. Risking a glance at her, I gathered my notepad, the page still blank where I'd failed to make notes, and hastily made my way toward the door. She didn't look up.

"Not you, Miss Edwards."

I stopped, not even making it out of the room before she called after me. Turning around, I watched as she packed her laptop into its case, gathering it with a multitude of reports and papers in her arms. She sauntered across the room toward me. For a moment I thought she wasn't going to stop, but she did, right in front of me, as close as we'd been when… I couldn't breathe. She was so close.

"My office," she whispered, stepping right up against me.

I didn't even see her hand move, let alone feel it land on my bottom until she squeezed it, hard. Transfixed, I couldn't look away from those dangerously twinkling eyes. She stepped back, breaking all contact, and stepped up to the door. She stilled, looking back over her shoulder at me.

"Now."

STRIPPED BARE

Robyn Nyx

Robyn Nyx is an avid shutterbug and lover of all things fast and physical. She writes lesbian fiction when she isn't busy being the chief executive of a UK charity and lives with her soul mate and fellow scribe, Brey Willows. They have no kids or kittens, which allows them to travel to exotic places at the drop of a hat for research.

"Jesus, Cree. You broke your belt across her back?"

I shake my head. "No, buddy. I broke *her* belt." When she raises her eyebrow as if my explanation doesn't change her reaction, I shrug. "Cheap leather."

Grant laughs. "That makes all the difference."

"Actually, it does." I tug at my own belt. "This is premium-grade cow. I couldn't break this across a tree, let alone someone's back."

"Still, that's pretty hardcore."

"She was a black handkerchief sub, she demanded it that hard. And anyway, I'd never give anything I couldn't take myself."

Grant leans forward on the couch. "Oh yeah? Prove it."

"What?"

"Go to Bedeviled, pick the biggest, baddest butch, and bottom for her. Let *her* go hardcore on *you.*"

"*I'm* the biggest, baddest butch in Bedeviled. And there's no way I'd go butch for that."

"But you would for a beautiful, long haired mistress?"

"I didn't say that. And who am I proving anything to, anyway?"

Grant grins and takes a swig of her beer. "Yourself…if you really believe you don't give out what you can't take. What about Valentina? There's always been something between you two."

I can't stop the low sigh that the mere mention of her name always evokes. "The Mistress of the House? I don't think so." It's my turn to take a swig from the beer I'd been warming in my increasingly heated grip. Valentina. The archetypal femme fatale. It's easy to believe that title was invented just for her.

"Ha, I knew it. I think she'd be exactly your type."

"My type? I don't have a type." And I really don't. I like all women, as long as they're warm and willing. There has to be a spark: It could be her eyes that promise something special, the way her mouth moves, a certainty in her smile. It can be in the hands or the way she walks. It's almost always to do with what's upstairs. She doesn't have to be physically perfect—whatever that's supposed to be—and she can be practically any shape, size, or color. But she has to have something that grabs me by the throat and demands attention. That said, I *am* a sucker for a femme fatale. Invariably and predictably, I'll do absolutely anything they want me to…*outside* of the bedroom.

"I haven't switched for two decades, Grant." Jesus, that hadn't been a successful first foray into S&M. The woman in question was winging it big-time. She had no pacing and wrenched the safe word out of my mouth barely ten minutes into the scene. After that, I got a taste for being a master. I never really looked back…unless you're counting fantasies in my head. I'll admit to hundreds of those taking me over the edge on nights alone with my trusty silver bullet vibrator for company. But that's all they are, right? Fantasies don't mean I actually *want* to bottom for some sexy femme fatale beauty with a bullwhip. Do they?

"So, you're chicken?"

I shake my head. "I won't be goaded into being a tickle toy for anyone…even a phenomenal femme like Valentina." I down the last of my beer, and Grant sensibly stays silent, but I'm still irritated. "You don't understand what I do. You're a tourist, and it intrigues you. That's why you come here and ask me to regale you with tales of my evenings but never actually do anything yourself."

Grant looks suitably chastised before she gets up from the couch.

"You're right, Cree. I shouldn't have pushed. I'll go."

I grab her wrist and pull her back onto the sofa. "Don't be an ass. Just understand that what I do is real. We call it play, but it's far from it. It's serious, and it's my life. I won't make light of it by bottoming for a bet."

Grant nods, picks up her beer, and clinks it to my empty bottle. Time for a change of subject. Grant's sex life was often just as interesting as mine in a completely different way. She liked to bed down with anyone and everyone. "Let's talk about your sex life instead. Who have you been fucking lately?"

❖

Grant has been gone for hours, but her challenge taunts me. She's right about the connection between Valentina and me, of course, which was why I'd snapped and given her hell. The moment she'd mentioned Valentina, flashes of her leather-clad flesh assailed my mind. I imagined looking up at her from the floor, her high-heeled boot pressed against my chest. I could practically feel my muscles stretching against leather restraints pulling my arms up and high, allowing her complete access to my naked back. What might it be like to hear her Californian lilt whisper, "Take it for me, boi."

I'd spent my adult life fulfilling fantasies, why would I deny the darkest of my own desires? Valentina's reputation as a Mistress was second to none. Was it time to revisit the persona that had first led me to this world? My first and only top wasn't worthy of the title and had set me firmly on the dominant path. Was I ready to stop hiding my boi under a bushel?

I side glance at my phone sitting on the oak table beside me. It won't take any effort to call. I have Valentina's number, and it's even in my VIP contacts. She's made it clear on more than a few occasions that she'd like to have me under her hand. I've always wanted her under mine, and she knows it. Up to now, it's been a stalemate. Maybe it's time to explore. But can I truly give up control after so many years as a Master…even if the boi in me is desperate to?

I pick up my phone and open the contacts. Valentina looks up at me, her eyes seducing me from the two-dimensional screen, challenging my ability to relinquish control, daring me to indulge my desires. I nibble on my lower lip and contemplate the best-and worst-case scenarios. Valentina is a pro, the best in her field, really. There *is* no worst-case scenario. Even if I can't handle what she has to give me, she is too much of a lady to reveal my sad failure. Mind made up, I press the call button and wait for the velvet tones of her smooth voice to caress my ears.

❖

The two bodyguards at the door look at the floor as I pass. I recognize them from a play party the previous month. I'd strung them up side by side and had a lot of fun practicing my coordination with dual whips. The fair-haired one bruised like a proverbial peach, but the darker, more muscular one begged for a far firmer hand. A sweet, sweet memory, to be sure.

"Sir," the darker one whispers as she opens the door.

I don't respond and step inside. If I acknowledge them as the bois they'd been for me, how could I hold on to the slight shard of submissiveness I'd cultivated since last night's conversation with Valentina? It had to be tonight. I didn't want to lose my nerve, and Valentina had cleared her schedule, such was her eagerness to finally claim my pain. The door closes behind me, immediately taking away any opportunity for a last-minute change of heart.

"You're precisely on time."

Ah, her voice. Smooth and even, but violent undertones beat beneath it, promising hell if I disappoint her. I take a deep breath through my nose. All I can smell is leather. All I feel is wet and swollen. Barely inside her honey trap, and my resolve to please her already reverberates through my core, surprising me with its instant intensity. Any thoughts that this might not be a good idea begin to fade.

"Why wouldn't I be?" I ask, taking the moment of pre-play to focus on her feminine flawlessness. Calf-high, lace-up, heeled boots hug sprayed-on leather pants. A matching black leather corset pushes up her breasts, rising and falling just a little faster than her usual controlled breathing. I've watched her in action enough times that I could identify her exact rhythm from a line-up, blindfolded, and the excitement throbs in my jeans.

"Indeed," she says. "You wouldn't want to start this by disappointing me."

I swallow hard at the threat as she devours the ground between us elegantly, her heels click-clicking on the shellacked stone floor in consummate cadence with my pulsating pussy. Her thick leather signature cat swings at her hip.

"Would you?" she asks.

Her mouth is at my throat, and her breath feels like it could burn the skin straight off me. "Of course not." My answer is slightly flippant, the delivery too forceful, but it's too late to rein it in. She wraps her hand around my throat, and her nails dig in before she drags them down over my collarbone and into the deep V of my chest.

"Take off your jacket."

She takes away her hand and waits as I follow her instruction.

"And if you give me attitude again, you'll be putting it back on and leaving. Do you understand?"

I nod and look down, cursing myself for testing her so soon. She told me last night that I was to come here willing to give her my everything, without reserve. I clamp my jaw tight, suppressing years of being the dominant master. I'm here because I want to be. Not because of a bet with Grant but because Grant's challenge made me realize how much I want to be under Valentina's hand. "I apologize. It won't happen again."

I look up, and she arches her eyebrow before she turns and beckons me to follow. I've only taken two steps when she spins around and places her hand on my chest.

"Crawl."

My eyes partly close and my breath leaves my body in a horny hush. Her clipped instructions destroy me. I take the appropriate amount of time to sink to my knees. Too fast and she can't fully appreciate the gesture. Too slow and I'm milking it. I press my palms to the floor, and it's unexpectedly warm. Under-floor heating in a dungeon is a thoughtful addition.

"Wait."

She walks away from me, and the distance is unbearable. How have I denied this for so long? How can this already feel so natural?

From my position, I see her turn in front of a huge leather armchair.

"Come to me, Cree."

I bow my head and begin to crawl to her. I'm desperate to be at her feet, but this approach is for her pleasure and can't be rushed. I've taught so many slaves the importance of this act and what it truly means to both players: its sweet submission. I hear her murmured approval and allow myself an internal smile, knowing that showing it on my face would most likely result in punishment.

She reaches down and pushes me back on my ass. I begin to place my hands behind my back, offering her complete and unfettered access.

"No." She shakes her head. "Hold out your arms."

I do so, and she fastens my wrists into thick leather restraints attached to chains hanging from the ceiling. She flicks a switch and the chains slowly retract upward, pulling me to my feet. She doesn't stop until my arms are stretched, my chest pulled taut from the tension. My feet are still flat on the ground. Small mercies.

She unclips the whip from her waist and steps behind me. Her hand is in my hair, yanking my head back, and her mouth is at my throat again. If it turned out there really was such a thing as vampires and Valentina was one of them, I'd beg to have the humanity sucked from me to join her in immortality. Every synapse in my body is jumping. Every muscle fiber is straining for her touch. She's barely spoken to me, but she already has me exactly where she's wanted me for years.

"I can give you what you need, Cree, what you hunger for. I can break you down and build you back up, stronger, harder. But for that, you will be mine forever."

The slow way she enunciates her words weakens me. She moves in front of me, and I can smell the almonds from her trademark drink of Disaronno. Her lips brush mine and I lean into her, but she pulls away. Her nails drag sharply across my forearm and bicep. She reaches my shoulder and bunches my tank top in her hand. Her other hand grips my throat. It's vulnerable, raw, but feels reassuring, restorative.

"How much do you need me, boi?"

I exhale, swallow. That word. Three letters with so much potential. A word I hear in my fantasies over and over. A word that brings me to my knees. It's not about gender. I don't want to be a boy, a guy. This is about power. Submission. Release. "More than you could ever know."

"I know a lot, sweet boi," she says and caresses my cheek. "Use your words. How much do you need me?"

I lick my lips and look into her darkened eyes, her desire reflected in mine. "I need you more than the earth needs gravity. More than my lungs need air."

She smiles and traces her tongue over my lips, the combination of almonds and cherries tempting me to strain toward her, but I remain steady. She never kisses anyone. I know that. She's told me it's the most intimate thing about sex. Then she's behind me again and cracks her cat in the air.

The first strike is an immediate release. We've been building this up so long, I could explode. All the spoken and unspoken taunts that have passed between us; all the times we've watched each other from the sidelines, silently wishing we were part of the play. Here, now, the self-imposed repression of our attraction releases itself in irrepressible rhapsody. I'm strung up so tight that there's little give and nowhere to hide. Not that I want to. The second lash I can fully appreciate. I can feel exactly where the tips hit, and though I can't see her, I know she's directly in line with my body. The third is different. She moves to my left and the cat feels more like a strap across the whole of my upper back. She's directly behind me for the fourth, and I can't help but let out a deep, guttural growl. Her rhythm is perfect. Her pacing, precise. I stop counting and simply enjoy her excellence, finally allowing myself to connect with the primal part of my being that has craved this for as long as I've been sexually aware.

"Boi," she says.

She pauses the thrilling tempo that has me breathless for her hunger, desperate to feed her my pain. "Mistress." I whisper the word she's effortlessly engineered me to say. I can almost hear her smile despite not being able to see her. Under her hand I feel uninhibited in a way that differs vastly from topping. In her chains, I've never been so free.

"Don't go off in your head." She accompanies her admonition with an elegant strike of her whip. "I want all of you present. Right here, in this moment. Your body...and especially your mind."

"I'm sorry. It's a habit."

Another lash dances across my shoulders.

"You're sorry, who?"

The next blow forces me forward. Her power belies her visually diminutive frame. "I'm sorry...Mistress." She comes around to face me, and I briefly maintain eye contact to reinforce my veracity before casting my gaze to her feet, just as I'd trained countless slaves to do for me and their future Masters. Those boots, though.

She grabs a handful of my hair and jerks my head back.

"Where are you now?"

Frustration echoes in her voice, and I'm struck again by my deepening determination not to disappoint her. "I was admiring your boots, Mistress."

She bites down on my shoulder.

"Are you thinking about how it might feel to put your mouth on them, pretty boi?"

I shake my head. That wasn't my first thought, but now that she mentions it... "No, Mistress. I was wondering how they'd feel on my chest. I was thinking about what you might look like from that angle."

Her hands encircle my body, and she pulls the front of my tank top over my head, leaving it bunched behind my neck. She's in front of me again, and I'm already in love with my mistress. She has me, and she knows it. Stripped bare, the illusion of control no longer in my grasp, she has the version of me she wants, the me no one before her has had.

She nudges my legs apart and my shoulders jar. I grimace just a little, but my desire for that feeling is a welcome friend, long denied but never truly absent. She's watching her hand on my body as she finger-traces an uninterrupted line from my neck, over my chest and stomach, to the top of my jeans. She slips her hand inside my shorts and locks her eyes on mine. She can't be seeking proof of her power. There's no ambiguity. It must be entirely visible on my face. A wicked smile plays across her full lips when she pushes my cock aside and reaches my swollen, sodden pussy. She explores for a while, never taking her eyes from me. I think I stop breathing. I know my mouth has dropped open a little, and I struggle not to close my eyes, not wanting to lose this connection.

She's inside me now, and I'm thankful for the straps keeping me secure. I catch my breath, but it's shallow and quick, unlike the slow and deep way she's fucking me, impressive given the confines of my jeans. My gaze slips from her eyes to her arm. It's been a while since I've seen one from this angle—that's the purview of long-term lovers—but I love to watch a woman's arm work this way. It's artistry in motion. And her arm is glorious. Her left hand grabs me by the throat and brings me back to face her. She withdraws her hand from my pussy and wipes my liquid arousal all over my abs before bending to trace her tongue over them. Then her mouth is on mine, and I can taste myself. This is always the most honest thing about sex. You can't fake it. And for her, I was hemorrhaging honesty.

Her hand slides around my back, and she pulls her nails from my shoulder to the small of my back. She breaks my skin, and it burns beautifully. She kisses me, soft at first, then harder before she breaks away and I'm left desperate, needing yet fulfilled. Her lips on mine mean so much more than the average kiss. She's giving me the piece of her she never gives anyone. Every moment since we met has been leading inexorably to this meeting of our minds and bodies, of our souls and desires, of our authentic selves. My knees buckle beneath me, weakened from the force of the revelation.

She takes the buck knife from a small holster on her waist, pulls my tank away from my neck, and slices through it. It falls to the floor, joining my long-ago relinquished control. Her hand rests on my naked hip while the other gently caresses my throat. I raise my head to meet her eyes.

"See how much better you can feel when you truly give yourself to someone…to me?"

I nod. "Thank you, Mistress…for showing me." My words aren't adequate. They might never be enough. But she knows. My body is answering every question she asks.

"How would you like to thank me, boi?"

Fuck. Her slow and deliberate delivery. Her husky tone is driving me wild. "With my mouth, Mistress, if you'll allow it?" Because, dear God, I want to taste her so bad. She smiles. She knows what that means. Just as she's never kissed anyone in play, I've never put my mouth between anyone's legs.

She backs away and flicks the switch to release my chains. She nods toward the floor to indicate that I should sink to my knees when my restraints allow. Finally, I'm positioned before her. She runs her hands over my shoulders and back.

"So powerful and yet so delightfully weak."

She extends her right leg so her boot pushes against my bare chest. "Remove my boot."

I begin to raise my hands, but she shakes her head.

"No, boi. Use your oh-so-clever mouth."

I move my face and her boot slides up to my shoulder, her heel grazing my skin. I get to work on the knot with my teeth, thankful it's not too tight. I twist my tongue around the loop and pull it from the eyelet. My nose is pressed up against the soft leather and the smell is intoxicating. Slow work, but I'm down to the ankle. I pause and pull back a little. How am I supposed to get it loose?

She cuffs me around the head gently, obviously irked by the momentary arrest in my progress.

"Stop thinking and just do it."

She digs her heel into the center of my chest for emphasis. I take the boot tongue between my teeth and draw it backward. I slip down so I'm practically doing a press-up to reach the heel of her boot. I manage to clamp my mouth around her heel and slowly pull backward. It's finally off and I rock back on my ass. Knowing that dropping her boot to the floor would be disrespectful, I await instruction. She takes it from me before I oblige with a repeat performance on her left boot.

She stands and works open her leather trousers. As she's pushing them down, along with her white panties, she reveals strong and finely shaped alabaster legs. She folds her clothes and places them on the table beside her chair. The pleasant leather I could smell earlier is replaced with the even more delicious aroma of pure silken sexuality. She's nose height and I'm eager. Restraint isn't a strong enough word to describe how I'm currently stopping myself from descending on her with ravenous hunger. But I remind myself I'm not in control here.

She sits down, leans back, and pushes her ass forward in the chair, opening her legs. I clench my jaw but that doesn't stop a husky breath rasping from my throat.

"Let's see if your mouth is bestowed with the same talent as the rest of you. Show me your gratitude, boi."

I don't need to be told twice. The beauty of her pussy matches the rest of her. She's smooth and slick and tastes like nothing that's passed my lips before. Her fist tugs at the short hair on the back of my head, and I evoke a distracted sigh into her pussy. She's found another one of those things that just melts me, and reality kicks the fantasy version of this situation out of the park.

"Focus."

She's a little breathless, and I'm with her immediately. My lips close around her clit, simultaneously sucking and licking. She grips harder, communicating that I'm on the right track. My hands, respectfully placed together at the small of my back, disengage, and with trepidation, I slowly rest them on her thighs. Her resultant sigh excites me more. I look up and can just see her face, her eyes closed. My left hand grips her strong upper leg, and I chance my luck, moving my right hand to her pussy. I slip one finger inside her and she elicits a primitive, throaty moan that courses through me. She's got me so fucking horny, so in touch with both our bodies, that I can't tell where I end and she begins. What I'm doing with my mouth and finger, though, is exactly what she wants. I risk slipping in a second.

"It's your mouth that's thanking me, boi." Her voice is all-commanding. "Take out your fingers and astonish me with your genius tongue."

I withdraw my fingers without taking my mouth away from the sweet paradise that is my prize. I carry on with what's so delighting her, and I'm enveloped in her powerful sex, reveling in my service to her. She wraps her legs around my head and rests her feet on my contentedly abused back. I can feel the intensity building in her swollen clit, hard and pulsating in my mouth. The force she's gyrating her hips against my face is escalating. She's so close.

So I ease off my rhythm until she too slows her body. I check her reaction. Her lip curls and she's snarling at me.

"You'll suffer for that."

It's hard to smile with my mouth so full, but I manage. I slow right down until her hips are barely moving. She's slick with her juices. I slip from her clit to tongue their origin and get a solid hit of her. She writhes beneath me, swears, and bucks her hips before I return to her clit to rebuild her ascent. A riot squad couldn't break my concentration and drag me away from her now. It doesn't take long before the winning combo has her twisting beneath my mouth again. She's so wet it's hard to keep the connection.

Her movements are getting faster and harder.

She's right there, about to fall.

And I slide off the gas again, pull her back from the brink. Her hands tighten in my hair and her feet press on my back. I chance a quick look and she's snarling viciously again, baring her teeth. She's even sexier when she's pseudo-mad.

"Three strikes and you're out, boi. Don't forget who's in control tonight."

God, the way she wraps her lips around that word. I've heard it in my head a hundred times, but out loud, in her voice, it has me maddeningly aroused.

I sigh deeply into her glorious pussy. *Damn, Valentina.* She's so fucking hot, I want to pleasure her forever. I squeeze my eyes and my thighs shut. I take a long, slow taste from the base of her pussy, over the hole where her juices are seeping out, and drag my tongue back to her clit. Her reaction is precious, and she tastes too good, so I repeat it. And then again.

"Boi. If you stop…again…I swear, I'll flog you to death."

I've never come before without some physical stimulation of my own body, but things are about to change. I suck and lick at her clit in the way she's immediately taken to, and her rise to the verge of her orgasm is quicker than last time. Her hands keep me firmly in place lest I forget myself, lest I forget who's in control again. I can feel her whole body shaking around and over me. The rhythmic rearing of her hips against my face quickens.

And she falls. Everything tightens. She pulls my head deeper between her thighs like she wants me to become part of her. *Happily so, Mistress.* Her orgasm shudders through her very core, starting at her pussy and erupting in her mouth. Mine joins hers, unassisted yet powerful. My mouth remains clamped to her clit as its beat steadily slows, pulsing out a Morse code thank-you. She pulls me up and kisses me as hard as her orgasm was. She shoves me back down to a kneeling position and gently runs her fingers through my hair.

"Next time, you can be in control," she whispers.

Next time. Thank God. I curl up closer to her and rest my head on her thigh.

I briefly think about how to thank Grant. Her challenge has led me home.

BOSSY

Raven Sky

Raven Sky is a polyamorous queer femme who hails from Canada and who is fueled by wanderlust, tea, books, and insatiable curiosity. She's published erotica in the following anthologies: *Best Lesbian Erotica Vol. 3*, *Escape to Pleasure: Lesbian Travel Erotica*, and *Lust in the Dust: Post-Apocalyptic Erotica*.

I am a smart, capable, accomplished woman. I tend to get what I want. At least nowadays. But getting here wasn't easy. Because I used to be a smart, capable little girl, and like most little girls, I had to learn how to get shit done without earning the dreaded label of being *too bossy*. "Bossy" confused the younger me, until I figured out, on some subconscious level, that it was something girls got called when they were too strong, too clever, too skillful. So I learned to hide those things about myself. To be just the right non-threatening amount of talented, and to direct attention for any of my success to other people's influence. For the longest time, I didn't even realize I was doing this.

A turning point came in my late thirties, though. Hanging out with friends of ours, another couple, drinking and ostensibly playing euchre, I stumbled into a rediscovery of the heady justness of being a woman who speaks her mind with zero fucks. Which is ironic, because it was an abundant literal giving of passionate fucks that led to this revival.

As I recall, I had been complaining about my latest haircut, explaining to my friends why I didn't tell my hairdresser that I was unhappy with it. That's when Kendra exploded.

"You're paying a *professional*; don't leave until you get what you want!"

Kendra is the femme half of our best friend couple. She's loud, larger than life, and unapologetic about being a big woman with strong opinions about, well…everything. Her boldness both scares me and draws me to her. Ash, her partner, is more even-keeled. Patient. The stereotypical strong but silent butch type. They fit well together. A study in contrasts.

"She even tipped her," Jade chimed in, mischievously, which earned her an irritated glare from me.

"Jen, seriously." Kendra gestured wildly with her empty wine glass. "You've got to learn to speak up. You can't go your whole life being afraid to express an opinion or ask for what you want. Like right now, I want a refill. You don't see me hesitating to say, 'Babe, top me up.'"

"I'm not afraid," I protested as Ash promptly rose to fill her glass with a good-natured grin. She grabbed mine on the way to the kitchen, too.

"Oh, please, Jennifer. I've been your friend for like what, eight years now? I've heard you tell the same story a million times. You just need to practice… Wait! Actually, that's it."

She was tipsy and her eyes had lit up, so I knew that whatever idea had just popped into her head, it was going to direct our evening, as her whims usually did, often with amusing results.

Ash returned from the kitchen, handed the glasses over, then settled back into her chair. Kendra stared fixedly at her until she said, "What?"

"I think our friend Jen needs an intervention. A lesson in asking for what she wants. How about you bois treat us girls to a little massage?"

We all looked at each other. "Sure." Jade got up to move closer to me, but as she passed her, Kendra grabbed her arm.

"No. You do me. Ash will do her. If everyone's okay with that?"

Heat flushed through me and I could see by Jade's face that she was having the same reaction. We had always found Kendra and Ash super attractive. They were bigger women who wore their curves well, taking up space confidently in a way that defied expectations. I always admired the way their fullness of flesh positively dared you not to find them sumptuous. As skinnier women who constantly worry about their weight, Jade and I both find that refreshing. And alluring. We aren't the kind of couple that hides things like that from each other. We share openly when we think someone is hot. And we had joked around in the past about how dangerous it would be to drink too much with them. I knew from Jade's face that she was remembering the same conversation. Her eyes sought mine and I nodded, and so did she, and so did Ash. And so…that was that. Ash made her way over and settled beside me on the couch.

Then Kendra started talking to Ash in French, an annoying habit they had of making jokes and sharing secrets in a language we didn't know. Or at least didn't remember. I mean, everyone learns French in school in Canada, but most Anglophones tend to forget it all upon graduation. Not Ash and Kendra, though. Usually, Jade would just join in, pretending to follow along and making up ridiculously pompous-sounding nonsense. "Bonjour, croissant ballet moustache." But this situation was too delicate for that kind of play. So we just awkwardly sat there, waiting.

Then Ash's hands were on my shoulders, kneading very gently. I knew she had strong hands. I'd stared at them often enough. But she was barely touching me. Did she not want to be doing this? Did she think I was too tiny or—

"How's it going over there?" Kendra piped up. "Are you enjoying Ash's touch, Jen?"

I mumbled a yes, not wanting the attention.

"Really? And how's the pressure? Too hard for you?" I noticed her eyes were twinkling playfully. Did she tell Ash to give me a piss-poor massage? Was that what she was up to? Making me ask for more pressure? Fine, I could do that.

"I could handle more pressure, um, actually," I said, awkwardly, suddenly afraid of hurting Ash's feelings. Kendra barked something out in French and Ash practically snapped my neck with the pressure. I gasped, and without hesitating blurted, "A little softer!"

Ash chuckled and whispered "Good job" in my ear before reverting to massage me at just the right amount of strong and knowing pressure.

Before long, I lost myself in the sensations, in the deliciousness of letting go, in the novelty of new touch, then I was startled to look up and see Kendra studying me intently.

"Your girlfriend has good hands," she drawled.

"Yes, she does," I admitted, smiling at my sexy girlfriend.

"Mine too though, wouldn't you say?"

"Definitely."

There was undeniable erotic tension connecting all of us now. I was sure that everyone could feel it. The bois kept kneading our flesh in silence, though, waiting, and I was incredibly anxious and excited, uncertain as to where Kendra intended to take this.

"That was a good start. But if you're going to be assertive like me, you need more experience bossing people around. Ash likes to be bossed around by a pretty woman, don't you, Ash?"

Ash didn't answer, but she made a sound in the back of her throat, and I assumed she was smiling.

"Okay, Jen, I'm the boss and you're my assistant. I'm teaching you to lead. And we're going to tell these handsome butches exactly how to please us. They're here to serve our every need. Sound good?"

"Sounds like every day," Ash muttered, and we all laughed.

"Now what shall we have them do?" Kendra challenged me.

But it was too much pressure. Too terrifyingly exciting. I couldn't even make eye contact. I just looked down and waited.

"I want to watch them wrestle," Kendra announced. "Who do you think would win?"

Jade and Ash both immediately stopped massaging us and started laughing and sizing each other up rather dramatically. I laughed along.

"Seriously, should we have them wrestle? Would you like to see that, Jen?"

"Yeah, definitely." Then I added without thinking, "But they should be topless!"

This got a huge reaction, and Jade bounded over to kiss me and playfully raised my glass to my lips, saying, "That's it. Keep drinking, baby."

Ash and Jade knew exactly how to play this up. They were super charming, hamming it up, being mildly silly but with fiercely sexy undertones. They liked being on display for a highly appreciative crowd of two. They postured and flexed. Jade removed Ash's belt, making a big production of it and snapping it loudly once it was off.

"I think our lovely ladies should do the rest," Jade said.

Ash nodded and waited to see which direction Jade would head. Jade looked at me, then made her way to Kendra. She checked in with her eyes. I smiled. Ash followed suit and knelt before me on the couch.

"Would you like to unbutton me?"

The memory is so clear; I can still return to the intensity of that moment. How I couldn't breathe. How the world shrank down to my hesitant fingers on her shirt, revealing her secret self, button by button by button by button. Until she was undone, exposed, and my heart was beating wildly. I risked looking at her face and saw immediately that she wanted to kiss me as much as I did her. My eyes lingered on her mouth, so tantalizingly close, her lips, so soft and inviting.

Ever conscious of our partners, though, we looked across the room to Jade, who had flung off her T-shirt with enthusiasm and was smirking and raising her arms above her head, offering Kendra the task of removing her black sports bra. Kendra wasn't one to hesitate. Her manicured fingers traced Jade's midriff, then worked their way under her bra, freeing her tight, pert breasts from their constraint. She flung the bra away with eager abandon.

Their eye contact smoldered. My girlfriend looked wicked hot, kneeling before another pretty femme. I've always loved the contrast she embodies, how her edgy short hair and androgynous clothing mask her wholly female body, like a secret waiting to be unwrapped. At times, the way she holds herself can suggest boyish cockiness, and yet the way she comports herself always expresses a gentle, feminine core. The interplay in her gender expression, the contradiction, is what tends to get me. This night was no different. She kneeled teasingly before Kendra, her dark eyes twinkling roguishly, hands firmly on her hips, her body open with self-assured poise to Kendra's keen, appraising gaze. I felt myself start to get wet, just watching them.

Then Kendra began directing the show. Ash broke obediently away to play her part and I was left bereft. Until she and Jade started grappling on the living room floor, that is. They grappled with each other in a memorably funny and exhilarating way. It was playful but edged with real eroticism as they tussled about before us, to my silent delight and Kendra's very vocal appreciation, instructions, and taunting. Their bodies came together in queer and inspiring configurations of straining muscle and bouncing curve. A new study in contrasts, with Jade's taut, athletic frame in ever-shifting juxtaposition with Ash's more voluptuous physique. Kendra hooted enthusiastically and I stared elatedly as they struggled for dominance. Ash is significantly bigger than Jade, though, so it was no surprise when she won, panting and sweaty, both of them smiling and proud.

But Kendra was a few glasses in, and more inspiration had clearly struck. She blurted out, "That was a good show, but I want to see you two make out."

My heart skipped a beat. Or five.

"What are we now, your porn stars?" Ash asked, smiling wryly.

"Yes, you're my porn stars. Exactly. I'm the director and you two have to make out however I say."

Jade grinned. "I thought this was about Jen learning to give orders. Why isn't she the director?"

"Because Jen is the fluffer, that's why."

"Lesbians don't need fluffers!" Jade exclaimed.

Kendra gave Jade her most condescending look. "Lesbians don't *need* fluffers, but that doesn't mean they don't *want* fluffers."

I watched Jade anxiously, curious about her reaction. All her partners had been feminine, so I wasn't sure what she would feel about making out with another butch. And indeed, I saw in her face that she was struggling with mixed emotions.

"I'd like to establish ground rules," she finally said. "Can we keep things above the belt? At least for now." Ash nodded and Kendra clapped her hands with determination.

"Okay, okay. Now what should we have you two do?" She was in her element. Giving orders, bustling about rearranging the set, and grabbing extremely random props. She was shouting orders to a nonexistent crew, using film terms that no one was sure she understood, but it kept everyone laughing. When we weren't holding our breath, that is. Because when Ash and Jade finally kissed, it was *toe-tingling hot.*

I'd never seen my partner make out with someone else and it was like falling for her all over again, watching the way she moved her toned, tanned body with such easy confidence. I didn't feel jealous at all. I was riveted. I felt lucky to call her mine. I felt reinspired to love every little bit of her. No matter how much you love your partner, over time it's easy to forget to really look at them. Incomparable intimacy comes with a quality long-term partnership, but the price of that close connection is the loss of the mystery and distance that fuel certain kinds of desire. Watching my partner make out with someone else helped me see her anew. It gave me the distance to recognize once again just how much I do and do not know her. For her touch with Ash was both different and familiar all at once. It was deliciously uncanny in a way that felt unsettling and stirring. Ash aroused new things in my girlfriend, and in me, as a result.

I'd also never really seen two masculine women together. It was thrilling to witness something so rare and powerful. It was everything I like in a dyke but…doubled…and I was wondering if this multiplication of the object of desire is why straight guys like girl-on-girl porn, when Kendra rudely interrupted my rapture at the vision with a harsh "Cut! Cut! I said 'Cut,' goddammit!" She had a hardcover book that she was using like a clapperboard to interrupt them. "This isn't working," she said imperiously. "Ash needs fluffing."

I realized with a start that she was calling me into the scene, and I froze in terror. I just wanted to watch and revel from the safety of the sidelines, but the spotlight was clearly on me now.

"Me too. I need fluffing too." Jade smirked, sidling up to me. "Come on, baby. Fluff me!" She laughed, but I couldn't. I didn't know what the hell a lesbian fluffer would even do. I started to sweat and freak out, but then Ash was behind me and my girlfriend was before me and *I* didn't have to decide anything because *they* had decided that I needed to be in the middle of a decidedly succulent butch sandwich.

They smelled delicious and their hands…so many hands, so many places, feeling me every which way and where. I couldn't focus. I didn't fight it. I just melted into the sensation of something so amazing that it had never even crossed my mind before that moment as a real possibility within the livable realm of sensual pleasure. Something so achingly beautiful and unique that I could intimately know. Something unthinkably, staggeringly, marvelous. *That's* a butch sandwich. Warm breath on my neck. Teeth on my earlobe. Hands cupping my breasts, rubbing my thighs. *Whose? Wow. Oh my God.*

At some point, I suddenly became aware of Kendra and her

crossed arms as she scrutinized the scene. I struggled to focus on what she was saying.

"This isn't in the script, but it's fine. It's fine. We'll fix it in post. A good director knows when to let her actors improvise." She moved to her chair and sipped her wine, watching us and unbuttoning her blouse. "Upstart little fluffer," she muttered as she reached her hand into her shirt, presumably to play with her nipples as she watched us. I heard Ash invite her in, but she demurred. "Nope. This is all Jen. Make her tell you what she wants."

"What do you want?" Ash whispered into my ear, her fingers waiting on the clasp at the front of my push-up bra. I looked at Jade and saw open enthusiasm. "I want you both to fuck me," I admitted, and Ash released the clasp and my tits burst free, seeming to free the last of our restraint along with them.

"That's my girl," Jade growled as she removed my pants and panties with Ash's eager assistance.

What happened next is almost beyond my ability to describe, because it's so much more than what actually happened. I mean, it wasn't just how our bodies came together—who did what to whom and how. I opened more than my legs; I opened my mind. Not only to new sensations but also to new possibilities of being. I mean, what literally happened is that two women I respect took turns worshipping my body. Worked together to see just how much pleasure I could take. Occasionally, they tried to outdo each other in a friendly, mildly competitive way.

But I learned things, too. A silly but surprising example: I always thought that scissoring was made-up bullshit invented by straight men. None of my lovers had ever placed their pussies on mine. Generally grinding, yes. Specifically scissoring like the chicks in girl-on-girl porn, no. So when Ash put one of my legs up on her shoulder and began moving herself, slick and rhythmic, against me, I was taken aback. Usually if my legs were dangling over some dyke's shoulders, there was a strap-on involved. I thought I might miss the sensation of penetration, but this was so novel, this warm, wet softness shared between us, that I felt no lack. Matching my breath and movement to the level of intensity she was emitting, my legs started to shake, sweat broke out on my skin, and I started to feel bold.

"I want to see you two kiss," I commanded.

They smiled and went for it with gusto. I watched them lock lips over me, one of Jade's strong hands grabbing the back of Ash's head, the other still squeezing my breast. Their kissing was fierce. Wild. A continuation of the wrestling in some strange way, as they met each other's power with equal power. *Fuck!* Why do we never see images like this? I wondered briefly, somewhere in the back of my mind, as I felt my wetness flood. This was exceptional. And I was blessed to be witness to it. This strange carnality of boi-on-boi competition.

Luckily, I was brought out of my head by Ash's physical insistence. I felt her pelvis push hard against me and not relent. It pulsated and began to spasm. A low growl escaped her lips and it was so very fine and feral that my body responded in kind, her sensuality and freedom inspiring my own speedy release as our bodies came together in perfect, rare harmony. An unexpected gift.

Then she crashed down beside me, struggling to catch her breath and craning her neck to check in visually with Kendra, who was clearly in the midst of her own rather flamboyant crescendo. I wasn't sure her chair was going to survive the tumult.

I looked to Jade, who had snuggled down on the other side of me, smiling slyly as she traced her hand along my face and kissed me sweetly. "You're so sexy," she whispered.

"I agree," Ash said.

"You're both amazing," I responded, truly in awe.

"Yeah. Okay. I admit it. Those were some pretty impressive moves," Jade conceded playfully.

"It's all in the hips," Ash replied, winking.

"Yes, yes, everyone's incredible." Kendra got up noisily and threw a blanket our way. "Who needs a refill?" She shuffled off to the kitchen to replenish our drinks, while the three of us snuggled under the blanket, giggling and giddy like schoolgirls. Drunk on more than the alcohol.

Have I mentioned that there were tits everywhere? So many tits. All over me. *Mine. Hers. Hers. Mine? Hers. More. And hands. Oh my God.*

By the time Kendra came back, we were already well into round two, which earned us a huffy "Wait till I shout 'action,' at least. Show some respect for film set protocol." We invited her in, but she was still into her game and wanted only to watch.

"Watching is kind of her thing," Ash explained, helping us to feel more comfortable with her voyeuristic distance.

"What do you want, Jen?" Jade murmured in my ear.

I didn't hesitate. "I still want you both to fuck me. But at the same time."

And they did. Taking turns placing their hands on my pussy. Working in tandem. Stroking my clit. Slapping. Penetrating. Thoroughly enjoying. Jokingly pushing each other's hands out of the way. Getting cocky.

"Watch this."

"Nah, you gotta use three fingers."

"It's all about the twist."

"You said it was all about the hips."

"Can't be a one-trick pony."

Eventually, Jade straddled my face, burying all my senses in her pussy. The sweet familiar scent, taste, and feel of her engulfed me as the sound of her moans filled my ears. Meanwhile, Ash's strong and nimble fingers filled my cunt with new sensations. Her mouth teased my clit. I found myself mimicking her rhythms and moves, so that everything her tongue played out on my clit moved its way through my flesh to Jade's. Quick, powerful, nonstop flicks of the tongue. Slow, sumptuous swirls encircling the inner lips. Vigorous head-shaking and direct pressure. Coy, warm breath playfully teasing my pussy. Whatever I was given, I passed on, feeling it both in myself and in my partner. It wasn't something I did consciously but a pattern that I fell into, one that felt wonderfully right. In time, Ash added in suction, drawing my clit into her mouth and holding it there, steady and strong, as her fingers thrust forcefully within me, pushing me to the edge of climax and holding me there in the most agonizingly blissful way.

"At the same time," I whispered. And they finally caught on, switching gears smoothly to meet me where I was. They both moved inside me and synchronized their rhythms. I didn't last more than three minutes, thinking of them both with their fingers inside me together, feeling them meet in my most intimate place. Fulfilling the deepest of my secrets, a desire so very deeply held.

I let out a long, luxurious sigh. Stretched like a cat. "Oh my God, I don't think I could possibly handle anymore. Who's next?"

"Done already, princess?" Jade teased.

"You can't be done yet," Ash said. "I haven't even had a chance to show off my signature move."

I started to protest, uncomfortable about being the center of attention for so long. I'd never shake a reputation for being a pillow princess if I kept this up. But on and on it went. Banter. Pleasure. Playfulness. Orgasm. And learning.

At one point, I turned to Ash. "Can I go down on you?" No beating around the proverbial bush. No needing to be prodded to ask for what I want. Just a confident, direct request. I was pleasing her with my mouth when Kendra finally decided to step in.

"You've got to pinch her nipples really hard if you want her to come." She put down her glass and walked over to us. Knelt. Looked hungrily at me. "Kiss me. I want to taste my girlfriend on your lips."

Hotter words were never spoken. And because I'm such a fast learner, I didn't hesitate to agree. "Okay, but only if you return the favor with my girlfriend." Like I said, I'm a smart, capable, accomplished woman. A bossy femme learning to reclaim her strong will. And I tend to get what I want.

MARKS

Nell Stark

Nell Stark is an award-winning author of lesbian romance, published by Bold Strokes Books. Her 2010 novel *Everafter* (with Trinity Tam) won a Goldie for paranormal romance. In 2013, *The Princess Affair* was a Lambda Literary Award finalist. Her most recent novel, *The Princess Deception*, came out in 2018.

I crave your marks on my skin.

In the mirror, I admire their edges with my fingers, my gaze. Sometimes, I beg you to take pictures of what you have done to me. I know that's dangerous, but I can't help myself. There is a part of me that wants the tiny railroad tracks of your teeth always to crisscross my abdomen, and the stripes of red lining my buttocks never to fade.

From a distance, you admire your handiwork with a blend of satisfaction and guilt. "I don't want to hurt you," you say. The gaze you turn on me has a beseeching quality to it.

I return to the bed and slide into the comforting circle of your arms. Your eyes are pools of melted chocolate. Your sharp, relentless desire has become a bed of banked coals, capable at any moment of flaming to life. The thought of you taking me all over again makes me wet.

"Yes, you do."

I try to say this gently, always gently. You aren't entirely comfortable with the part of yourself that wants so badly to possess me that bruises are the by-product. But that's what I want. What I *need.* And I also need you to feel at peace in your desires—especially because you are the only one who has ever helped me find peace in mine.

For so long, I was afraid of what I wanted, and how much. My fear was undifferentiated—I was so starved for touch, for intimacy, that I couldn't appreciate its subtleties. The raw force of my desire seemed alarming; its magnitude monstrous. Then I met you. You never flinched from my need, never wanted me to dampen my own fire. Slowly, you convinced me I shouldn't fear myself.

"Only because it's what you want," you insist.

It wasn't always what I wanted. Until you, I didn't even recognize myself as submissive. From the Latin *submittere,* to submit. Literally, "to send under." That prefix, *sub*, is what I crave. I love being under you, pinned to the mattress by your weight, looking up into your eyes that burn like stars and promise to catch me up in their conflagration. I love being helpless beneath you. I love giving myself to you, granting you permission to do whatever you wish to my body. "Trust" is a powerful word, but sometimes it doesn't seem adequate to describe the strength of the faith I have in you, the security I feel when I am with you.

"You are what I want," I say. "I love you. All of you. Especially this part."

You stare at me for a long moment. When you finally kiss me, gently but thoroughly, I'm reminded of our wedding day. Like so many others, the first thing we did as a couple was to share a kiss. That act—witnessed by people who loved us—sealed our vows to each other. Since then, the way we express that love may have evolved, but its core remains the same.

When you pull away, I make a small, disappointed sound. I could kiss you forever. You smile, then brush your thumb across my lips. "Turn onto your stomach."

Do you know the pleasure I take in obeying you? My pulse quickens with excitement even as contentment flows through me like syrup, sweet and thick. I roll over and pillow my head on my forearms, waiting. The air is deliciously cool on my back. Outside the window, birds are singing. The stressors of reality loom in the back of my mind like thunderheads, but for now, they are held at a distance by your commanding presence.

Your fingertips are gentle against my buttocks, and I realize you are tracing the red lines you put there earlier. The crop you used has made my skin deliciously sensitive, and I shiver at your caress.

"I didn't go too far?"

I raise my head and crane to look at you. "You didn't go too far. I won't let you, remember?"

You stroke my hair, then gently push my head back to my arms. "I know. It's just hard not to worry."

"I trust you to stop when I tell you," I say. "You have to trust me to decide when that is."

"I do. I will."

Your fingers continue their stroking motion. My breaths slow. My pulse slows. Lazily, I wonder why birds sing. I'm glad they do.

"You are so beautiful like this," you murmur. "I love how the red contrasts with the white." You make a sound that's something between a sigh and a laugh. "Could you ever have imagined you'd enjoy being hit?"

"Not until recently." I reach one hand back toward you, and you intertwine your fingers with mine. "My parents didn't spank me often, but I lived in fear of disappointing them that badly. This, though—this is completely different."

"You are *not* a disappointment," you say, quietly but with vehemence. "Not in any way. I don't do this to punish you. I do this because you want it."

I look back at you again. Your brow is furrowed. I don't want you to worry about this, but I love you even more because you do.

"Yes. And part of *why* I want this is that you enjoy doing it. It's symbiotic." I squeeze your hand. "Don't be afraid."

Be thou not afraid. The words the angel Gabriel said to Mary at the Annunciation. Maybe I should feel like I'm blaspheming, but I don't. Our love has become my religion. Where most religions rely on interdictions to define themselves, our religion relies instead on affirmations. *Thou shalt worship thy lover with thy body. Thou shalt give thyself to thy lover without reservation. Thou shalt covet thy lover and receive satisfaction.*

What I have learned since being with you is that my satisfaction comes primarily, though not exclusively, from surrender. The word itself is problematic, weighed down by the baggage of white flags and the stigma of quitting. Surrender means giving up, giving in. Walking away. But when you wrap your fingers around my neck and I melt beneath you, surrender feels like victory. The fierce possessiveness of your expression is a goad to my pleasure.

I remember the first time I wanted to give you power over my breath. We were kissing, deeply, and you traced the contours of my throat with your fingertips. Your touch was teasing, but even the tiniest movement of your fingertips sparked a strange new need.

I did my best to express how I was feeling. "You can put your hands around my neck, if you want," I said. My voice trembled on the last few syllables, but not from fear.

You pulled away, flustered and protesting. I realized, then, that I knew something you weren't yet prepared to know. I kissed you gently. Later, you made love to me with consummate tenderness. Maybe you thought you were comforting me, but I knew you were reassuring yourself.

For days, and then weeks, I waited. In the meantime, I gave myself up to you in every way you would allow. And then, finally, one night you pushed me up against the wall. Time slowed to a crawl. I took deep breaths, feeling the pressure of your thumb against my windpipe. I wanted so badly to lose myself in the sensation, but I also knew we had to be careful.

"Wait."

Immediately, your grip loosened. But when you would have removed your hand entirely, I held it in place. I looked up and saw you nervous, nearly fearful. When I smiled, you frowned in confusion.

"I want you," I said. "I want you this way, so much. But if we're going to do this, we need to be safe." I raised my free hand to caress your shoulder. "Two taps." I demonstrated quickly. "If I do that, you let go. Okay?"

"Okay." You spoke the syllables so solemnly.

I cupped your cheek in one palm, and you leaned into me a little, like a cat. "Put your hands back where they were."

For an instant, you seemed surprised. Then you collected yourself and raised an eyebrow. "You don't give the orders."

A low, needy sound came from my mouth. I hadn't intended it to escape, but I wasn't sorry. You smiled your Cheshire grin and proceeded to tease me with kisses, your lips skating across the expanse of my sternum while your fingers tormented my nipples. Only when I was writhing beneath you did you finally return your hands to where I wanted them.

As you squeezed, every cell in my body relaxed.

Do you know how rare that is? From the instant I wake until the moment I sleep, my mind gnaws at itself. Relentlessly. Everything I haven't done, everything I should have done better, everything I should want to do but don't have the will or focus to accomplish. Guilt, fear, insecurity, despair. At best, it's an irritating buzz, a wasp hovering just out of reach. At worst, waves of anxiety and panic crash over me without rhythm, sucking me under without warning. It's all I can do to catch a quick breath before being plunged back beneath the surface.

But when you kneel above me and press your thumbs into the hollow of my throat, the chaos subsides. The waters still. Maybe that's because every cell in my body is preoccupied with melting into your touch. I don't know the reason, and I don't really care. All I know is that your possessiveness both excites and soothes me. Heals me, even.

Sometimes, afterward, you ask why I love you. I think you do this because you are still afraid that what you enjoy, what you *need,* is in some way monstrous. I will never, ever tire of reassuring you. The trust you show me in those moments of vulnerability only makes me feel more tender, more devoted to you. Never less.

I love you in so many ways, for so many reasons. I love the curves of your body and the brilliance of your mind and the generosity of your soul. And beneath it all, I love the energy crackling between us, arcing and billowing like a magnetic field. At times, that energy is nearly dormant, like cosmic background radiation—a comforting murmur reminding me I'm not alone. At other times, it flares brightly, a quasar pouring its fiery heart into the void. I never feel more alive than when the invisible filaments between us crackle with electricity, drawing us into tighter orbits around each other.

That's what happened on the afternoon we discovered edge play. You were using your favorite pocketknife to open a package. I was telling you some inane story—I can't remember about what. I turned around at the same time you stood up, knife in hand. I looked at the knife and then at you. You looked at me, then at the knife.

Suddenly, inexplicably, I wanted to feel it against my skin. I knew you could tell. Energy surged, arcing like a solar flare.

"Take off your shirt."

Once I obeyed, you approached, holding the knife between us. My heartbeat accelerated, but I wasn't afraid.

"I'm not going to cut you." Your voice was low and intense, inflected by a note of command that soothed and excited me all at once. "I could never do that."

"I don't want you to," I whispered.

"But you do want me to do this?"

You reached out, slowly, and touched the blade to the skin above my left breast. I watched the metal gleam, felt the cool slide of its edge. The world seemed to pause. My breaths slowed, deepened. Relief flowed across the surface of my mind, smoothing out the jagged edges.

You stopped, then looked at me. Dimly, I realized you had asked me a question.

"Yes. Please, yes."

As if by prior agreement, I didn't touch you. I watched you, though. Your gaze flickered between me and your hand as you dragged the knife slowly, so slowly, across my skin—down and around, tracing the contours of my breasts like a topographical map. And then you raised the blade, severing our connection.

I bit back the plea on my lips. *Don't go*, I wanted to say. A whimper escaped instead. Your smile was triumphant, and it made me wet.

Your hand shifted, holding the knife so it was angled toward my body. I licked my lips as you guided the sharp point downward. At first, the contact was barely perceptible. Testing. Then you let gravity take over until the knife's tip barely pricked my nipple, bridging pleasure and pain. My hips ached to thrust toward you, but the precarious position of the knife held me still. I groaned softly.

"You like this," you said, voice saturated with wonder.

I stammered out an affirmative, breathless reply. You held the point still for another moment, then pulled it back and collapsed the blade. I stood there, hands at my sides, suffused with pleasure. You tossed the knife onto the table and wrapped me in your arms, cradling my head against your neck.

"You are incredible," I said against your skin. I pulled back just enough to meet your eyes. "Where did that come from?"

"I have no idea. It just…happened. I looked at you, and you had this expression on your face, and…" You shook your head. "I don't know. But it wasn't too much?"

I cupped your face in my hands and kissed you lightly. "Did you miss the part about being incredible? I'm not sure how we read each other's minds, but I am *not* complaining."

You kissed one corner of my mouth, then the other. "We're so good together. I just don't ever want to scare or hurt you."

"You didn't. You won't." I smiled at you, and you offered me a tentative smile in return. "Don't be afraid."

These are the memories I savor as you continue to stroke and pet me, your soft fingertips skating across my back, along my thighs. You avoid my buttocks now, and I know why: The marks you've made are sensitive, and you're trying to lull me into sleep.

I don't realize I've drifted off until I open my eyes and our bedroom is filled with shadows. The birds are no longer singing, but they'll be back in the morning. At first, I think you've left me alone to nap, but then I raise my head to the sight of you, propped against pillows, reading something on your phone. You are so beautiful, so beloved. My heart thumps in my chest like a dog wagging its tail.

I haven't said a word, but you look up and smile. "You slept."

It's rare for me to feel relaxed enough to nap, and I enjoy the pride in your expression. "You get all the credit."

"Mm. Come here."

I go willingly. When I am securely enfolded in your arms, and you in mine, I press lazy kisses against your shoulder. I inhale deeply, absorbing your scent into my lungs, my blood. Our lovemaking has left me relaxed and satisfied. Reality is often overwhelming, but the oasis of your embrace comforts and sustains me.

You kiss the top of my head. "How's your ass feeling?"

I wriggle experimentally. I'm pleasantly sore. All too soon, the sensation will fade. For now, I'll savor it to the fullest.

"Feels great." I kiss your chin. "How are you so good at this?"

"At dominating you?" You twist to meet my gaze. "You tell me what you want. Not in words, necessarily, but in the ways you react. I watch and listen to what you like and what you don't. I pay attention."

For a moment, it's hard to breathe. You understand me better than anyone, and you use all that knowledge to discover new ways of caring for me. "You are a gift I'll never take for granted," I say, sealing it with another kiss.

We can't stay in bed forever, of course. As much as we might joke about wanting to, we both have goals and ambitions to chase. In the morning, I'll polish the memory of tonight and tuck it away like a precious jewel, to be retrieved and admired in secret meditation. And as we both go through the ups and downs of our daily routines, I'll live in anticipation of the next time that incredible energy charges the atoms between us.

It could be tonight. It could be tomorrow. It could be as elaborate as you tying me up and having your way with me, or as simple as you pushing me up against the wall for a quick, hard kiss.

The choice, my love, is yours.

About the Editor

Victoria Villaseñor has been an editor with Bold Strokes Books for over a decade. She loves playing with words and helping authors create the best version of their books possible. She lives in England with her wife and fellow author, Robyn Nyx. They travel on a whim and love every minute of the life they share.

Books Available From Bold Strokes Books

Face the Music by Ali Vali. Sweet music is the last thing that happens when Nashville music producer Mason Liner and daughter of country royalty Victoria Roddy are thrown together in an effort to save country star Sophie Roddy's career. (978-1-63555-532-5)

Flavor of the Month by Georgia Beers. What happens when baker Charlie and chef Emma realize their differing paths have led them right back to each other? (978-1-63555-616-2)

Mending Fences by Angie Williams. Rancher Bobbie Del Rey and veterinarian Grace Hammond are about to discover if heartbreaks of the past can ever truly be mended. (978-1-63555-708-4)

Silk and Leather: Lesbian Erotica with an Edge, edited by Victoria Villaseñor. This collection of stories by award-winning authors offers fantasies as soft as silk and tough as leather. The only question is: How far will you go to make your deepest desires come true? (978-1-63555-587-5)

The Last Place You Look by Aurora Rey. Dumped by her wife and looking for anything but love, Julia Pierce retreats to her hometown only to rediscover high school friend Taylor Winslow, who's secretly crushed on her for years. (978-1-63555-574-5)

The Mortician's Daughter by Nan Higgins. A singer on the verge of stardom discovers she must give up her dreams to live a life in service to ghosts. (978-1-63555-594-3)

The Real Thing by Laney Webber. When passion flares between actress Virginia Green and masseuse Allison McDonald, can they be sure it's the real thing? (978-1-63555-478-6)

What the Heart Remembers Most by M. Ullrich. For college sweethearts Jax Levine and Gretchen Mills, could an accident be the second chance neither knew they wanted? (978-1-63555-401-4)

White Horse Point by Andrews & Austin. Mystery writer Taylor James finds herself falling for the mysterious woman on White Horse Point who lives alone, protecting a secret she can't share about a murderer who walks among them. (978-1-63555-695-7)

Femme Tales by Anne Shade. Six women find themselves in their own real-life fairy tales when true love finds them in the most unexpected ways. (978-1-63555-657-5)

Jellicle Girl by Stevie Mikayne. One dark summer night, Beth and Jackie go out to the canoe dock. Two years later, Beth is still carrying the weight of what happened to Jackie. (978-1-63555-691-9)

My Date with a Wendigo by Genevieve McCluer. Elizabeth Rosseau finds her long-lost love and the secret community of fiends she's now a part of. (978-1-63555-679-7)

On the Run by Charlotte Greene. Even when they're cute blondes, it's stupid to pick up hitchhikers, especially when they've just broken out of prison, but doing so is about to change Gwen's life forever. (978-1-63555-682-7)

Perfect Timing by Dena Blake. The choice between love and family has never been so difficult, and Lynn's and Maggie's different visions of the future may end their romance before it's begun. (978-1-63555-466-3)

The Mail Order Bride by R. Kent. When a mail order bride is thrust on Austin, he must choose between the bride he never wanted or the dream he lives for. (978-1-63555-678-0)

Through Love's Eyes by C.A. Popovich. When fate reunites Brittany Yardin and Amy Jansons, can they move beyond the pain of their past to find love? (978-1-63555-629-2)

To the Moon and Back by Melissa Brayden. Film actress Carly Daniel thinks that stage work is boring and unexciting, but when she accepts a lead role in a new play, stage manager Lauren Prescott tests both her heart and her ability to share the limelight. (978-1-63555-618-6)

Tokyo Love by Diana Jean. When Kathleen Schmitt is given the opportunity to be on the cutting edge of AI technology, she never thought a failed robotic love companion would bring her closer to her neighbor, Yuriko Velucci, and finding love in unexpected places. (978-1-63555-681-0)

Brooklyn Summer by Maggie Cummings. When opposites attract, can a summer of passion and adventure lead to a lifetime of love? (978-1-63555-578-3)

City Kitty and Country Mouse by Alyssa Linn Palmer. Pulled in two different directions, can a city kitty and a country mouse fall in love and make it work? (978-1-63555-553-0)

Elimination by Jackie D. When a dangerous homegrown terrorist seeks refuge with the Russian mafia, the team will be put to the ultimate test. (978-1-63555-570-7)

In the Shadow of Darkness by Nicole Stiling. Angeline Vallencourt is a reluctant vampire who must decide what she wants more—obscurity, revenge, or the woman who makes her feel alive. (978-1-63555-624-7)

On Second Thought by C. Spencer. Madisen is falling hard for Rae. Even single life and co-parenting are beginning to click. At least, that is, until her ex-wife begins to have second thoughts. (978-1-63555-415-1)

Out of Practice by Carsen Taite. When attorney Abby Keane discovers the wedding blogger tormenting her client is the woman she had a passionate, anonymous vacation fling with, sparks and subpoenas fly. Legal Affairs: one law firm, three best friends, three chances to fall in love. (978-1-63555-359-8)

Providence by Leigh Hays. With every click of the shutter, photographer Rebekiah Kearns finds it harder and harder to keep Lindsey Blackwell in focus without getting too close. (978-1-63555-620-9)

Taking a Shot at Love by KC Richardson. When academic and athletic worlds collide, will English professor Celeste Bouchard and basketball coach Lisa Tobias ignore their attraction to achieve their professional goals? (978-1-63555-549-3)

Flight to the Horizon by Julie Tizard. Airline captain Kerri Sullivan and flight attendant Janine Case struggle to survive an emergency water landing and overcome dark secrets to give love a chance to fly. (978-1-63555-331-4)

In Helen's Hands by Nanisi Barrett D'Arnuk. As her mistress, Helen pushes Mickey to her sensual limits, delivering the pleasure only a BDSM lifestyle can provide her. (978-1-63555-639-1)

Jamis Bachman, Ghost Hunter by Jen Jensen. In Sage Creek, Utah, a poltergeist stirs to life and past secrets emerge. (978-1-63555-605-6)

Moon Shadow by Suzie Clarke. Add betrayal, season with survival, then serve revenge smokin' hot with a sharp knife. (978-1-63555-584-4)

Spellbound by Jean Copeland and Jackie D. When the supernatural worlds of good and evil face off, love might be what saves them all. (978-1-63555-564-6)

Temptation by Kris Bryant. Can experienced nanny Cassie Miller deny her growing attraction and keep her relationship with her boss professional? Or will they sidestep propriety and give in to temptation? (978-1-63555-508-0)

The Inheritance by Ali Vali. Family ties bring Tucker Delacroix and Willow Vernon together, but they could also tear them, and any chance they have at love, apart. (978-1-63555-303-1)

Thief of the Heart by MJ Williamz. Kit Hanson makes a living seducing rich women in casinos and relieving them of the expensive jewelry most won't even miss. But her streak ends when she meets beautiful FBI agent Savannah Brown. (978-1-63555-572-1)

Face Off by PJ Trebelhorn. Hockey player Savannah Wells rarely spends more than a night with any one woman, but when photographer Madison Scott buys the house next door, she's forced to rethink what she expects out of life. (978-1-63555-480-9)

Hot Ice by Aurora Rey, Elle Spencer, and Erin Zak. Can falling in love melt the hearts of the iciest ice queens? Join Aurora Rey, Elle Spencer, and Erin Zak to find out! A contemporary romance novella collection. (978-1-63555-513-4)

Line of Duty by VK Powell. Dr. Dylan Carlyle's professional and personal life is turned upside down when a tragic event at Fairview

Station pits her against ambitious, handsome police officer Finley Masters. ((978-1-63555-486-1)

London Undone by Nan Higgins. London Craft reinvents her life after reading a childhood letter to her future self and, in doing so, finds the love she truly wants. (978-1-63555-562-2)

Lunar Eclipse by Gun Brooke. Moon De Cruz lives alone on an uninhabited planet after being shipwrecked in space. Her life changes forever when Captain Beaux Lestarion's arrival threatens the planet and Moon's freedom. (978-1-63555-460-1)

One Small Step by MA Binfield. In this contemporary romance, Iris and Cam discover the meaning of taking chances and following your heart, even if it means getting hurt. (978-1-63555-596-7)

Shadows of a Dream by Nicole Disney. Rainn has the talent to take her rock band all the way, but falling in love is a powerful distraction, and her new girlfriend's meth addiction might just take them both down. 978-1-63555-598-1)

Someone to Love by Jenny Frame. When Davina Trent is given an unexpected family, can she let nanny Wendy Darling teach her to open her heart to the children and to Wendy? (978-1-63555-468-7)

Uncharted by Robyn Nyx. As Rayne Marcellus and Chase Stinsen track the legendary Golden Trinity, they must learn to put their differences aside and depend on one another to survive. (978-1-63555-325-3)

Where We Are by Annie McDonald. A sensual account of two women who discover a way to walk on the same path together with the help of an Indigenous tale, a Canadian art movement, and the mysterious appearance of dimes. (978-1-63555-581-3)